A Little Bird Told Me

Rachael Gray

BLOODHOUND
— B O O K S —

First published in 2024 by Bloodhound Books.

www.bloodhoundbooks.com

Print ISBN: 978-1-917214-42-1

For Steve, Mum, Dad, and Mell

A SWEET AND STICKY ENDING

'Don't look at me like that. You knew this could only ever be a short-term thing. If we're not careful, he'll find out, and then where will we be?' She paused, head tilted. 'I know, but he is the vicar, and how would it look if people knew you were fraternising with me behind his back?'

He stared at her for a beat, then returned to licking his bottom.

'I see. That's how it is, is it?'

The ginger moggy who'd taken up residence in her potting shed finished his ablutions and manoeuvred his ample frame in preparation for another protracted nap.

'Not this time. Off you go.' She nudged the trug and when that didn't work, she used her trowel to lever out the rotund feline. Rudely displaced, he meowed piteously for a moment before slinking off in search of another sunny corner where he might snooze undisturbed.

She watched him go with a chuckle. The vicar had the poor thing on a diet and so she really shouldn't have been encouraging him with tidbits, but, like her, he was getting on in years so the odd treat wouldn't hurt.

With secateurs and gloves at the ready, she popped on her sun hat and headed out into the garden. All week she'd been itching to tackle the flower beds, but the rain had persisted day after day until, finally, that morning, the late September sun had made a welcome reappearance.

After thirty minutes, she had dead-headed her 'Lady Emma Hamiltons' and was working her way through the equally fragrant lavender when a shadow fell over her. With a sigh, she rested back on her heels. She'd had no visitors all week and now, the minute she got on her gardening gloves, someone called by unannounced. She looked round to see a figure silhouetted by the light. Squinting, she offered a tepid smile. Usually, she took pleasure in time with friends and neighbours, and she always enjoyed a good gossip, but not today. She hadn't even started on the snapdragons and rain clouds were gathering in the distance.

She moved so the sun was no longer in her eyes. Now she could see her visitor's face. 'Oh,' she sighed. 'Hello again.' She was debating how best to get up from her awkward position when her guest held out a hand. It might have been well meant, but she hated the presumption. She was old, not infirm, and it got right on her marigolds when people assumed otherwise. She wanted to bat the hand away, but in the end, the aches in her back and knees persuaded her not to be churlish.

'I suppose you'd better come on in,' she said once she was fully upright. She set off across the lawn, through the open door into the pleasant coolness of the kitchen where she busied herself making drinks. Despite the unexpected nature of the visit, she couldn't unlearn eighty-some years of good manners.

As she poured, holding the jug of lemonade with both hands to compensate for that blasted tremor she'd developed, a bakery box appeared on the counter in front of her. She put down the jug, keen to lift the lid of the box and reveal what delicacies were inside. *I'm no better than that cat,* she thought. *Never could resist a sweet treat.*

'It's a bit early in the day, but that's very kind, thank you. What's the occasion?'

A shrug was the reply.

Well, whatever the reason, she was going to enjoy this fruit tart, call it compensation for the interruption. She gathered a couple of plates and cake forks and waved the visitor ahead of her through to the front room.

She settled into her favourite chair and balanced the plate on her lap. She hoped this would be quick. She had things still to do and at her age life was too short to dilly-dally.

She lifted the first mouthful to her lips.

Delicious.

She was being watched closely as she ate a second piece, and a third.

Her visitor smiled.

Chapter One

'She's dead.'

Laurel gave a start; she'd thought the lane was deserted. She looked for the owner of the voice and found her in the front garden of the cottage on her right. Only then did the words sink in. 'What! Who's dead?'

Dressed in the distinctive livery of the Royal Mail, the postwoman gestured to her. 'The old dear who lives here. Or lived here, I suppose I should say. See?' She pointed to the window.

Despite a flicker of uncertainty, Laurel picked her way up the garden path and peered into the property. In a chair facing away from them was a body. All she could actually see was the top of a grey-haired head and a bare arm hanging at an odd angle. But there was something about the stillness, the angles.

'See, she's gone.'

Laurel cast around for a response. 'Yes?' Her stomach flipped over as she looked again at the lifeless form. She was no stranger to death, but she hadn't anticipated coming across a recently deceased person whilst on a sunny afternoon stroll.

Her palms were sweaty, she rubbed them on her jeans, but she couldn't do anything about the buzzing in her head.

'Best call someone, I suppose.'

Knocked back into action, Laurel dug in her bag. 'It's okay, I've got my phone with me.' When she clocked the lack of bars, she let out a shaky breath. 'No signal.' She showed the screen to prove it.

The postwoman clucked her tongue. 'Never is round here.'

Laurel's fingers trembled as she shoved her mobile away. 'Should we try to get in? Just in case...?' It was always best to double check. 'Is there a defibrillator in the village?' Her training was hard-wired: ABC, airways, breathing, circulation. Call for help. CPR, defib if appropriate. The NHS liked a checklist.

'I'm sorry, love, there's nothing we can do to help her now.'

'We should call the police.' They had to do something.

Her companion patted her on the arm. 'Good idea.' She pointed up the lane. 'You nip up there to the school and ask them to call Ben. He's one of our local coppers. He'll let the doc know and will let him in when he arrives. Until then, I'll wait here with poor Mrs Armitage. There's no rush.'

After the ambulance, and police, and fuss, Laurel was on her way home, still dazed, when a stranger fell into step with her. An older man, he was wearing a bizarre combination of red wellies, denim shorts, and a T-shirt with a red velvet waistcoat.

'I've got a magnificent Gingernut Ranger, if you're interested?' he said.

Her nose wrinkled as she tried to process his words. She studied him, this unknown person by her side. The afternoon sun traced shadowed lines across his leathery skin and his dusty glasses reflected the trees beginning to shift from summer green to autumn bronze. In his tanned, sinewy hand, the man held a piece of string, and attached to the string was a rabbit. He tugged on the makeshift lead, coaxing the animal to keep up.

She blinked. 'Sorry?' Already wrung out, and confused by the unexpected rabbit, Laurel decided she must have misheard.

'For your hens. I've got a splendid young cockerel if you ever want to raise some chicks.' He paused. 'Aroon.'

On autopilot, she replied, 'Nice to meet you, Aroon. I'm Laurel, Laurel Nightingale.' How did he know she owned chickens?

'Oh no, forgive me. I'm Albert, your new neighbour. Aroon's the cockerel.'

'Right...' She remembered him now. He'd waved to her from next door when she'd arrived that morning. A better response was needed. 'Hi, Albert.' Not great, but the best she could summon for now.

She felt his attention as he observed her while he ambled along. 'I'm sorry about the upset you've had, my dear. Not the introduction to the village you were hoping for, I shouldn't think?'

She shook her head. No, it was a death that had brought her to Elderwick, but not this one; she certainly hadn't planned to find the dead body of a senior citizen on her first afternoon in the little hamlet.

'And you'll find the news travels fast in this neck of the woods, especially with Lou involved.'

'Lou?'

'The lady with whom you found poor Lily.'

Of course. Her brain was two steps behind. It hadn't even crossed her mind to ask the postwoman her name as they'd stared through the window. Lou had disappeared as soon as the police officer arrived, presumably to complete her round. Laurel had hung on outside the cottage. It had felt right to wait until the doctor had been in to see the late Mrs Armitage.

Albert's voice brought her back. 'It's such a shame. She was a lovely woman, Lily.'

Laurel's mouth was dry as she reached for the appropriate condolence. 'I'm sorry for the loss of your friend.' She cringed at the platitude. Were there ever words for such a situation?

Albert didn't reply but rummaged in his trouser pocket, pulled out a white hanky, and wiped his eyes.

They'd reached her garden gate and stood in silence for a moment.

Laurel watched the rabbit.

The hanky disappeared and Albert clapped his hands. 'Anyway, you're new here, and that's exciting. Let's not dwell on loss for the moment. There'll be time enough for that. From the city, are you? Escaping the cut and thrust for the quiet life?' He parried an imaginary blade, then waved towards the cottage behind her. 'You've picked a delightful spot.'

Her new home and intended refuge was a burnt-orange brick building tucked neatly away on a quiet lane that led to nowhere. A low hedge and wooden gate bordered a tidy front garden bisected by a short flagstone path to the door. The door was a heavy, solid affair, with one small pane of wavy glass at eye level, the wood painted in the same sage green as the frames around the four windows. And yes, there were chickens in the back.

Albert continued, 'As long as you don't mind Aroon. He's a bit of an early riser, and you'll be hearing him about 4am most mornings. He's a looker, but not all that in the brains department, that bird.'

Her mouth dropped open, but she caught the twinkle in his eye.

'Ah, I'm only pulling your leg. Aroon doesn't start until at least 5am.' Albert bobbed on his toes as he chuckled, his face creasing along well-worn laughter lines.

Her lips curved in a matching response, and the tension in her body eased, if only a touch. She hadn't thought she was up to talking, but it was helping a little to be distracted by the gentle rhythm of small talk with an undemanding conversationalist.

'I'm from Somerset, so hardly the big smoke,' she offered. 'Near Taunton, to be more specific.'

'Welcome to Yorkshire! "Along the banks of crystal Wharfe, Through the vale retired and lowly..."'

'Wordsworth?' she hazarded. A half-buried memory dredged from her school days.

He nodded. 'Was there ever a poet who better captured the glory of our wild spaces? God's own country. It is grand indeed, and vast. As for Somerset, I've been down West Country way many a time, but mostly in my younger days.' He gestured to his thick, white fluff of hair. 'It's softer down there.'

'It is beautiful.' She felt a pang of loss at being so far from the landscape that had shaped her life thus far.

'I can tell you miss it,' he said, as he bent down and eased the string out of the rabbit's busy mouth. 'But Yorkshire has many treasures to charm you. Do you know the East Riding well?'

'Not really. I went to Beverley Races once, but I don't remember much about it.' She glanced away from him, and looked instead along the lane that stretched beyond, heading off between the fields and blinked away the prick of tears. It had been the last trip she'd taken with her mum, and she couldn't cope with any more upset today. She turned back with her smile held in place.

'So, what prompted your move *oop* north to our quiet little backwater?'

'Have you lived in the village long, Albert?' With a little nudge, most people were quick to talk about themselves.

He caught her eye, crow's feet crinkling. 'I have. I was born and brought up here, but I was away teaching at university in London for some time. Once I retired, I was ready to leave the city and come back home to fresh air and wide-open spaces.'

Keen to know what he'd taught, she didn't have a chance to ask before a rustle interrupted them. The rabbit, having nibbled through his bonds, was munching his way through Laurel's flower beds.

'Lago?' cried Albert. 'What the bugger are you up to? You're an embarrassment!'

Laurel opened the gate and Albert lunged towards the animal. After a brief tussle, he retrieved his errant pet, with three stems of late blooming sweet peas being the only casualties.

He held the escapee tightly in his arms. 'Apologies, apologies. I shall mete out suitable punishment as soon as I get him home. Rabbit pie perhaps, I'm a dab hand at a flaky shortcrust. And you must let me replace what he's destroyed.'

'No, please, there's no need.' Her stomach lurched. She was reasonably sure he was joking about the pie; she didn't want to think of the curious rabbit becoming dinner.

'You hear that, Lago? She has pleaded for clemency on your behalf. Very well, I will spare you. Still, we must away before you cause more mayhem.' Turning again to Laurel, he added, 'I'm popping out for a short while, but after that I'm only next door if you need anything. I hope you're soon feeling better after your upset, and I look forward to us learning more about each other in better times. Take care now.' He reattached the string, gave her a wave and set off along the lane, Lago lolloping along behind.

Was it only rabbits that could lollop, she wondered, watching the odd couple as they disappeared round the corner.

As she turned to head indoors, a piece of paper caught in a sudden breath of wind scurried across the path. She snagged it before it disappeared into the hydrangeas. Torn with smudged ink, she could make out the words *Stop the development* and *devastate our village* along with a date and time. The estate agent hadn't mentioned anything about a new development in the area and none of the legal searches had turned up cause for concern.

A dull pressure pulsed in her temples. First a death, now destruction?

Chapter Two

Late the next afternoon, surrounded by moving boxes, hands sticky from packing tape, Laurel stopped to survey the chaos in progress. Despite finding Lily's – her mind stuttered over the word – body, her new home, Myrtle Cottage, hadn't lost the charm she'd fallen in love with. Her conviction that this was a place she might find solace was restored. The creaking stairs and odd corners, old and bubbled glass giving on to views of green life and blue sky. It was a world away from the modern house she'd had on a small development in Taunton. Her old house had been a place to grab a bite to eat and in which to sleep, little more. Before, work had been her life. Here in Yorkshire, her priorities would be different. They had to be different.

She considered the contents of the box she'd just unsealed. Nestled inside, tightly packed, spines upwards to protect them, were her books from work. They used to sit, pride of place, in a glass-fronted cabinet in her office at the hospital. She'd read every one, multiple times, and most had coloured tabs or scrap paper page markers littered throughout. They charted her career from the early days in mental health services on to more specialised roles in acute hospitals: bipolar disorder to breast cancer, OCD to COPD. She lifted out a chunky paperback, *Psychology: The Science of Mind & Behaviour* by Richard Gross, her A-level text, the weighty tome she'd started with twenty years ago.

Whether she would return to clinical practice or try something altogether different, she didn't know. There was a question she needed to answer before she could make a decision. The idea of no longer being a psychologist was dizzying; it was all she knew, and she was afraid she might discover it was all she was.

The sound of her landline interrupted her reflection. It couldn't be anyone she knew, but perhaps it was the police finally contacting her about the death of Lily Armitage. She'd been expecting a call ever since getting home the previous day.

With some reluctance, she negotiated her way into the hall and snagged the handset from where it sat, out of place on the third stair. She carried it back through to the living room and found herself a box-free gap in which to sit.

'Hello?'

'Hi?' The voice was hesitant. 'Sorry to bother you, it's Rose. Is Sally there, please?'

Laurel frowned. 'No, sorry, you must have the wrong number.' She fiddled with the receiver, expecting the caller to say goodbye and hang up. Then it clicked. 'Wait, do you mean Sally Belvedere?'

'Yes.'

'She's moved. I'm the new owner. Sorry, I don't have her forwarding details or anything.'

'Oh. Oh no.' There was a long pause. 'Oh dear, well, I don't really know what to do now.'

Curious, Laurel asked, 'Can *I* help with anything?' Seconds passed, making her wonder if Rose had hung up.

'No, that's very kind, but I-I'm sorry, it's just that my mum died yesterday.'

Laurel stifled a gasp. The woman on the phone must be Lily's daughter. She shouldn't have answered the phone. The unkind thought zipped through her mind. Not because she didn't feel for the woman on the end of the phone, but it was all a bit too close to home.

'Sally's a good friend of hers– *was* a good friend,' the voice continued. 'I was hoping she could help me because I'm in New Zealand so... Sorry to bother you, though. I'll let you go.'

'No, it's okay.' Laurel couldn't just shrug her off, that would be cold. 'You might not know, but I was one of the people that found your mum.' In her mind, she replayed the scene: the chair; the unmoving arm; the unnatural tilt to the head. She swallowed back her distress.

Rose heaved a sigh. 'I didn't know.'

'I'm so sorry for your loss.' Again, the words felt inadequate. 'I don't want to assume anything, but I'm guessing things must be pretty hard for you right now?'

'It's awful, you know? I can't stop thinking about it. It's come as such a shock. I still can't believe it, that she could be gone just like that.'

Laurel wondered what the police had told Rose about her mum's death. Neither the officer nor the doctor had been willing to share any details with her whilst she'd been outside the cottage. 'Look, if it would help to talk, I'm Laurel and I'm a pretty good listener.'

'That's lovely of you to offer, but I can't impose. You don't want to hear a stranger blub on.'

Laurel was certain the caller would very much like to talk, but was doing the usual polite dance of not wishing to burden others with her sadness. 'It wouldn't be an imposition, I promise. I used to work in palliative care, so I know how useful it can be to talk… but only if you want to.' It was hard not to slip into her professional mode, a habit of many years now.

'That must have been a tough job. Were you a nurse?'

Not that she wanted to mislead, but telling people you were a psychologist could shut down a conversation quicker than a Freudian could ask about your mother. 'No, my job was to support people: patients and their families.' Not exactly a lie.

Another pause.

'If you're honestly sure? I'd kind of built myself up to talking to Sally. I have friends here, but no family, and no-one who knew Mum.'

'You don't have any other family?' Laurel understood how it was to be alone. Her dad had died when she was six from a quick and brutal brain tumour. She missed him every day. Only seventeen short years later, she lost her mum to cancer too – pancreatic, equally cruel – making her an orphan long before she was ready to face the world lonely and untethered.

'No, it's… no, it's just me.'

'Then talk for as long as you need. I'm here for you.'

Laurel settled back into the oversized cushions of the sofa and curled her feet up under her. She listened as Rose talked about how her mum, Lily, had made Elderwick her home five years ago and had loved every second she'd spent there. She'd moved after her husband, Sebastian, Rose's father, had died following a brief illness. Sebastian and Lily had long talked about downsizing to a little place in Yorkshire close to where he'd grown up.

'After Dad was gone, Mum was determined to move anyway, just like they'd planned.' Rose sniffed loudly. 'I had an accident last month, so I've been laid up. I'll be over as soon as they say I'm okay to fly, but… argh, I should be there!'

'Until you can get over… If there's anything I can do?'

There was another gap in the conversation and Laurel pictured Rose considering this offer from a total stranger.

'You know, actually there is a small thing. Mum always had a key hidden in the garden in case she locked herself out again. I told her so many times that it wasn't safe, that it's not like it was when she was younger. See, she was too trusting. She never listened to me. Stubborn woman. I don't want it left where anyone might find it. Would you be able to pick it up and keep it safe for me?'

'Of course, I'd be happy to. Only is it okay to go to the house? Won't the police be there?'

'No, why would they be?'

Laurel opened her mouth but held back the words. She frowned. 'No reason, I suppose. I just... never mind. I can get the key. It's no problem.'

'And I was wondering, if you're going over there anyway, and only if it wouldn't be too uncomfortable, could you pop inside and make sure all the windows are closed and everything is switched off?' Rose sounded calmer now she was making practical arrangements.

'Absolutely.' Laurel's thoughts were churning.

'Thank you. Can I give you my email address, if you wouldn't mind letting me know when you've been and if there are any problems?'

Laurel grabbed a pen and jotted it down, double checking the spelling, then asked for a contact number too, just in case she needed to reach Rose urgently.

'You know, I think this conversation has done me some good. I'm so glad it's you I ended up speaking to today.'

'I'm happy I could be here for you, and that I can help.' It was true, it was nice to feel useful again, but the conversation had sparked a serious question.

After saying goodbye, Laurel hung up the phone and sat,

brow furrowed. Why had she jumped to that conclusion that Lily's death was suspicious? Elderly ladies died all the time, from all kinds of ailments and illness. If there were anything untoward, the police would have informed Rose, but Rose had given no indication of that being the case.

She replayed the moment Lou had called her over and how together they'd looked through the front window to see the unmoving figure in the chair. There had been nothing in sight to spark such misgivings... had there?

In the absence of any evidence, then, *why* had she assumed Lily was the victim of foul play?

Chapter Three

Spurred on by her suspicions, and as the sun was still warming the afternoon from a washed-out sky, Laurel wasted no time heading back to Lily's cottage, Church View. The tickle was becoming incessant. She had to work out what she'd seen that had made her uneasy.

All the way there, she ignored the warning voice in her head. *This is different, and I'm not getting involved. I'm simply curious.*

Rose had told her to use the gate on Church Lane, which opened into the back garden of the cottage. The gate, set into the stone wall, was old and weathered. It filled the gap in the wall so there was no way of knowing from the outside what lay beyond. She ran her fingers over the silvered oak panels, then grasped the handle and lifted the latch. It made a fitting creak as Laurel pushed her way through and she shivered.

Closing it behind her, she felt a million miles from another living soul. She couldn't see the house; her view was obscured by towering rhododendron. She followed a shady woodchip trail winding between the bushes, which brought her into the sun and to the edge of a mossy lawn studded with daisies and love-in-a-mist; their delicate white, blue, and purple heads bobbing in the gentle breeze.

The far side of the lawn lapped against the back wall of the cottage where deep-set mullioned windows draped in climbing roses glinted in the light. The thatch on the roof looked new, the edges still crisp. By one of the two chimneys was a straw sculpture of a hare, a descendant of the dollies that superstitious farmers once upon a time placed on hayricks to ward off evil spirits and witches. It had to be the only thatched property in the village, probably one of very few left in the whole of East Yorkshire.

Following Rose's directions, she found the worn and heavy key beneath a pot overflowing with red geraniums to the left of the door. It was such an obvious hiding place. It turned smoothly in the lock, and she pushed open the door to be surprised by a bright, modern kitchen-diner. She took a moment to check her shoes were clean before crossing the threshold and letting her eyes roam around the space. Hanging on a hook was an apron still with a faint dusting of flour and a cookbook propped on a stand open to a recipe for toad-in-the-hole. She could almost imagine the owner had only stepped out for a moment.

There was a cream Aga in a recess, a butler's sink, oiled wooden worktops, and at the far end a large dining table on which stood a vase of wilting greenery. She approached the table to look at a box sitting alongside the vase. It was empty save for a few pastry crumbs. The writing on the side said The Plump Tart. Laurel recognised it as the name of the local bakery, a business she was eager to visit.

She checked the windows were all latched and took a moment to snap to the off position the few switches that were on, except for the fridge-freezer, and resolved to drop Rose a line asking if she would like the contents clearing. Taking a look inside, there was little to see: a pint of milk, almost full; some butter; eggs; veg in the crisper drawer; a pack of sausages. The freezer contained a pint of ice cream – an expensive brand – and a bag of frozen broccoli florets, unopened. Stuck on the outside was a calendar with the weekly WI meetings marked and a note about an appointment at the hairdressers a week on Tuesday.

Laurel had stalled for long enough. It wasn't the kitchen she most needed to see. It was time to go into the front room. The room where the body... Lily had been.

The focal point was an inglenook fireplace with logs stacked high and a comfortable chair on each side. On the small occasional table by the seat facing the window lay a bookmarked copy of *The Green Witch* and a pair of glasses, bent and missing a lens. She tried to picture Lily sitting by the fire in winter, warmed by the glowing embers while hunkering down with a good book, of which there were many more on four large bookcases.

She felt the tickle of a draft around her ankles and watched a small black and white feather dance in the fireplace where eddies of ash whispered around the hearth. *Maybe I saw the crumpled glasses?* She thought. *That must have been all that was bothering me.* She had to admit, now she was in the room, nothing looked out of place and broken spectacles meant little. But the itch didn't abate.

She moved to stand by the window and regarded the room from the same angle as she'd viewed it for the first time, outside with Lou. Lily had decorated her walls with framed family photos and three large paintings. On the mantelpiece stood a clock in a wooden case ticking away undisturbed. Nothing peculiar. She squeezed her eyes shut and tried to summon the scene as viewed from outside. Try as she might, she couldn't identify the source of her unease.

She opened her eyes and blew out a breath. There was nothing here. The stress of her recent move and seeing someone so recently passed away must have pushed her imagination into overdrive. She should know better. Marginally reassured, she turned to the stairs. She would confirm the first floor was secure and then head off.

Upstairs were four doors off the landing. The first opened into the bathroom, the second was Lily's bedroom, the third had been set up as an artist's studio with an easel and paints all carefully stored, and the last was an office. She thought of the days after her own mother's death when, swamped by grief, the mundanity of paperwork had been a life raft onto which she'd clung. Rose wouldn't be able to do the same.

Again, everything was shut tight, and Laurel was ready to leave when a movement caught the corner of her eye. She flinched; she was being watched.

The telegraph pole was the perfect height for the magpie, who regarded her with its intelligent eyes. It cocked its head and chattered, the noise harsh and indignant. She rubbed at the goosebumps on her arms and stepped back, out of sight of the bird. Magpies had always unnerved her. She remembered the feather in the fireplace and wondered if the bird had somehow been in the house.

She'd done what she'd come for and now thoroughly spooked, she was eager to leave. She retraced her steps downstairs, passed through the living room to the kitchen, and back outside. The afternoon had kept its warmth, but still she shivered. With a shaking hand, she locked the door before popping the key securely into her pocket.

As she exhaled the breath she'd been holding, she heard the creak of the garden gate. She froze. Soft footsteps were just audible on the sun-baked earth. The fear that Lily's death hadn't been natural reasserted itself with conviction. What if this was a killer returning to the scene? She pulled her phone out of her jeans pocket, not sure who she was going to call. Glancing at the screen, she saw there was no signal. *Damn it!* Her heart thumped in her chest. She cast around for an alternative escape route but was rooted to the ground, unable to move as the intruder drew closer.

A young man carrying a wicker basket emerged from the undergrowth. He gave a start as he saw her and came to an abrupt halt.

She watched his Adam's apple bob in his throat as neither of them spoke.

'Hi,' he said eventually, and set down his basket. 'I'm so sorry. I didn't think anyone would be here. Who are you?'

'Who are you?' she shot back, ruffled despite his calm demeanour.

'I'm Hitesh.'

'Hitesh?' She blinked and inched further away.

'I'm so sorry. I didn't mean to surprise you.' He shuffled his sandaled feet. 'I'm not trespassing. Lily and I were friends. We talked often in her garden and about the garden and I just wanted to come and make sure it's okay. She would hate for it to be abandoned.'

Laurel wasn't sure about his claim. Whether or not it was true, she wasn't about to confront him alone.

'Okay. I'm Laurel, a friend of Lily's daughter. She asked me to come round and pick up a few things.' The slight exaggeration came easily, but she withered when he glanced at her empty hands.

'Ah, yes, Rose. Lily spoke about Rose a great deal. She missed her very much after she moved to New Zealand.' He pulled a red handkerchief from his pocket and passed it over his eyes.

'And the basket?' she said, gesturing to the battered wicker carrier resting by his feet.

'To collect some early cobnuts. They're very creamy at this time of year and delicious in a salad.'

Laurel screwed up her nose and she considered this. 'I've never tried cobnuts before; I thought they mostly grew in Kent?'

'Possibly, I don't know. But they grow here also, and Lily has a tree. Or do you say *had* a tree? That's ridiculous, *had, has* what does it matter...' He trailed off and sighed, wiping his eyes again. 'I apologise. It is very sad that she died.'

'You were close?' Laurel softened at the sorrow in his voice.

'I like to think so, yes. When I first moved here, she was one of the first people in the village to stop and chat with me and we became friends. We both like to grow things, and eat what we grow, and be kind to animals and nature, so we had common ground.'

'Have you been here in the village long?'

'It's been quite a while now, but I don't live in Elderwick exactly. I live in Drumble's Hive, the commune just up the track past Little Wick. It's a wonderful place. You'd be very welcome to come and visit sometime. Or if you would rather not, you should definitely try some of the food and drink we make to sell in the local shop and café. The cloudy apple juice, in particular, is very good.'

'I'll do that.' Laurel didn't commit to whether she meant the visit or the apple juice.

Indicating his basket, Hitesh said that he'd better be getting on. Sensing that he was upset and might want to be alone – and thankful for a reason to leave – Laurel added that she too had better be getting on.

'It was good to meet you, Hitesh. I'll maybe see you around sometime.'

He sketched a wave, picked up his basket, and melted away into the shrubbery.

Feeling shaken, Laurel headed for the gate and let herself out.

Chapter Four

As Laurel stepped through the gate, back into the lane, she patted her pocket, ensuring Lily's key was safely stowed, then turned to retrace her steps home. Rounding the corner from Church Lane onto Wayback Lane, she saw a woman approaching. She ducked her head, but the newcomer called to her.

'I heard you'd been spotted up this way,' she said. 'You must be Laurel?' In a sky-blue tunic and blonde hair in a perfect chignon, she drew closer and held out her hand. 'I'm Maggie Wright, wife of Councillor Wright. Sorry to accost you, but I thought now was as good a time as any to welcome you to the neighbourhood.'

'Nice to meet you.' Maggie had a firm handshake. Laurel admired her nails, polished in flawless pearlescent pink, whilst wondering how to get away as quickly as possible. She had things to think about.

Maggie's voice dropped to a whisper as she nodded towards Church View. 'Terrible news about Lily. Albert tells me it was you and Lou who found her?'

Laurel wasn't sure if the breathless tone was because Maggie was angling for an inside scoop on all the details. She kept her expression neutral and said, 'It was quite a shock.'

'I can't believe she's gone.' Maggie sniffed as her eyes welled up with tears. 'Oh gosh, sorry, sorry, don't mind me. She was such a lovely woman and...'

Laurel rummaged to find a clean tissue to offer her and revised her uncharitable assumptions.

Maggie nodded her thanks as she took it and wiped her eyes. 'I hope all this doesn't colour your first impressions of Elderwick? It is such a quiet little village where everyone looks out for their neighbour. Lily will be missed.' She inhaled a shaky breath and tried on a smile. 'I know it doesn't make up for her loss, but at least she lived a long and happy life.'

Laurel wanted to reach out to comfort her, but held back. 'Rose mentioned Lily was very happy here.'

'Her daughter? You've spoken to her?' Maggie brightened. 'I think I met her when Lily first moved in. Charming woman. Turned a few heads during her stay, if I recall, but she was already set on a new life in New Zealand. She'll be coming over for the funeral, I expect.'

Laurel summarised her conversation with Rose and explained Rose's arrival was likely to be delayed given her recent injury. 'It was quite by accident I ended up speaking with her, but I'm glad I did.'

Maggie touched the back of her hand. 'And I'm sure she appreciated it.'

Laurel's stomach chose that moment to rumble. She felt her cheeks heat up until she caught Maggie hiding a grin. 'Sorry, I haven't had chance to get any proper food in yet.'

'You know, if you've got a minute, let me introduce you to The Plump Tart. If anything can cheer the soul, and satisfy the stomach, it's the divine creations Hetty and Constance produce. They're sisters; it must be something in their genes.'

Much as Laurel wanted to retreat to Myrtle Cottage, she really was very hungry. When Maggie assured her it was a short walk to the bakery, she relented and trailed along as Mrs Wright kept up a running commentary of who lived in which house, who did what, or not. Tasty morsels of gossip.

'It sounds like everyone knows everyone else around here?' Laurel hoped she didn't sound critical. She was interested to know how active the village grapevine might be. She had the idea it was lively.

'It's true what they say, I'm afraid; nothing is a secret here for more than five minutes. For example, there was a sighting of Ryan Gosling in The Snooty Fox beer garden once, and within ten minutes, seventy-five percent of the population of Elderwick were craning their necks to get a peek at him. It turned out to be a case of mistaken identity, of course. It was just Fred, the milkman's son, back from inter-railing round Europe. It was fun for a few minutes though and I heard the bar had record takings that day. Two weeks later, when Sheryl Crow was also spotted at the pub, I rather suspect Sam, the bar manager, was trying to create a repeat performance.'

Laurel smiled as Maggie's chatter continued down North Street, towards the village centre and the bakery.

The bell over the door jingled as they stepped into the warm embrace of apple and cinnamon scented air.

'Maggie! And how are you this wonderful day?'

Maggie smiled at the striking woman standing behind the counter. 'Hetty, good morning to you, too. I'm very well, thank you. I've brought Laurel to show her your wonderful bakery. She's new here.' The way Maggie spoke – she may as well have winked at Hetty – gave Laurel the distinct impression her arrival in the village had been discussed well in advance.

Hetty grinned and Laurel felt her lips curl into a smile in return. This was the image she'd had in her head when she picked the small Yorkshire village as her new home: friendly people, a warm welcome, and cake. Cake always put her in a sunny disposition, and the array of pastries on display was sublime. The cabinet was a treasure trove of tarts, cream slices, croissants, *pain au chocolat*, and chocolate éclairs.

Hetty must have seen her looking. 'Can I tempt you?' she asked, her tongs hovering tantalisingly over one of the perfect bundles of golden choux, thick, rich cream and a silky robe of glossy chocolate.

Laurel licked her lips and hesitated. 'I don't think I can say no.'

'Maggie?'

'Now you know they're my favourite, but I'd better not, thank you. I've got to watch my figure.'

'And a very fine figure it is to watch too.' Hetty giggled. 'Listen at me! Am I allowed to say that?'

Laurel saw a blush creep up Maggie's cheeks.

'Will you and Constance be going to the meeting about the development?' Maggie asked Hetty, changing the subject. 'Laurel, have you heard about it?'

She nodded. 'I saw a flyer, but I don't know the details.' Perhaps this was an opportunity to find out a little more. Between the news about a development and finding a dead body, she could practically feel her fight-or-flight response limbering up. Maybe she should get two éclairs?

Hetty was looking behind her, checking that the door through to what Laurel assumed was the kitchen was closed. 'I'll be going, but I think you and I, Maggie, are very much in the minority of those who support it.'

'I wasn't sure if you *were* in favour of it?'

'It'll mean we can expand our business. The new hotel

and restaurant will be a big daily order. We'd be fools to pass it up and let some other business benefit. Constance doesn't agree. She thinks we should stay small and keep on as we are. What she doesn't appreciate is that if it's another bakery supplying the hotel, we're going to end up in direct competition and it could shut us down. That would be seriously crap after we've worked so hard to establish ourselves and our reputation.'

'With it being partly my husband's project, naturally, I am supportive,' said Maggie. 'However, I understand the concerns people have. I would hate for the character of Elderwick to be lost. But Nicholas has reassured me it won't change the village, it will be *revitalising*.'

Laurel didn't know these people well enough yet to point out that, in her opinion, revitalise was just a fancy word for change and not necessarily good change at that.

A wheelchair banged through the door behind the counter. Identical expressions of guilt flashed across Maggie and Hetty's faces.

'*Revitalise* my arse, that's just management speak for mucking up something that's perfectly fine as it is. I'm no fan of Derek Fisher–'

'Neighbourhood nosey-parker and local regulations tyrant,' Maggie explained to Laurel.

'–but at least he's standing up to the Hartfields.'

Laurel pressed her lips together so as not to laugh. This must be Constance. She liked Constance.

Poised on the brink of a verbal battle, they were distracted by a sour-faced, grey-haired older lady who clattered in through the door and elbowed her way between Laurel and Maggie. Laurel winced as she caught a bony prod in the ribs.

'If you're not too busy jibber-jabbering, I need some bits,' she demanded.

'Dorothy, I'll be right with you once I've finished helping these two ladies.' Hetty nodded to Laurel and Maggie.

'I haven't got time to faff about while you all cackle on like a gaggle of geese. I've got a last-minute guest in at Tulip Cottage, arrived yesterday, some friend of Mr Fisher's. All very inconsiderate,' she huffed. 'And just what was it you were saying about Mr Fisher as I came in? It's rude to gossip, you know.'

Maggie turned to Laurel. 'This is Dorothy. She lives over the way and has a holiday cottage.' To Dorothy she said, 'I thought you'd be glad of a new guest. Didn't you say only the other day how quiet it's been?'

Dorothy harrumphed and didn't reply. Instead, she poked her finger in the air, directing Hetty to the items she wanted. Hetty gave in and served her, while Constance retreated to the kitchen.

'I'd better be getting on, too,' said Maggie. I've got a dinner to prepare for some of Nicholas' colleagues from the bank. One last thing though, I run the WI in the village and we would just love you to join us. We're always interested in having new members.'

'I'm not sure that the WI is really me.' Laurel's brain stuttered as she tried to think of a better excuse. 'I can't bake for toffee and I'm strictly a jam from the supermarket kind of girl,' she added in desperation.

'Maybe you'd meet me for tea and cake one morning then, instead. I can at least tell you a bit more about us and we can get to know each other? There's a wonderful café called The Pleasant Pheasant. Hetty and Constance provide all their cakes, so we're guaranteed another delicious treat.'

The prospect of cake was always tempting.

Maggie took her silence for consent. 'Shall we say Thursday at 10am, unless you'll be at work?'

'No, Thursday will be fine. I'll see you there.'

As she walked home, enjoying her éclair – she hadn't been able to wait to tuck in – she reflected that whilst she hadn't learnt much more about the development, it was clear emotions ran high amongst the locals, and not everyone was on the same page about it, not by a long shot.

Chapter Five

After a night dreaming of magpies, the sound of the phone in the hallway dragged Laurel from her unsettled slumber. She struggled to untangle herself from the sheets, and lurched out of bed, banging her shin on the bedside table as her legs wobbled, not yet as awake as their owner.

She reached for the door, hauled it open, staggered along the landing and down the stairs, grateful that she managed to avoid going head first and breaking her neck on the flagstones at the bottom. She snatched up the phone. It was a second before she could speak. She needed to get an extension upstairs.

'Hello,' she gasped.

'Laurel? It's Rose. I'm sorry to bother you... oh heck, what time is it there? I hope I didn't wake you? I still get a bit mixed up with the time difference between there and here.'

'Rose, hi, no, it's fine. How are you?' Laurel sat on the bottom step and rubbed her leg where she was sure a bruise was already forming.

'I'm really sorry to phone again, but yesterday the coroner's office called and I'm confused about something. I haven't been able to stop thinking about it and what it might mean. Can I talk it through with you?'

'Of course. What's happened?' The hairs on the back of Laurel's neck tingled.

'So, when the police first rang me to tell me Mum had... passed away, they told me the ambulance crew believed she'd had a heart attack. There was nothing to suggest otherwise and given her age... but now they say her case has been referred to the coroners because she hadn't seen a doctor for a while. She didn't like seeing the doctor as a rule, and she was always in excellent health. Anyway, they've done a post-mortem, and it's come up with something.' Rose paused. 'Now they're saying Mum might have died from poisoning.'

'Poison?' Laurel hesitated, lost for words. 'Oh, my goodness... gosh, I'm... I don't know what to say.' She'd been right. Something *had* been off about Lily's death.

Silence fell as they each contemplated this news.

'It's not really sunk in yet,' said Rose finally.

'No, of course, that's understandable.' Whilst she didn't want to pry, curiosity pawed at her. 'What do these results mean, exactly?'

'I'm struggling to know,' admitted Rose. 'They were trying to be sensitive, but I think what they were saying was the poisoning must have been accidental or... or that she took it deliberately.' Her voice wobbled.

Laurel pressed the handset closer to her ear. 'Do they mean as in suicide?'

'That's what they were getting at.'

Sensitive to Rose's grief, she was careful with her tone of voice. 'Do you think it's possible?'

'That's the thing though,' Rose's tone was puzzled, 'I don't believe that; Mum would never kill herself.'

Laurel pursed her lips. It didn't feel like the right

explanation to her either, but she had no basis for her belief. She considered the most delicate way to phrase her next question. 'Was it possible that your mum was depressed but was protecting you from knowing about it?' It didn't fit with what she'd heard about Lily from Maggie or Albert, but you could never truly tell what was going on in other people's lives.

The reply came quickly. 'No. I mean, I thought about that, of course I did, but Mum was happy. She had so much going on, she loved it in Elderwick. She missed Dad, but I think she had a whole new lease on life and she wasn't lonely. She was a member of every organisation and club going from the University of the Third Age to the WI. No, I can't believe that it was suicide. But the alternative doesn't make sense either. How could she have accidentally taken poison, and it's not like she was allergic to anything?'

'Okay...' Laurel's mind was racing. This new information was only adding to her unease over the situation. She thought back to the scene in the cottage and added the suspicion of poison: the sudden death of an otherwise healthy woman; a broken pair of glasses; an empty cake box. She caught her breath. The cake box... was that important?

Rose cut into her contemplation. 'I've been doing some quick research online and I think she should have what's called a forensic autopsy now, done by a forensic pathologist. Do you think I should call back and ask about that? They left a number in case I have any questions.'

'It couldn't hurt to speak to them again. Did they talk to you about the next steps?'

'I get the feeling they're stuck on the idea it was deliberate or an accident. Apparently, the police didn't report anything suspicious when they found the body: the doors and windows were all locked, nothing looked as though it had been disturbed.'

Laurel searched her mind for the bits of knowledge she'd

gained from her work with the terminally ill and those occasions in which the coroner's office had been involved. 'Are they sending samples to toxicology?' she asked.

'I can't remember. They might have said that. I was finding it hard to follow after the poison stuff.'

If samples had been sent for testing, it could be some time before the results came through. Another question presented itself. 'Rose, if they're thinking poison, surely, they would have expected the police or the ambulance crew to have found the source of the poison in the house? Then again,' she answered herself, 'they wouldn't have been looking because they thought it was a heart attack.'

'I don't see what Mum could have had in the house. She didn't like to use any chemical products. She used natural whenever she could, like vinegar for windows, bicarb for cleaning. Nothing poisonous.'

'I didn't see anything suspicious when I visited, but again, I didn't know to look. But if it wasn't deliberate or an accident...' Laurel let the unasked question hang.

'I don't know what to think anymore,' murmured Rose.

Laurel was tempted to leap to the conclusion pinging around in her brain. She was trying to look at the fresh evidence objectively, but all it did was reinforce her conviction. For a few seconds, she managed to hold back before breaking the silence to blurt, 'I don't want to say it, Rose, but what if your mum was murdered?'

Chapter Six

For the remainder of the day, Laurel alternated her time between unpacking yet more boxes, and searching online for information about common household poisons, procedures in the coroner's office, and the effects on the body of various noxious substances. If Lily had been murdered, she couldn't stand by and do nothing.

As the day faded into a blustery evening, she reluctantly closed down the fascinating webpage devoted to The Poison Garden at Alnwick and turned her attention to the Elderwick community meeting due to begin in a half hour.

Unsure of how to dress, she opted for jeans, a smart blouse and a pair of white canvas shoes that were easy to slip on. She eyed herself in the hall mirror before leaving the house and ran a hand through her short, bobbed hair. She considered again whether it was time to ditch the hair dye and go gracefully from brunette to grey, but at forty-one, she didn't think she was quite ready for that.

When she reached the village hall, she tried to time her approach to blend in with a group of five chatting locals, hoping to slip in unnoticed. She was sure the people present for the meeting were delightful, but with any introductions, there would be questions about why she'd moved to Elderwick. She knew she couldn't avoid the enquiries forever, but she was still assembling the narrative for herself. Unfortunately, Albert appeared in the entrance and hiding was out of the question. That evening, he had gone with an eye-catching combo of purple corduroy trousers paired with a pale pink shirt.

'Laurel! Lovely to see you. Good of you to come along.' He waved her inside. 'I didn't like to bother you with this nonsense when we met the other day, but you maybe heard about it in the village?'

'Actually, I found a leaflet that I think you dropped in my garden when you were rescuing my flowers from Iago.'

'You mean Lago? Lago from Lagomorph: rabbits and hares. Yes, indeed. Dropped it, did I? Ah, well, good, good. Here you are. Come with me.' He motioned to the front of the hall. 'There's a seat down near the stage for you. Our local county councillor is here already, so I expect they'll be starting soon. Oh, but grab yourself a coffee at the back first if you like. I've even brought some nut juice, if that's what you're in to?'

'Um, nut juice?'

'Yes, what do you call it, almond milk for the vegans and lactose intolerant?'

'Oh right. No, I'm okay, thank you.' She followed Albert down the aisle and he pointed to a lone vacant seat before bustling off on some other business.

Feeling conspicuous, Laurel studied the stage where two people sat alongside an empty chair. In the middle seat was a man of around fifty years of age. His posture was stiff, his blond hair in a side parting and swept back with an attractive hint of silver at the temples, not a strand out of place. Councillor Nicholas Wright, she guessed. She looked around for Maggie but didn't spot her, nor could she see Hitesh, but Hetty and Constance were a few rows back.

Laurel tried to picture Nicholas and Maggie together and failed. For all her polish, Maggie's warm nature shone out, whereas he had an arrogant air and a mean slant to his lips. His eyes remained glued to his phone as he ignored the man speaking heatedly to him from his left.

The second man was very different. Whey-faced and small in stature, his head topped with a few strands of sandy hair. In his beige suit, he was a dull counterpoint to the polished councillor. Accountant would be her guess. That or tax inspector. The lines on his face cut deep with evidence of displeasure and his hands fluttered ineffectually in the air as he spoke. Every so often he would reach out as though to touch the councillor but would draw back before making contact, not quite daring to be so bold.

A few minutes later, Albert hopped up the steps onto the stage and seated himself in the third chair. He nodded to his colleagues alongside him, but was ignored. He caught Laurel's eye and grinned as he shrugged.

The murmuring amongst the gathered crowd quieted as the bland man stood to speak.

'Ladies and gentlemen, thank you for coming along this evening to my emergency community meeting.' His plaintive voice cut through the chatter in the packed hall. 'I think you all know me, but for any that don't and for the minutes, my name is Derek Fisher. I am chair of the parish council, co-ordinator and lead of the Elderwick Neighbourhood Watch and lead for the Neighbourhood Watch team North Street to Little Wick, liaison to the county council, liaison with the community policing team and long-time resident of Elderwick.'

'He forgot to mention scourge of the allotments and all-round nosy parker,' someone whispered just behind her followed by a snort of laughter.

Derek paused and looked like he might have heard, but after a hard stare in Laurel's direction, he resumed. 'I would especially like to thank our esteemed county council representative and resident of our wonderful village, Mr Nicholas Wright, for joining us. We're also joined by Albert.'

Albert didn't rate a proper introduction, it seemed.

'Now, let's get on. We're here today to talk about how we stop the proposed development of Elderwick Hall. I am of the belief that Mr Wright, on hearing our concerns, will agree this abominable plan should be halted.'

Laurel thought she saw Nicholas' mouth twitch in displeasure, but she wasn't close enough to be sure.

Derek railed for over twenty minutes, giving a comprehensive rundown of the drawbacks to such a project. His description of the planned building works and expected disruption alone didn't paint a pretty picture. Not once did he invite the audience to participate or voice their opinions, but by the time he was finished, there was little he hadn't covered. There had been muttering around the hall throughout his speech and Laurel could tell that whilst people may not feel warmly towards Derek, many were equally concerned to preserve their tranquil corner of the world. She pictured her own little cottage on the quiet Birch Lane and felt her agitation rise.

When Derek took a long enough pause for breath, Nicholas stood and raised his hands, asking for quiet. He waited a beat longer than necessary.

'Thank you, Derek. Whilst I understand that this isn't an official parish council meeting, I have agreed to say a few words in the hope that we can stop all these unhelpful rumours.' He glared at Derek. 'As you all know, Elderwick Hall and the grounds haven't been open to the public since the early 1930s...'

There was an audible grumbling.

'...so there will be no loss to the village. The existing rights of way will be maintained, in a *sensitive* manner in keeping with the development. However, what this development *will* bring to Elderwick is significant. New jobs will be available for our young people who have been leaving in droves. There will be new jobs for any residents who want them, and I believe Marcus Hartfield, the gracious steward of Elderwick Hall, has already approached several of you to discuss possible employment in the hotel, the grounds, the restaurant, the golf club, and the personal development centre. With this abundance of new facilities, we expect to attract quality visitors and new residents to the village.'

Laurel's eyebrows rose. The subtle stress Nicholas had placed on the word quality felt deliberate and insulting. From the tightening around his eyes and his compressed lips, she could see Albert hadn't missed it either.

'Besides which,' Nicholas continued, 'Mr Marcus Hartfield, whose family has supported and cared for this village for hundreds of years, applied for approval in the correct manner and this has already been granted by the council. So, we can look to building a bright future together or we can waste our time and rail against something which is going to happen, anyway.' He sat down and resumed his focus on his phone, unconcerned with what any in the audience or on the stage might have to say in response.

Derek looked like he'd sucked on a lemon.

'Hartfield couldn't even be bothered to be here,' shouted a voice.

'Afraid to face us,' exclaimed another.

More people were joining in, expressing their disgust.

There was the occasional dissenting voice, people speaking up in favour of the prospect of new jobs, but they were drowned out.

'Silence! Order!'

No-one paid Derek any attention, and it was Albert who calmed the rabble, getting to his feet as he called, 'Please, ladies, gentlemen.' It took a moment until it was quiet enough for him to speak and be heard. 'It seems from what Mr Wright has told us that Mr Hartfield has engaged with the proper processes. However, it also seems that these processes moved at an astonishing rate. And I don't believe we were aware until now that approval has already been given.'

There were scattered shouts of agreement.

'Perhaps, therefore, the questions we should ask are of the county council: why such a short, as to be almost non-existent, consultation period? Why did they not respond to any of our objections? And on what basis has this proposal been approved when our local off-grid community couldn't even get permission to erect a temporary fruit and vegetable stand on the empty plot on the allotments at Turnip Corner? Let alone the recommendation we put forward last year to the council requesting a focus on providing affordable housing for our youngsters.'

He sat down to raucous cheering.

Laurel wasn't sure Nicholas had even been paying attention until he swivelled in his chair to face Albert and replied, 'I hope you're not suggesting what I think you're suggesting? In fact, I don't have to stay and listen to this. The decision is made, we should all be grateful, and that's an end to it.'

And with that, the honourable councillor was up and heading for the door. The audience watched him go, and a few hurled some choice words at his departing back.

Following Nicholas' exit, the clamouring built until Derek

declared he would follow up on the behaviour of the council. This earned a smattering of applause.

'Before we all return to our homes,' he continued, 'I have a few announcements that I will use this opportunity to share. First, remember people, put your bins out after 6am on collection day and make sure you take them in by 7pm. There have been too many put out the night before and it makes our streets look untidy.'

Oh, good grief. Laurel ducked her head. She was guilty of that and it was only her first week. She wasn't sure, but thought that Derek was glaring at her again. She slid down a little in her seat, willing him to move on.

'Second, if we want to have a chance at most picturesque village next year, then we need to do much better with our flower beds. It seems someone, or a group of someones, has been vandalising displays. The Neighbourhood Watch has been on high alert and will endeavour to catch the culprits. Furthermore, I don't want to single anyone out, but, whilst they haven't been vandalised, the beds outside the post office are looking distinctly untidy.'

'Oh, come on. Really? You know it's the primary school children who look after those!'

The outburst came from a tired-looking young woman a couple of rows back. Laurel suspected she might be the teacher of said children. It was a pretty low blow to criticise the youngsters. Derek was not endearing himself to her.

'Third,' Derek picked up his thread as if he hadn't heard, 'the annual Autumn Festival, which this year will be on Saturday 21st October, is fast approaching. All entries for the painting competition must be submitted by 10am on Wednesday the 18th, and all entries to the fruit and vegetable, and home baking categories by 8am on the day of the festival. There will be an archery display this year and a chance to have a go yourself. Though goodness knows why; it sounds like an accident waiting to happen. The equipment is being delivered in a week or so and will be kept in the smaller storeroom here, in the village hall, which will therefore be kept locked and out of bounds to all other users for the duration. The festival will open at 10am.

'Lastly, I think you'll all have heard about the passing of Lily Armitage. I know that many of us in the village knew her and enjoyed her company. She will be missed.'

'Here, here,' sighed Albert.

Derek bowed his head, and a hush fell over the room. 'Thank you, everyone, that's all for this evening.'

Chapter Seven

Laurel hesitated on the steps and shaded her eyes so she could scan the faces of the people on the terrace.

'Laurel,' Maggie called. 'I'm so pleased to see you again.'

Laurel spotted her waving from a sun-bright corner nestled between plant pots. She smiled at the warm welcome and weaved between the tables to take her seat opposite Mrs Wright. She'd been apprehensive before setting out, but now, mellowed by the warmth, she dropped her shoulders and took a steadying breath. The chill of frosty autumn days wouldn't be far away, but on this morning the soft edges of summer lingered.

The terrace of The Pleasant Pheasant Café overlooked the village green with its war memorial, pretty flower beds, and wooden benches dotted around. To the right, across North Street, was an attractive village pond, populated with a dozen ducks floating on the green water, and book-ended by two magnificent weeping willows. The road around the green was quiet enough that customers weren't disturbed by traffic and could enjoy the tranquillity of Elderwick over a cup of herbal tea or, judging by the mouth-watering aroma, a bacon sandwich.

The café was housed in an attractive double-fronted building with sparkling windows and a hint of pretty curtains inside. The red bricks were swathed in wisteria which would bloom around the doorway in showers of purple in spring. Although those flowers had faded, the soft pink roses in pots around the terrace were abuzz with honeybees and still going strong.

'I hope you'll like it here,' said Maggie. 'Jo, the owner, makes soup to die for, especially the pea and mint, and she gets all her cakes and pastries from The Plump Tart, as you'd expect. Of course, it's too early for lunch but you can get an avocado toast or smoked salmon and scrambled egg until 11am. If you've got a sweet tooth like me, I can recommend the scone with jam and cream and a home-made elderflower cordial.' She paused for breath.

Laurel smiled. Maggie's enthusiasm for the food was engaging.

'I love food,' Maggie continued, as though reading her mind. 'If my life had been different, I would like to have been a cook in a little café. I can rustle up a mean quiche.'

Though she had already eaten breakfast, the talk of food was making Laurel's mouth water and the smell of bacon wafting from the kitchen was enough to make a dead man hungry. 'Where has your life taken you?' She studied her companion over the top of the menu. Maggie was wearing cream linen trousers, a fuchsia pink top, and a lime green scarf. Many people would shy away from such bright colours, but on Maggie they worked.

'I've been a full-time mum and now I'm a full-time wife of the councillor. Oh, and I run the WI, which is effectively another full-time job. What about you? I hear you're a psychologist. Have you got a new position down here?'

In anticipation of the question, Laurel had prepared a bland answer. 'I'm taking a bit of a time off. I've been in palliative care for about twelve years now and it was time for a break and a change of scenery.' Feeling a twinge of guilt over the evasion, she steered the conversation away. 'I intend to try the whole self-sufficiency thing, maybe go a bit *The Good Life*. I've already got the chickens.'

'You've certainly picked the most beautiful place to do it. I adore Elderwick; everyone is friendly, and it's so quiet and peaceful.' Maggie closed her eyes for a moment and beamed. When she opened them again, she asked, 'How are your chickens?'

'Not great,' Laurel admitted. 'They haven't laid a single egg since I got them.' It was her first time caring for poultry and she didn't like to admit she had no idea what she was doing wrong, despite devouring all the books she could find on caring for hens.

Maggie nodded, as though this was no surprise. 'You need to talk to Albert, your neighbour. He'll know what to do. You've met him, haven't you?'

'I have. He seems like an interesting chap, very friendly.' She wondered if she should ask Maggie about his unique dress sense.

Before she could find the right words, a tiny brunette, who looked to be about sixty, bustled out to greet them. In a smart white pinny, hair piled atop her head, and a pair of glasses perched on her nose, she exuded efficiency. 'Maggie, great to see you and your new friend...?'

'Jo, this is Laurel. She moved into Sally Belvedere's old place, and she was kind enough to meet me for a drink this morning. I was just telling her how tranquil life is here.'

'Tranquil, if you don't count Derek's crazed flowerpot vandals,' Jo chuckled. 'He'll be on the warpath today;

someone has pulled all the plants out of the tub by the village hall.'

'Oh, what a shame. They had some lovely pansies in there. Hardly the crime of the century, though.' Maggie shook her head, an indulgent smile on her lips.

Laurel enjoyed the gentle back and forth. She hoped she was wrong to be suspicious about Lily's death, because if displaced flowers were the worst crime in the village, then she had chosen the right place to rediscover her equilibrium after years in her stressful profession.

Jo mirrored the head shake, then got down to business. 'Now, what can I get for you lovely ladies?'

After they'd ordered – an elderflower cordial and scone with cream and jam each – Maggie resumed the questioning. 'I hear you've moved here all on your own. That's very brave. Oh, and then poor you, finding Lily like that. I don't know what I would have done, gone to pieces I expect. You seem very capable, but don't you miss having a man around?' She leaned towards Laurel. 'Don't you get frightened at night?'

Laurel was tempted to laugh at such an old-fashioned notion. 'Not remotely. In fact, I've never been used to having a man, or a woman, around and can manage perfectly well on my own.' She hadn't meant to sound so sharp.

Maggie sat back and her hand fluttered against her chest. 'Oh, I'm sorry, you mustn't take any notice of me. I think it's wonderful you have your career and you're self-sufficient. I just thought you'd be wanting to settle down to have children soon?' A little frown line appeared between her eyes.

Laurel considered letting it pass without comment, but it was the twenty-first century.

'Maggie, you seem very nice, but please don't assume every woman wants to be a mum.'

Maggie's cheeks went pink. 'No, of course, you're right. I'm sorry. It's just that Nicholas, my husband, is always saying that women are leaving it too late to find husbands and have children these days and he's so happy we settled down together while we were young. It's brought me such great happiness too, so...' she trailed off.

'Let's change the subject, shall we?' Laurel didn't want to start an argument. She wasn't sure she and Maggie were destined to be friends, but she was new to the area and didn't want to fall out over a couple of old-fashioned opinions. Best to move to a safer topic of conversation.

'Tell me more about yourself.'

'Oh, why would you want to know about me?' Maggie furrowed her brow.

'Because you've been very kind and invited me for tea and cake when I don't know anyone else yet. And because I'm interested to get to know you.'

'Okay, well, let me see. I'm married to Nicholas, as you know, and we have two wonderful children, Vanessa and Conner, both adults now, of course. We live at The Grange, just off South Street, Nicholas and I that is, the children live in London and Manchester and both are very successful.' Her eyes shone as she spoke about her children.

When Maggie offered nothing further, Laurel asked, 'And what about you?'

'Well, that's it, dear.'

For a second, Laurel was flummoxed, but then tried a different approach. 'You mentioned you like to cook. Where did you learn? What do you like to make?'

She brightened. 'My mum taught me. She was a superb cook, and she was completely self-taught. She wanted to do the food for my wedding, but Nicholas said we should hire caterers.'

Back to Nicholas already. 'Did you consider becoming a professional?'

'Oh goodness me no, not really. I enjoy cooking for Nicholas, and I did for the children when they were at home, but nothing more than that.' Then, in a hushed voice, as though it was some dirty secret, she added, 'In fact, for a time, I wanted to join the police.'

'Wow, that's different.' This woman had hidden depths. Laurel tried picturing her in uniform, walking the beat, but couldn't quite see it.

'Yes, you wouldn't think it, would you. I don't suppose I quite look the part?' She patted her hair.

'Why didn't you join?' Laurel thought she could take a good guess at the answer.

'It wasn't for me. It was a silly notion I had from watching too much *Cagney and Lacey* or some such. Besides, Nicholas felt it was better for me to stay home with the children, and he was right.'

There it was.

Jo arrived with their order, and they fell quiet for a few moments as they savoured the still warm scones topped with immoderate helpings of jam and cream.

'Maggie, these are delicious. You're a star for introducing me to this place, but my hips won't thank you!'

Maggie gave a wicked grin. 'Anyway, enough about me. Tell me more about you. You're not a criminal psychologist, I suppose?'

People often had funny ideas about psychologists and were disappointed when she explained what she did in reality. She was forever stuck between those who viewed her as a type of mind-reading mystic, and those who saw therapy as nothing more than a cup of tea and a good chat.

'No, clinical. I worked in a hospital. I work with– *worked* with people who have life-limiting conditions like cancer and motor neurone disease. My role was to help people to manage their illness, sometimes to come to terms with it if they were struggling with that or to find a way to improve their quality of life even if it was going to be much shorter than expected.' It made her cringe to talk about helping others to manage when she'd made such a mess of things herself.

'Goodness, what an important job to do, but how do you keep from being upset all the time?'

'It is hard,' Laurel agreed, 'and it does take a toll. It really does.'

'If it's not too indelicate to say, maybe it was good you were the one to find Lily. I suppose you're... I mean... oh dear.'

Laurel guessed what Maggie was trying to say. 'You mean because of my work I'm more used to death? I guess that's true. Mind you, Lou, the post-lady, she didn't seem fazed at all.'

'And on your first day in Elderwick.' Maggie touched her hand.

'You asked about criminal psychology. Is it something you're interested in?' Eager to change the subject again, Laurel brought the focus back to Maggie.

She clasped her hands and leaned in, narrowly avoiding a spot of jam on the table. 'I find it fascinating! I watch all the TV programmes where they have psychologist profilers, and I love the Tony Hill books by Val McDermid. I think I would have made a good detective. Well, I'm not sure I could be tough with the criminals, but I'm good at spotting clues and figuring things out. You're probably good at that too, being a psychologist?' Maggie seemed to be warming to the topic and hadn't mentioned Nicholas again yet.

'I'm not sure about that,' said Laurel with a grin. 'Speaking of books though,' *another nice redirect*, 'I'm rather partial to a good police procedural or psychological thriller myself.'

Maggie looked delighted. 'You know, I was thinking of

starting a book club. One dedicated to exactly those kinds of books, and maybe some cosy murder mysteries, too.'

'That could be fun. You should do it. I'd join.' Laurel was warming to Maggie, after all, and it seemed they shared at least two passions: food and books. A reading group could be a useful way to build on her socialising skills – goodness knows, that would be a better item on her *new life* agenda than running around playing amateur detective over a death.

Maggie pulled a face. 'You might be the only one. There was a club in Elderwick before, but Gladys and Doris only ever wanted to read romance novels or Catherine Cookson and everyone else just went along with them. I mean, I like Catherine Cookson, but a bit of variety would have been nice.'

'Mmm...' Laurel mumbled through another bite of scone.

'I had to stop going in the end because we were all meant to take turns in hosting the meeting, but Nicholas wouldn't allow us to meet at our house, so it didn't seem right for me to stay in the group. If it were just the two of us, though...' She hesitated. 'Perhaps one day when Nicholas is out at work, you could come round? It would have to be when he's out because he doesn't like to be disturbed at home. Or maybe it's a bad idea?'

Maggie glanced away, but not before Laurel saw the hope in her expression. She bit her tongue. Not wanting Maggie to lose courage, she offered a solution. 'I'll tell you what, why don't you come round to mine instead? We can even get some cakes from the bakery. We can start our own crime fiction book club.'

Maggie looked thrilled. 'Really? That would be wonderful. I'll need to check with Nicholas first, but let's swap numbers so we can arrange a date. I don't have a mobile since there's never any signal in this village, but remind me when we've finished eating and I'll give you my landline.'

'What book should we start with?' asked Laurel.

'Well, I know it's rather old-fashioned, and hardly a

psychological thriller, but how about *Murder is Easy* by Agatha Christie? I've read most of her books, but never that one. If you'd prefer something else though?'

'No, that's a good suggestion. What's it about?'

Maggie's impish grin resurfaced. 'Murder in a little country village.'

Chapter Eight

A couple of days after Rose's second phone call and Laurel was still mulling over the strange events that had happened since her arrival in Elderwick. A good long walk was called for. The perfect activity to help her step back and get her thoughts in order.

Before her purchase of Myrtle Cottage had completed, she'd researched local walks in anticipation of upping her exercise and adopting a healthier lifestyle once she'd moved, and she knew exactly which walk she wanted to try first. The route took her out of the village and along a shady track where the blackberries were plentiful and copper leaves were only just beginning to stipple the canopy. She crossed a bridge over a disused rail line and turned down a farm track before veering off through a kissing gate to start a lung-stretching climb up Elder Hill. Her legs were aching as she gained the top and paused to catch her breath.

She'd come out onto a plateau of wild grasses where skylarks burst upwards to hover silhouetted against the sky. A few yards on there was a thoughtfully placed bench on which she sat with a sigh, letting the liquid melody of the small brown birds wash over her as the breeze cooled her skin.

So far, her relocation north hadn't gone quite as planned. In fact, that was an understatement. Finding an elderly, deceased lady on day one was not the ideal start, but to follow that with suspecting murder based on zero actual evidence. Was she being crazy, or – she felt a twist in her stomach – was this part of her need to make amends for what had happened *before*? Sometimes, being a psychologist was a pain; why couldn't she let herself do something illogical *just because*, why did she always have to analyse it?

She sprang to her feet and set off at a brisk pace, hustling down the hill. She pushed energy into her feet, steadied her breathing, and kept her attention on the sheep in the fields, the clouds barely moving above... anything but death.

Arriving back in Elderwick, with sweat making corkscrews of her hair, she passed the pub, The Snooty Fox, and heard raised voices. A hulking black Range Rover with the personalised number plate MAH 1 was slewed across two parking spaces outside. Could it belong to the Marcus Hartfield of Elderwick Hall she'd heard mentioned at the village meeting?

On the spur of the moment, she detoured across the road and pushed through the door and into the bar. Inside, modern fixtures and décor were married with exposed stone walls and original oak beams creating a bright, clean space that maintained an old world charm. Apart from a man behind the bar, the place was deserted. She ordered a half of local cider on the barman's recommendation and was surprised at the raging thirst woken with the first sip. She made short work of the drink and asked for another.

'I'm Sam,' he said, as he refilled her glass. 'And you must be Doctor Nightingale?'

Laurel shuffled her feet. It was unsettling to have people know who she was before she'd met them.

Sam grinned at her. 'Don't worry, you'll get used to it, everyone knowing your business.'

She wasn't sure she would, but she didn't want to get a reputation for being unfriendly. 'I'm sure I will.' She pulled her mouth into a smile and started on her second cider. 'I didn't realise Yorkshire was a cider place, but this is delicious.' Being from Somerset, she knew a good cider when she tasted one, but had always associated the drink with the South West, never Yorkshire.

Sam wiped a cloth over the bar, then refilled a container with cocktail umbrellas. 'It's gaining ground up here. There's a place near Market Weighton does a lovely drop, but mostly we sell what they produce up at our very own Drumble's Hive.'

'The commune?' she asked. 'I met someone from there the other day, Hitesh. Do you know him?'

'Yes, I know him, he's the one who brings our cider over for us. It's quite famous, you know, the cider and the commune.' He put away the cloth and turned to her with a sparkle in his eyes. 'Speaking of famous, we once had Ethan Hawke in here. How's that for celebrity?'

She levelled a stare at him and injected a teasing note of doubt into her tone. 'Really?'

'Oh, there's lots of famous people around these parts, not as they like you to know that, but they all recognise a good hostelry with a warm welcome when they find one. If you come in from time to time, you might be lucky enough to meet some of them.'

'That would be lucky.'

An angry shout from somewhere outside made Laurel turn to look through the windows.

Sam grunted. 'Speaking of warm welcomes, that's Mr Hartfield, enjoying a *quiet* drink out the back with Mr Wright and Barclay. People keep showing up to heckle him about his development. I was out collecting glasses a minute ago and it was working up to be a bit tense. Not that he can't take care of himself, mind.'

'Out back?' This could be her chance to get a look at the elusive villain of the village.

'Up the passage.' Sam pointed.

She excused herself and followed a narrow corridor through to the garden at the rear. On emerging into the golden evening light, her eyes were first drawn to the swell of bronze hills stretching to the horizon. She gasped at how beautiful it was and would have remained transfixed if not for the angry mob.

There must have been twenty people on their feet facing a tall dark-haired man, well dressed but casual in jeans and a black T-shirt, standing on a bench, calling for people to quieten down. Marcus Wright, presumably. Laurel joined the back of the crowd and rose onto her tiptoes to get a better look.

'If I can just say a few words, then we can all return to our drinks and get on with our evening.'

Near Marcus, she spotted Nicholas Wright, hair and teeth perfect as ever, and there was a striking brunette seated to his left. *She looks familiar*, she thought, but couldn't put a name to the face.

'I appreciate that there's a great deal of concern about our development plans, but I can assure you everything will be done with the utmost care and ultimately to the benefit of you all.' Marcus gestured to Nicholas. 'I understand that Councillor Wright–'

Someone booed.

'–has explained we have been through all the proper channels and have the necessary approvals. However, the plans can only ever tell part of the story and won't be able to show you just what a wonderful destination we're building. So, I would like to invite you all to visit Elderwick Hall and grounds next Saturday to discover for yourselves just what it is we intend to create.'

'Fancy pictures and presentations aren't going to convince us,' called a man from near the front.

'Perhaps not, but what have you got to lose by looking? We will bring new jobs to the area. A new restaurant for a start. One in which we hope to offer produce from our local commune, Drumble's Hive, and bread and cakes from our wonderful village bakery. We want this development to be for everyone. It's not just about new people moving in; it's about revitalising our local economy to the advantage of all. Not only that, but we plan to host a wide range of events and activities that locals can enjoy. Everything from yoga and meditation, to foraging workshops, and self-defence classes.'

It was quite the sales pitch, and Laurel saw a few heads nodding amongst the masses.

He turned serious. 'Please, don't forget, my family has lived in Elderwick since the late 1700s. I love this village and only want the best for it. Now if you wouldn't mind, my wife,' he gestured towards the brunette, 'and I are here for a quiet drink on a lovely evening. If you could all go about your business, it would be much appreciated. And as a token of my thanks, please have a drink on me.'

That got a few cheers. Some people were easily bought. As the majority made a dash for the bar, Laurel spied Albert sitting at a table and went over to ask if she could join him. *No rabbit with him today*, she noted.

His face lit up when he saw her. 'Laurel, sit, sit. It's good to see you. Been for a walk?'

'I have, up around Elder Hill and back.' She settled herself down and brushed a strand of sweaty hair off her forehead.

'Did you arrive in time for the show? This must be the first time you've seen Marcus. What are your impressions?'

'He's bad at parking, but he appears to be very charming. Bit of a smooth talker, perhaps.' She omitted her thoughts on how attractive he was. Quite at odds to the older, portly gentleman in tweed she'd pictured when she'd first heard his name.

'Hmm. And of course, you've already seen Nasty Nicholas in action at the community meeting.' He clapped a hand to his mouth. 'Sorry, I shouldn't be bad-mouthing folk. I should let you form your own opinions.'

Laurel found it hard to believe Albert said anything by mistake. She barely knew him, but he was a smart man. Besides, following her meeting with Maggie, her opinion of Nicholas aligned with Albert's.

'It's not my place to say,' he continued, 'but I'm glad you've palled up with Maggie. I think it'll do her good. She's becoming far too quiet and timid. She needs a confidence boost.' Albert was watching her. 'You'll see, when she's with Nicholas, she's a whole different woman.'

Laurel didn't doubt it, but felt it was too soon, and she was too new to the village to pass comment. She chose to be diplomatic. 'I'm enjoying getting to know her, and you. You've both been so warm and welcoming.'

He twinkled at her. 'I'm glad to hear it. It can't be easy, moving to a whole new part of the country?'

'No, and I don't make friends easily.' *Why did I say that?* She wanted to take back the words but found herself adding, 'I haven't always made enough time for friends, and I want to change that.' It was embarrassing to admit, as an adult, she'd never mastered the art of making and maintaining friendships, but why was she telling this veritable stranger?

'You seem to be making a pretty good job of it so far and I'm not prying, but if you ever want to talk, you just come and find me. Aroon and I always have time to help set the world to rights.' He gave the back of her hand an affectionate tap. 'You must always let me know if there's anything I can do. I might be clocking up the years, but I like to be of service where I can.'

Feeling vulnerable after her unexpected admission, and touched by Albert's kindness, she swallowed hard and focused on her drink until she could think of a safer subject. *Old habits die hard.* 'Actually, it's probably not what you mean, but I could use some chicken advice, if that's okay? Maggie tells me you're the man who knows.'

'By all means, ask away. I've spent my life surrounded by chicks, so I know a thing or two. What's the problem?'

A snort of laughter escaped, which she tried to cover with a cough. Albert didn't seem to have noticed. 'They're not laying any eggs,' she said when she had herself under control. 'I've read all the books. They've got a comfy house, the right food. What am I doing wrong?'

'Well, it all rather depends, and... you know what, this could take a while. Shall I fetch us each another drink and then we can see what's to do? Might as well make the most of Marcus' generosity.'

She nodded with enthusiasm. He got up and headed inside to the bar and Laurel was drawn back to the view. Her new cottage had a pleasant outlook over trees at the front and fields at the back, but this was special. Lost as she was in the moment, she felt a prickle on the back of her neck. It took her a second, but she found Marcus' wife was looking at her. When their eyes met, she gave a faint smile and made her way over.

'Do you mind if I sit? Marcus is talking shop with Nic, and it's boring the bloody pants off me. Plus, I think Derek Fisher is heading their way, and I can do without that. I'm Petra. You're new around here, aren't you?'

Flustered to be looking so dishevelled and grubby against

the young woman's effortless style and poise, Laurel put on her best smile and held out a hand. 'I am. I'm Laurel. It's nice to meet you.' They shook and Laurel, seeing her close up, was finally able to place her. 'You're Petra Pipenko! You do the vlog about young women starting their own businesses. I saw you on *Question Time*.' She hoped she wasn't gushing. Had the cider gone to her head? She was usually far more reserved.

'That's me.' Her half-smile broke into a wide beam. 'Hi, Albert.'

'Hello there, Petra.' Albert put down a tray on which were balanced two orange drinks and two shots. 'Good old Sam knows to keep us seniors happy and not keep us waiting at the bar. I thought we could try Porn Star Martinis.'

'Okay, wow,' said Laurel. 'I didn't think this was a cocktail kind of place, but I'm up for a new experience.' She sipped the lurid liquid while she tried to work out what to do with the shot of what must be Prosecco.

'It was my idea,' said Petra, 'I told Marcus that all pubs these days should have a cocktail menu. Just because we're in Yorkshire doesn't mean everyone only drinks ale. And see, now even Albert's drinking them.' Her face lit up as she smiled at him; it was obvious what Marcus saw in her.

'Petra, my dear, I'm always open to novelties,' Albert replied, his eyes crinkling. 'But look, where are my manners? You don't have a drink. I shall nip back and get you one.'

As he left again, Laurel caught Petra's eye and mouthed 'Porn Star Martini'. They giggled.

'He's quite the charmer, isn't he?' Petra agreed.

'Who do we have here?'

The voice from behind her left shoulder made Laurel start. She turned and found herself eyes to chest with Marcus. Up close, he was even more attractive with soft lines at his eyes, and were those dimples?

'Speaking of charmers...' Petra offered her cheek for him to kiss. 'This is my husband, Marcus.'

'I don't think we've met?' he said, holding out his hand.

'I'm Laurel, it's a pleasure to meet me... I mean you.' *Stop talking!* A pretty face wasn't usually enough to make her go giddy. Perhaps it was the effect of the cocktail.

He gripped her hand in his own. 'The pleasure is indeed all mine.'

Her heart fluttered and her cheeks warmed.

Letting go of her hand, which she could have sworn he held for a beat longer than necessary, Marcus turned to Petra and told her he was leaving soon with Barclay, if she would like a lift.

'I've got a meeting back at the Hall. The local plod thinks we might be troubled by the locals opposed to the development and he wants to check our security measures from the ground to the roof, if you can believe it?'

'You're going to humour him, though, aren't you?' Petra stroked his arm.

'Of course, dear, but if you're not coming back with me, he's going out on the roof on his own. Hope he's got sense not to get himself stuck like Barclay did, because he'll not get me out there to bloody rescue him.' He shuddered.

Petra rolled her eyes and said she was going to stay at the pub for a while longer. Waving her husband goodbye, she waited until he was out of sight before turning back to Laurel. 'He's cute, isn't he?'

Laurel grinned. This is what she'd been missing for so long: good company, idle chatter, and no stress. The disquietude troubling her mind since she'd found Lily was lifting. It had been ridiculous to imagine the death was in any way sinister, and she needed to put such notions from her head.

Chapter Nine

An hour later, Laurel was concentrating hard on getting her key into the lock of her front door. Her fingers were clumsy and her vision blurry, but she had a pleasant buzz thrumming in her head. For once, her shoulders were relaxed, and she wasn't frowning or clenching her jaw. About time, too. For years, work had been everything. Even her days off were spent either in the office, on her laptop or reading work-related journals. It had sustained her, got her through the dark times after her mum's death, but eventually the stress had been too much. She'd taken it too far.

Inside, she headed for the kitchen and put the kettle on for a cup of camomile tea, only to be interrupted by a knock. She wasn't expecting anyone. She stuck her head round the corner to look through the wavy glass in the door, but all she could see was a distorted figure. Still mellow, but no longer tipsy, she went to see who was calling on her.

'Ms Nightingale, we haven't met properly,' he declared. 'I'm Mr Derek Fisher.'

Anxiety bloomed in her chest. 'Derek, hi. How can I help? Do you want to come in?'

He nodded and followed her through to the kitchen.

Unlike the kitchen in Lily's house, Laurel's was small and quite dark. She was trying to think of it as cosy, but the oppressive dark wood cabinets didn't help. She intended to change them or to paint them a lighter colour, at least. If they were cream, they'd lift the room and would look great with the pale green she planned to put on the walls.

Derek sat at the tiny table for two, nestled against the wall between the fridge and the door to the garden. He smoothed his thinning hair, placed his hands on the well-worn surface and waited for Laurel to sit. He turned down her offer of a tea or a coffee.

'Ms Nightingale–'

'Laurel, please.'

'I'd rather keep things formal, if you don't mind.'

'Okay.' He sounded serious. She couldn't for the life of her think what he was there to talk about, *formally* or otherwise, unless this was about the bloody bins.

'Ms Nightingale, I understand you are a counsellor or psychologist or some such. Is that correct?'

Laurel's heart beat a little faster. 'I'm a clinical psychologist, if that's what you mean?'

'Quite. Now, I'm led to understand that um, *clinical psychologists*,' he said it the way a business owner might say *tax inspector*, 'work privately, often from their own homes.'

'Yes, certainly some do.'

'Well, I am here to ensure you understand that such a thing is not permitted here.'

She tilted her head. 'I'm sorry?' Why did he think he could tell her what she was and wasn't permitted to do in her own home?

'You are not permitted to operate a business from these premises.'

'I don't think that's accurate.' She held her hands palm up. She didn't want to appear defensive or show her agitation. 'My solicitor went through all the covenants connected to this building and whilst I'm not allowed to raise pigs or hang washing after midnight, I'm pretty sure I can run a business if I want to.' She hadn't yet decided if she wanted to establish her own private practice, but this jumped-up, self-appointed village superintendent wasn't going to tell her what she could or couldn't do.

He ignored her and continued. 'Should you attempt to operate a business from these premises, I will have no choice but to report you to the council and you will be asked to cease and desist.'

She pulled a face. 'I don't understand. On what grounds could I be forced to *cease and desist?*'

'It's not something we want happening here in the village.' He was getting red in the face and was clasping his hands together so tightly his knuckles were turning white.

What is going on here? 'I still don't understand. What is it you think I do? What would be so objectionable that you'd try to stop me?'

'It could be any number of things.' He ticked them off on his fingers, his voice getting louder with each. 'Your patients could be dangerous to residents. We don't want people with mental problems coming into the village. We don't want comings and goings at all hours. There's nowhere here for people to park without blocking your neighbours, and...' he hesitated, '...and it's not proper for a young woman to be entertaining strange men in her home.'

Had she gone back in time? What with Maggie telling her she needed to be married and having babies, and now Derek telling her how to behave like a *proper* young woman. And she was offended by the disparaging way he used the term *people with mental problems.* She inhaled and held back the retort on the tip of her tongue. Her patients often felt anger and fear, and it wasn't unusual for them to misdirect those feelings onto her. Was that happening here? Derek's *reasons* didn't explain the anguish she could see playing out across his face.

'Derek, what's this really about?'

He went rigid. 'Don't you dare try to turn this on me with your questions. I'll say it bluntly if that's what it takes. Don't be peddling your quack science here.' He stood, his chair scrapping across the floorboards. 'There'll be consequences if you do. I'll see myself out.'

Laurel's heart thudded as adrenaline flooded her veins. As Derek opened the door and stepped outside, she caught up to him. 'Derek, you don't get to come round here and tell me what I can and can't do in my own home. Seemingly the only basis for which is what you personally think is right and proper. I am a clinical psychologist, a professional. I try to help people and if I want to do that from here, then I'm damn well going to do it! And it's *Doctor* Nightingale to you,' she shouted.

Derek paused, his hand on the gate. He turned and spoke in a loud but shaking voice, 'You don't help people. People like you say you want to make people better, but you lie, you manipulate, and you made everything worse. You destroy lives with what you do!' He wrenched open the gate and stormed off up the lane.

Laurel slammed the door shut and burst into angry tears. He didn't know her, couldn't possibly know her work. The professional in her could see he must be railing against a wound in his own life – *made* everything worse, he'd said – but that last retort had cut close to home.

Chapter Ten

Maggie arrived at 10am with a box bearing the name The Plump Tart. The same type of box Laurel remembered seeing in Lily's kitchen. Maggie untied the decorative purple ribbon and lifted the lid, motioning Laurel to come and look. Inside were two perfect fruit tarts with crisp pastry bases and rich crème patisserie loaded with sliced strawberries, deep pink raspberries, and plump spheres of blueberries, all glossy with apricot glaze.

Laurel's stomach rumbled. 'Maggie, you shouldn't have.'

'Well, if you don't want yours...' Maggie teased.

'Now, let's not be hasty. I definitely didn't say that, and it would be rude for me to refuse.' Laurel opened the fridge, grabbed a pitcher of cloudy lemonade she'd made for the occasion, and plucked two plates and dessert forks from the dresser. 'Let's take them out to the garden since it's such a glorious morning. We can try out my new bistro set and enjoy the sun.' She had intended to tell Maggie about Derek's visit, but it was such a lovely morning, and she didn't want to ruin the mood.

The kitchen door was blocked with disassembled boxes

ready to be put out for recycling, so they went through the living room and out via the French windows.

The stone terrace where the table and chairs waited was shaded by climbing roses winding up and around a wooden pergola. Across the lawn, at the far end of the garden, where it would get both sun and shade, was the coop she had bought for her newly acquired brood of chickens. To Laurel, there was no sound more relaxing than the soft clucks that came from her three hens as they scratched about in the dirt, looking for insects.

Laurel and Maggie sat in companionable silence for a moment, enjoying the peace and the lemonade.

'We should probably get down to business and talk about the book,' said Maggie as she rummaged in her bag and pulled out her copy of the novel they were to discuss. Rather than open it, however, she pushed it to the side and started instead on her fruit tart.

'I have to admit, I haven't quite got to the end of it yet.' Laurel licked cream from her fork. In truth, she'd only managed the first chapter before getting distracted by a new Jasper Fforde novel instead.

'Oh, I'm so glad you said that. Me too.' Maggie gave a nervous laugh. 'I've had so much on my mind. The vicar has asked me to help with the arrangements for Lily's funeral until her poor daughter, Rose, arrives from abroad.'

'Rose?' Laurel speared a strawberry. 'She phoned again the other day.' She popped the last raspberry into her mouth while she thought about how much to tell Maggie. Rose might not thank her for sharing the coroner's conjecture about suicide.

'What did she say?'

Despite her hesitation and the resolution she'd made in the beer garden of The Snooty Fox to forget her suspicion of murder, the idea hadn't quit. Perhaps it would help to run it by Maggie. 'Can we keep this between us?'

Maggie gave an emphatic nod.

'Rose said Lily might have been poisoned.' It didn't sound so plausible anymore. Why would anyone poison an elderly lady?

'Oh, goodness me.' Maggie's hand went to her mouth. 'That's dreadful. I thought it was a heart attack?'

'Rose heard from the coroner's office who said it looks like Lily died from poison. They believe it was an accident or maybe suicide.' She watched Maggie's face, interested to see her reaction.

'Suicide? No, it must have been an accident. Lily wouldn't have taken her own life.'

That was interesting: two people, both of whom had known Lily, couldn't believe she would have harmed herself. 'Rose doesn't accept the suicide angle, either. I appreciate there's no way anyone can tell for certain when someone is considering ending their life, but Rose is convinced her mum was settled and happy. She's just as certain that there's no way her mum would have taken something poisonous by mistake.'

'I agree. Lily was always cheery, and sharp as a tack. No, the coroner has it wrong.' A line between her eyebrows deepened, and she chewed on her lip. 'What if... this is ridiculous – and maybe reading Agatha Christie has something to do with it – but what if there was foul play?'

Keeping her voice neutral, Laurel asked, 'You think it's possible that someone deliberately poisoned Lily?'

Maggie shrugged. 'I'm not saying that, but maybe it's a possibility and since we're here and Rose isn't...'

'We should check it out for her?' Laurel finished the sentence. So much for her hesitation to get involved. Without wanting to sound too eager, she suggested, 'We could take a trip over to Lily's house to see if there's anything there that might give us a clue about what happened. I've got the key; Rose asked me to keep it safe. I could call her and ask her if she would be okay with us looking around. I'm sure she would be.'

'Maybe.'

Laurel's stomach gurgled again. What did it say about her that her hunger held such sway even when discussing a potential murder? Then she gave up wondering and attacked the rest of the tart.

'I know I was waffling about foul play a moment ago, but I am struggling to believe someone harmed her on purpose. Lily was lovely.' Maggie took a bite of her own tart and chewed, tapping her fingers on the table.

'Tell me about her?'

She smiled. 'From the moment she moved here, Lily fit right in. She was sparky, did amazing things with her garden, and was always the first to volunteer for community projects and events. Everyone who knew her liked her. Even Derek liked her! Liked, not just tolerated like he does the rest of us. I can't, try as I might, think of a single person who would have wanted to harm her. No-one who lives here, that's for certain.'

'Were she and Derek...?'

'No.' Maggie shuddered. 'Can you imagine... Friends only. She was quite a bit older than him.'

'Could it have been someone from outside the village, then?'

'I'm not sure she had many visitors. Not much goes unnoticed around here. Between them, the ladies in the WI know most of the gossip, so I would probably have heard from them if there was anyone suspicious hanging around or any dodgy characters knocking on Lily's door. And I don't think she has family other than her daughter, and she's in New Zealand.'

'How about Hitesh? I bumped into him in Lily's garden. Do you know him?'

'A little. Lily mentioned him a few times. He used to help

her out in the garden with the things that she couldn't manage herself. When I've spoken to him, he's always been friendly.'

'He said he's been at the commune place for a while, but I don't suppose you know anything about where he was or what he did before moving here?'

'I don't.'

'It might be useful to talk to him then. To ask if he knows anything and to find out a bit more about him. We could see if we can find out who knew about her key too. She used to leave a spare key where anyone could find it. Rose told me. It was in such an obvious place.'

'You sound serious,' said Maggie. 'Do you really think someone killed her? Things like that don't happen in Elderwick.'

Maggie was right, she was getting carried away, but she just couldn't shake the feeling that there was something odd about Lily's death. 'It is strange though, isn't it? It's difficult to poison yourself inadvertently these days when everything has a warning label on it. Plus, if she had eaten or drunk something by mistake, surely whatever poison she took would have been seen by the police? Although...'

'Although, what?'

'They might have missed it if they weren't specifically looking for a source of poison.'

'I suppose that's possible. Since they thought it was a natural death.' Maggie sounded doubtful.

If she didn't do something, she knew the niggle would linger, burrowing its way into her brain and lurking like an itch she couldn't scratch. 'This is going to bug me unless I go back and look round at Lily's. How would you feel if you and I go round there with Rose's permission? Hopefully, we'll find proof it was just an accident after all.'

Maggie tucked a loose strand of hair behind her ear. 'It couldn't do any harm.'

'And we should talk to Hitesh and Lou, the postwoman, in case they can tell us anything useful,' she couldn't resist adding. 'But that's it. Then we're done.'

'I have a dinner in London with Nicholas this evening. We're catching the train this afternoon and staying overnight. Could we go tomorrow?' She looked at her watch. 'Fiddlesticks, I'd better go in a minute. I haven't packed Nicholas' case yet and he won't want to risk being late getting to the station.'

Laurel didn't think she'd ever heard anyone say fiddlesticks in real life. 'Of course. I've got some things to be getting on with. I need to read up about chicken rearing, see if I can find out why they're not laying. Plus, I should unpack the last few boxes that are still in the spare bedroom. How about we get together tomorrow for a late lunch at the café, then we can go to the house?'

Maggie put her hand to her cheeks, a curve creeping into her lips. 'I know I shouldn't be saying this because someone has died, but this is a bit exciting. We're like a real-life Rosemary and Thyme.'

Chapter Eleven

Laurel dashed up the street, her umbrella losing the battle against the downpour. The clear blue skies and sun of the previous afternoon had disappeared, replaced by heavy clouds swollen with enough rain to wash away any memory of summer.

Inside The Pleasant Pheasant, she found Maggie waiting for her.

'Don't be mad.'

'Why would I be mad?' Laurel asked as she dried her hands on her jeans and sat down.

'I might have arranged a blind date for you.' Maggie gave her a nervous smile.

'I see.'

'Now, I know you're going to say you don't need a man. I understand all that, but hear me out.' Maggie fiddled with her napkin. 'He's a police officer.'

'Okay.' She drew out the word. She'd only just told Albert she wanted to make more friends, but was she ready for a blind date?

Maggie leaned in and whispered, 'We're investigating a

possible murder. Imagine how helpful it could be to have an investigator whose brains we can pick.'

Laurel had to give her points for the strained justification.

'It's only a drink, but I understand if you don't want to go.'

Be open to new opportunities. It was meant to be her new mantra. 'Okay, tell me a bit about him, but no promises.'

Maggie clapped her hands. 'He's a lovely man. His name's Nathan Tillow, he's forty-seven years old, divorced two years ago, no children, he lives on the edge of the village in the little row of cottages between here and Little Wick. He's a very hard worker and very attractive. And it's just one drink in The Snooty Fox.'

'And how do you know Nathan?'

'Oh, he's one of our local policemen and well known around here. Plus, he's the son of Nicholas' colleague on the council. We bumped into Nathan on the train yesterday. Well, I did. Nicholas was in First Class and I needed to stretch my legs so I went for a wander down the carriages. We had a friendly chat between Doncaster and Retford and I just mentioned that I had a new, young, attractive single friend and he said he would like to meet you.'

Laurel winced, picturing the poor guy trapped on the train with no escape, agreeing to a date because Maggie wouldn't take no for an answer. He would probably call and cancel before they ever met.

'He said that he would like to meet me? You didn't suggest it?'

'Not at all. He said that he would be delighted to make your acquaintance. Well, he maybe didn't say that exactly, but I'm sure he will be. I said that you'd meet him on Thursday evening at 7pm.'

'If you've already arranged a date and time, it's something of a fait accompli.'

Maggie gave her a sweet smile.

Laurel pinched the bridge of her nose as she thought. 'I'll make a deal with you. I will meet Nathan, but on the condition that you and I will also have an evening out together sometime. A chance to let our hair down and enjoy a meal that neither of us has had to cook. Deal?'

'I could do that one evening when Nicholas is dining out for work, perhaps. I'll need to check with him.'

It was all Laurel could do not to roll her eyes.

'As long as he says it's all right, then you have a deal,' Maggie concluded.

'Good. I won't forget you know. I have an impressive memory, especially when it comes to food!' She grinned. *What have I let myself in for?* 'Now our social lives are sorted, let's get down to business, shall we?'

'Speaking of food, can we order lunch first? I'm quite hungry.' Maggie was already inspecting the specials board.

They deliberated over the tempting dishes on offer until Laurel plumped for a bacon and brie sandwich on freshly baked bread, and Maggie opted for the quiche of the day: roasted red pepper and goat's cheese. It sounded so delicious that Laurel almost changed her mind, but stuck with the sandwich. When it came, she was glad she had and savoured the perfect combination of soft melting brie and salty, crispy bacon. Heaven.

'I've been thinking,' said Maggie between bites. 'In terms of interviews, we could start by speaking to Lou? She'll be easy to track down this afternoon. Around 2pm, her round takes her past Lily's place, and since she's not a suspect – we don't suspect her, do we? – getting the information we need should be straightforward.'

Laurel wiped her fingers. 'I mean, everyone is a suspect at this stage and murderers have been known to involve themselves in the aftermath of their crimes... which I admit I only know from books, so that might not be true. Okay, so she's an unlikely suspect.'

'We could wait for her at Lily's house and watch out for her coming up the street. That way we can be out of the rain and can look round the house while we wait.'

'Good idea. Plus, being back near the house when we see her might jog her memory, and if Hitesh turns up in the garden again, he can be our second interviewee. Though, with this weather, I doubt he'll be harvesting cobnuts today.' She took another bite of her sandwich and almost groaned at how delicious it was.

'I have my WI meeting on Thursday evening. If you like, I can have a chat with the ladies about Lily and see if anything comes up?'

'Good idea,' Laurel replied with her mouth full.

'*Do* you think something bad happened to her?' Maggie asked again.

Laurel mulled over the question. 'Probably not. Things like that don't really happen. I mean, they do, but not like this. Probably. Anyway, I couldn't get Rose on the phone, but I emailed her to let her know our plan and in her reply she seemed all right with it. As long as we're not accusing anyone of anything, I don't think we're doing any harm.'

Plans made, their conversation turned to food, with Maggie listing the different desserts available that day in order of preference. It was no contest, and two salted caramel brownies were ordered and polished off.

When Jo had cleared the plates, Laurel reached for her bag to get her purse. 'My treat today. Oh.' She blushed. 'Oh Maggie, this is embarrassing. I thought my purse was in here, but it's not. I must have forgotten it at home.'

'Don't fret, you can treat me next time.'

'Thank you,' said Laurel, having another rummage through her belongings. She could have sworn her purse was in her bag. *So much for boasting about her memory.*

Chapter Twelve

C hurch View looked very different in the rain under the glowering skies as Laurel approached with Maggie by her side. She knew it was just her imagination, but it felt sinister now, as though the house had secrets it didn't want to share. Before, in the sunlight, it was easy to imagine that the owner had popped out for a while and would be back shortly. Now, the house was an empty husk.

At the back door, Laurel pulled the key from her pocket and inserted it in the lock. At first it wouldn't turn. The door had swollen in the damp and was reluctant to open.

'What are we looking for?' Maggie whispered when they made it inside.

'I'm not sure, but hopefully we'll know it if we see it.' Laurel couldn't help dropping her voice, too. *Stop being so fanciful*, she admonished.

'It's spooky in here.' Maggie echoed Laurel's feeling. The gloom wasn't helping. The bright airy kitchen of her last visit was cast in semi-darkness.

'Can we put a light on?'

Laurel flipped the switch, and the stark lights banished the shadows. 'Well, the kitchen is the most likely place to find poison. Shall we check it out?'

They went through each cupboard, the fridge, freezer, inside the oven, and even the microwave. The cupboards contained boxes of cereal, jars of dusty spices, and various tins, but nothing of note. Under the sink were the usual collection of cleaning products, all eco-friendly as Rose had said, with very few warning labels. Even if any were lethal, it seemed unlikely that Lily had drunk from one then put the bottle back before sitting down to die.

On the worktop was a cookery book and an empty biscuit tin standing lonely beside the kettle. Maggie plonked herself down on a chair at the dining table, looked in the empty bakery box, and poked at the dried-out stems in the vase on the table.

'It's upsetting to think about Lily being here one minute, picking flowers for the table and then gone the next.' She snapped her fingers. 'Just like that.'

Laurel regarded her, a small line furrowing her brow. 'You okay to carry on?'

'Yes.' It came out more of a sigh than a word. She cleared her throat. 'Yes,' she repeated. 'I'm fine. It brings it home though, doesn't it?'

Not trusting herself to answer, Laurel cast around, looking for anywhere they hadn't already searched.

Maggie hoisted herself up from the chair and shuffled back towards the door. 'Do you think there might be something in here?' She'd pulled back a curtain covering a cubby behind the door in which sat two bins. The bin for general rubbish was empty, without so much as a bin liner, but the recycling was half full.

'Tip it out and let's have a look.' Laurel helped Maggie pull it out and upend the contents onto the floor. They sifted through the boxes and cartons.

'It doesn't look like there's anything in here that's in any way poisonous.'

'No.' Maggie rested back on her heels. 'Just some sleeves from ready meals and another box from The Plump Tart. Lily loved their cakes and pasties almost as much as I do.'

Laurel grinned. 'I'd noticed.' She made a mental note to go back to the bakery herself as soon as possible. If everything they made was as incredible as the éclairs and fruit tarts she had already tried, she could see significant weight gain in her future.

'What's this?' On hands and knees, Maggie was peering into the space where the bin had been. She reached in and snagged a box that had lodged in a gap. 'Oh, it's an empty box of mint tea. I don't suppose that means anything.' She threw it onto the pile with the rest.

'Not unless Lily was allergic to mint tea?'

'I don't think so.'

'Okay, we're not finding anything in here. Let's try the living room.'

They scooped up the recycling and Maggie put it back in the cubbyhole.

The living room was darker still. Laurel flicked the switch for the ceiling light.

Maggie moved towards the framed photos on the wall and Laurel joined her to study the subjects captured in happier times. The pictures showed Lily and a man, presumably her husband, Sebastian. He was tall and dark-haired, with intense blue eyes. They made a handsome couple and looked happy together. In many of the prints, they stood either side of a dimpled youngster whose fierce smile shone out from the picture.

'That's Rose,' said Maggie.

It was sad to know that both parents were gone and that soon their daughter would be there to clear everything away.

With a sniff, Laurel turned to scan the bookshelves. Lily had eclectic tastes in reading, everything from *Jane Eyre* to a well-thumbed copy of *Walks in Mysterious Yorkshire* tucked away in a bottom corner. She picked up *The Green Witch* from the occasional table next to one of the armchairs and flicked through it. The book was a guide to using plants, flowers, and herbs for healing. Had Lily maybe made a mistake and ingested something harmful, believing it to be benign? It was a possibility.

Putting it back where she'd found it, she lifted up the mangled glasses she'd pondered on her last visit. With them in her hand, she puzzled over the missing lens. She hadn't thought to look for it before, but it must be nearby. She crouched down to see if she could find it.

'What are you looking for?'

There it was. The light caught a sliver of glass as she moved her head. 'This,' she said, pulling the loose lens from under the curtain. It wasn't broken, so maybe it had just popped out if Lily had perhaps sat on them by mistake. *Goodness knows*, thought Laurel, *I've done that with my sunglasses more than once.*

'Maybe you shouldn't have touched that? Oh, my goodness, maybe we should be wearing gloves?' Maggie dropped the book she was holding. It tumbled to the floor. 'Oh no, I didn't mean to do that.' She stooped to pick it up, stopped, pulled her hand away, then stood and stared at it where it had come to rest. 'What do I do?'

'It's all right.' Laurel picked up the book and set it back in the bookcase, then placed the glasses frame and loose lens back on the table. 'Technically, it's not a crime scene. We'll finish in here, then nip upstairs and that's it.'

Maggie didn't look convinced, but she nodded.

On the mantelpiece, behind the clock, Laurel noticed the edge of a piece of paper. Nudging it into view, she saw it was a leaflet advertising an exhibition of works by local artists at Burton Constable. Paper-clipped to it was a ticket for the event which, according to the date, was for the coming weekend.

'What do you think of this?' She held it out towards Maggie. 'Lily had a ticket for an exhibition. She was planning for the future.' She remembered the calendar on the fridge door. 'And she'd made an appointment at the hairdresser for next week. That makes it even less likely she took her own life.'

'Do you think... Would the police even listen to us if we passed this on to them? I think we should talk to them.'

'Rose said they're convinced that if it wasn't something taken deliberately, then it was accidental. This is unlikely to persuade them otherwise. Still, I'm glad that we found it. It fits with our theory that this was no deliberate act by Lily.'

'It looks that way, doesn't it? I mean, we're not finding any evidence, but then what do they say? An absence of evidence isn't evidence of absence. I read that somewhere.'

Laurel gave a wry smile. She and Maggie both knew the lingo, but how far could they get with next to no actual information? 'When the results come back from the toxicologist about the type of poison, it will give us a better idea of what to look for.'

'I hadn't thought of that. That should tell us one way or the other, then.'

At that moment, the rain intensified, rattling against the windows and what little daylight there was dimmed in a premature dusk.

Maggie closed the last door in the sideboard and said, with a tremor in her voice, 'I suppose we had better go upstairs and get this over with?'

They eased through the doorway and started up the stairs. Maggie walking so close behind Laurel she was almost stepping on her heels. It got darker with each step. The hall light threw out precious little illumination. Even as they approached the upper floor, the small windows along the landing did nothing to dispel the gloom. Laurel gained the top stair and checked outside for any sign of the magpie. Thankfully, he wasn't to be seen.

Maggie edged up behind her. 'Let's check out the bathroom,' she hissed in Laurel's ear.

It was spotlessly clean, with a toilet, small basin, and a bath with a shower. There was a cabinet above the basin containing the usual detritus found in bathrooms.

Frowning over the tube of Fixodent, Maggie took off the top and sniffed. 'I suppose someone could have put something in here, or in any of the other normal stuff like the toothpaste.' She held out the tube to Laurel. 'Should we test it?'

Laurel pulled a face. 'I'd rather not.'

In the end, the bathroom didn't provide any obvious clues and nor did Lily's pretty bedroom. The double bed was neatly made with a floral bedspread and lots of pillows. On the single bedside table were stacked four more books next to an old-fashioned clock that ticked loudly in the stillness. There was another framed photo of Sebastian. He looked vaguely familiar to Laurel, like a film star she couldn't quite place. He really had been quite handsome. In the drawer were a pencil, a book of crosswords, and a half-empty bag of Revels. She sniffed and guessed it was the orange ones that had been left behind.

In the office, they had a quick rifle through the drawers and cabinets, but there was nothing unusual to be found, and Laurel was close to admitting they were on a wild goose chase.

The only room remaining to be explored was set up with Lily's art supplies.

'Lily's paintings!' said Maggie from the doorway. 'She loved to paint. She was an art teacher before she retired. I think that

Marcus Hartfield even spoke to her about her giving art classes at his new development centre, or whatever he calls it.'

Lily had kept her art supplies carefully stored and ordered. She had a colourful selection of watercolour paints, a substantial collection of oils, and some charcoal. There was a desk set up for drawing and an easel in the middle of the room directly under a Velux window on which the rain was hammering down.

Stacked against one wall of the room were around two dozen canvases of varying sizes. The larger ones were all countryside scenes, probably local views. In one, Laurel was sure it was the spire of the Elderwick church, Saint Stephen's, nestled amongst green treetops. The smaller works were botanical and labelled in ink: *Cobnuts ready for harvest; Iris; Honeysuckle* and finally a playful and charming painting titled *Cat in the catmint – again.*

A sudden loud thump from downstairs made them spin round. Maggie wobbled, Laurel grabbed her arm and steadied her. She could feel Maggie shaking and her own heart was racing.

'What was that?' hissed Maggie as Laurel crept to the door of the art room and peered through the shadows towards the stairs.

'It's too dark,' she squeaked back at Maggie. Clearing her throat and putting on a voice far deeper than her usual tone, she called, 'Hello? Is there someone down there?'

'What if it's the poisoner? What if he knows we're on to him and he's come to shut us up?' Maggie was flapping her hands and had her eyes squeezed shut.

Laurel ignored her, took a deep breath, and started back down the stairs. There was a second thump.

Maggie gasped, and it was all Laurel could do not to squawk in fear. She steeled herself and rushed round the bend in the stairs so that she could see down into the hall.

The breath she'd been holding whooshed out. 'Oh, thank goodness. Maggie, quick, come down. Everything's all right.'

'What was it?' Maggie shouted back.

Laurel eyed two hefty packages on the mat by the door. She laughed at herself for being so silly and getting carried away. 'A couple of catalogues, by the look of it. Lou must be out there. I'll try to catch her.'

Laurel looked around and saw some keys on hooks on the wall. Grabbing the most likely looking one, she got lucky and flung open the front door. There was no-one there, but a red van was still idling outside the garden gate.

'Hello!' shouted Laurel, running – nearly slipping – down the path. 'Excuse me, have you got a second?' She wasn't sure she'd be heard over the rain.

The window came down to reveal a young man with a shock of red hair and an uncanny resemblance to Ron Weasley from the Harry Potter films.

Caught on the back foot, Laurel stammered, 'Oh, sorry, I was hoping to speak to Lou.'

'Yeah, she's gone,' he called back.

'Gone?'

'Gone. Her round's been moved. I'm filling in for this week and you'll get someone new next week.'

'Right, only we were hoping to speak to her about the lady who used to live here.'

'Sorry, can't help you with that.' He revved the engine.

'Do you know where her new round is?'

'Nope.'

'Can you find out?'

'Nope.'

'Please, we just need a few minutes of her time.'

'Look, I don't know where she's gone. If it's that important, you'll have to call the sorting office in Beverley, but I don't know that they'll tell you anything.' With that, he put the van in gear and drove off.

Maggie, recovered from her fright, joined Laurel by the front door.

'Ron Weasley was not helpful,' Laurel said to her, but Maggie wasn't listening.

'Why is there no other post on the mat? It's been a few days now since... well, you know. There should be some junk mail at least, and the village newsletter was delivered yesterday. Where is it all?'

Laurel ran a hand through her hair, annoyed she hadn't realised sooner when they had the chance to quiz the Ron lookalike. 'That, Maggie, is an excellent question.'

Chapter Thirteen

Finished with clue hunting for the day, Laurel and Maggie relocked the front door and let themselves back out through the kitchen, then picked their way through the dripping garden to exit into the lane.

A figure in red wellies and blue and white check trousers approached, face obscured by a large black umbrella. The brim jerked upwards to reveal a startled Albert. 'Ladies, you gave me quite a fright there. Oh, but you look quite shook up yourselves; is everything all right?' He peered through the downpour.

'We're fine, we had a little scare, but it was nothing,' said Maggie.

'Lily's daughter, Rose, asked us to collect a couple of things for her from the house and check on the garden.' Laurel wasn't ready to tell anyone else about her theory and their search for evidence. She kept her fingers crossed that Maggie wouldn't contradict her.

'Ah yes, poor Lily. She and I had many a long chat about gardens, you know. You'll have seen how wonderful hers is, of course, given whence you've just appeared. If you're speaking with Rose again, please pass on my sincere condolences.' His umbrella drooped. 'Strange business, though.'

Laurel caught Maggie's eye. 'What do you mean?'

'Oh nothing, nothing, just an old man and his musings.'

'Albert, you're one of the sharpest people I know. Tell us what you're thinking,' Maggie urged.

'I'm just a retired gent minding his own business, but Frank, the undertaker who will be taking care of dear Lily, mentioned something that has me vexed.'

He paused, and Laurel was certain he was doing it for effect.

Maggie didn't disappoint him. 'What did Frank say?'

'I'm not one who wishes to repeat bavardage, especially on a matter so delicate.' He moved closer, inviting them under the shelter of his huge umbrella. 'But Frank heard she might have been poisoned.'

'Poisoned?' Laurel squeaked.

Maggie joined in. 'My goodness, what a shock!'

Albert looked askance, and said, 'I suspect by your reactions you are already in possession of these facts?'

Laurel flushed and Maggie looked at the ground.

What the heck, in for a penny. 'It might be that we had heard something, yes.' She told him what Rose had said in her phone call and what she and Maggie had, or rather hadn't found, in Lily's house.

'Curiouser and curiouser, as Alice would say,' Albert murmured when she was finished. 'I may have one other piece of information which could be pertinent. Lily wasn't allergic to mint tea, but I know without a shadow of a doubt that she hated the stuff and would never drink it. I suggested it to her once when she was having some stomach problems – it's quite effective at relieving digestive discomfort – but she wouldn't hear of it.'

'She could have kept it in for a regular visitor?' suggested Maggie. 'The box we found was empty, so someone was drinking it.'

Laurel considered this. 'But there was no fresh box of mint tea in any of the cupboards. When I'm getting to the end of something, I nearly always restock before I'm completely out. Does this mean that she no longer needed mint tea? If there was a visitor, had they stopped visiting?'

'Or maybe she simply forgot to get more,' said Albert.

'Well, yes, or that.' Laurel allowed she was making a bit of a leap.

The rain, which had eased a little, renewed its assault.

Albert adjusted his umbrella and said, 'I must away before we're all bobbing like ducks. I wish you well with your mystery, and as the King of Hearts would say, "Begin at the beginning, and go on till you come to the end: then stop".' And off he went.

Head on one side, Laurel watched him go. Rabbits on string and literary quotes, Albert was a fascinating character. However, amiable character or not, their extended pause in the lane had left her soaked to the skin and, looking at Maggie, she was faring no better.

'This rain isn't letting up, is it? Nicholas is out, so shall we go back to mine and review our evidence?'

As interested to get somewhere dry as she was to see the inside of Maggie's house, Laurel readily agreed.

They squelched up to South Street and along the delightfully named Whirligig Lane to Maggie's home, The Grange.

'Let's sit in the kitchen,' said Maggie. 'It's the nicest room, much cosier than the drawing room and the conservatory is too cold on days like this. Not to mention the sound of the rain on the roof would be deafening.'

Laurel looked around with a smile as she made herself comfortable at the big farmhouse table, running her hands over the smooth, worn wood. She was sure she could smell flapjacks and pictured her new friend with a wooden spoon in one hand and a tin of golden syrup in the other.

Maggie bustled around, getting drinks before she produced an impressive lemon meringue pie that she placed on the table with a knife and two plates.

'Blimey, Maggie, I swear you're trying to fatten me up.'

'It's brain food,' she said with a smile before cutting them each a generous slice.

'You've got to tell me, how do you enjoy these cakes and treats and stay so slim?'

Maggie blushed. 'As the wife of a councillor I have to look after my appearance. I don't do anything special, it's just that by the time I'm finished cooking on an evening I'm not always that hungry. I don't eat many big meals. Nicholas likes his food traditional, meat and two veg and I've never been much of a carnivore. I'd like to be a vegetarian, but it's too much work and expense to cook two meals every day.'

Laurel could hear Nicholas' words in Maggie's voice.

'Oh, I nearly forgot,' Maggie changed the topic, 'I've got us each a notebook for our sleuthing.' She jumped up and took two beautiful Moleskine notebooks from a drawer in the dresser. 'Which would you like?' One was a pumpkin orange and the other duck-egg blue.

'Thank you, that's so thoughtful.' Aware of the blue walls of the kitchen, Laurel plumped for the orange and from Maggie's smile guessed she'd chosen well.

Maggie caressed the cover, then opened to the flyleaf where she printed her name and address. 'Should we approach this with a list like Agatha Christie has the detective do in the book we're reading?'

'Capital idea,' Laurel said with a grin. 'Let's start with the evidence, although I don't think we have much of that.' She opened her notebook and began to write:

> *Evidence*
> *Lily died. Possible cause – poison Not verified*
> *Unlikely to be heart attack Acc. to Albert*

Once she'd copied the same into her own book, Maggie set down her pen. 'Hmm, we don't actually have a lot of evidence, do we?'

'True. Let's recap what clues we've found. Maybe that will help.'

> *Clues*
> *Empty box of mint tea – Lily didn't like mint tea*
> *Who emptied the rubbish bin?*
> *Empty cake box – source of poison?*
> *Tickets for art exhibition & appt with hairdresser*
> *– future dates*
> *Missing post*
> *Broken glasses*

'That doesn't add up to much either, does it?'

'No.' Laurel's shoulders slumped, but she tried to rally. 'It does raise some new questions, though. Let's try one last list and look at who we've spoken to and who we still need to question.'

Persons of interest

Post-lady: Lou – Did she see anything Laurel missed? Is it strange she no longer has the post round in Elderwick? Where is the missing post?

Hitesh – Does he have a motive? Not been in Elderwick that long, what's his background, how did he come to know Lily?

Lily – Could she have accidentally ingested poison? Did she take her own life? – Why?

Albert – He seems to know an awful lot (*but that's just Albert)

Derek – He doesn't like anyone but seemed to get on well with Lily.

'Can you see any of them having a motive to murder Lily?' asked Laurel. 'From what you say, everyone liked her.'

After a minute of thinking, Maggie replied, 'The only possible thing I can come up with is the development at Elderwick Hall. Lily was against it, and she was so mad when Marcus tried to sweet-talk her by offering her the chance to teach some art classes to guests. But that doesn't explain why someone would murder her.'

Laurel added Marcus' name to her list.

Maggie hugged her arms across her chest. 'What a horrible word: murder. If that's what it was, because looking at this, I'd say we're missing all the key ingredients: who; when; where; and most importantly, why? The only thing we do know is the *where*.'

'Where...' Laurel repeated under her breath. 'Maggie, that's it!' She smacked her hand on the table. 'That's what has been bothering me from the start. I'm such an idiot, it's so obvious, but I didn't realise.'

'What?'

'The chairs. When I saw Lily from outside, on the day she died, she was sitting in the chair facing *away* from the window. When we were in the house though, her table with her books and glasses on, they were by the other chair, the one *facing* the window. Why wasn't she sitting where she usually does?'

'She could have fancied a change?'

'She could, but I can tell you, people almost always stick with the same seats, in classrooms, in therapy rooms, and in their own homes. I know I do.'

Maggie looked down at the chair on which she was sitting. 'You're right. You are so clever. I would never have thought of that.'

Laurel allowed herself a brief smile. 'It's curious, but not what you'd call cast-iron evidence. I'm not sure it takes us any further forward.'

'You know, now you mention the chairs, I wonder... poison isn't an easy way to go. I don't know much about it, but have you ever seen the film *Arsenic and Old Lace*, with Cary Grant?'

Laurel shook her head.

'Well, I won't give away the plot, but this gentleman has been killed with poison, and then his body is set up in this window seat so that the vicar doesn't realise the man is dead.'

Laurel scribbled a note as a reminder to see if it was on Netflix.

'When someone is poisoned, they tend to be sick and in pain and they don't just sit there and die quietly.'

'I see what you mean, I think. No wait, are you saying that Lily was poisoned, and someone sat her in the chair after she was dead?' Laurel massaged her temples. She could feel a headache coming on. Every time they thought of something new, it only looped them around to three more questions. Nothing was clear.

'You have your date with Nathan coming up. Do you think you might talk to him about all of this?'

Laurel groaned. She'd been trying to forget about Maggie's matchmaking plans. They weren't making much progress on their own, though. Maybe it was time to speak to an expert. 'I suppose it wouldn't hurt to run it by him.'

Chapter Fourteen

With her upcoming date in mind, Laurel sat down to do a little preparatory research and was impressed by what she learned. Nathan Tillow was an admirable man. Regularly in the local news for his work with disadvantaged youngsters, he'd set up several outreach schemes and even spearheaded a youth council to allow teenagers a voice on how their local areas could be improved and how the police might build productive relationships with the younger community. According to the *Hull Daily Mail*, he was also well known in the nearby villages for giving talks to the WI, and for advising residents on how to keep themselves and their properties secure. Along with most of the articles were photographs, including one showing him outside Elderwick Hall. She looked closely, he ticked all the boxes: tall, dark brown hair with a touch of grey at the temples, and she could tell he kept in shape. Knowing he was attractive *and* accomplished made the butterflies in her stomach flutter.

She went back and forth, trying to decide what to wear, torn between a floaty summer dress and sandals, or a classic casual look of jeans and a white T-shirt with ballet flats. In the end she went for the jeans but with a silk blouse, casual but not too dressed down. She wanted Nathan to know that she'd made an effort but didn't want to look out of place given they were just meeting in the local pub. A quick swipe of blusher and a dab of lipstick and she was done.

She looked at herself in the full-length mirror on the back of her bedroom door. 'You'll do.' She told her reflection. The jeans were tighter than she remembered, but that was probably down to all the delicious treats Maggie had been encouraging her to sample. The blouse was dove-grey, a colour that she'd always thought brought out the blue in her eyes.

When it came time to leave, she stepped outside, relieved to see it was a clear evening. The waxing crescent of the moon wasn't yet visible in the sky, and when it was, it wouldn't be bright enough to help her navigate home through the dark lanes. She didn't worry particularly about walking through the village at night, but it still paid to be cautious, and to be able to see where you were going since most of the lanes didn't have streetlights. She must buy a torch.

It was a short distance to the pub through the chill of the early autumn evening. As she approached the building, she could hear lively conversation and laughter spilling out from behind the doors. With a final check that the buttons on her blouse were fastened correctly – it wouldn't be the first time she'd been misaligned – she put on a smile and pulled open the door.

She spotted Nathan immediately. He looked like a rabbit caught in headlights. Swallowing her own nerves, she walked over and introduced herself.

'What can I get you to drink?' he asked when they'd exchanged names.

'I'll have a small white wine, Chardonnay if they have it? Thank you.' It might not be the most sophisticated of drinks, but it was still her favourite, and was worth the occasional comparison to Bridget Jones.

Balancing their drinks – a pint of Bumblehoney cider from the local commune for Nathan – they looked for a table and grabbed one near the fireplace. The nights had only just turned cold, and Laurel was glad of the warmth coming from the glowing embers in the hearth.

'Don't look now, but I think you have an admirer,' said Nathan, looking over her shoulder.

She spun round but couldn't see anyone.

'Never mind, he's gone. Is he your escape plan if we don't hit it off?' His laugh was easy, but his jiggling foot betrayed his nerves.

'Whoever he is, he's nothing to do with me. Besides, Maggie is convinced we're going to get on a like a house on fire. In fact, I'm surprised she's not here making sure of it!'

'Um...' began Nathan, 'on that note I want to apologise that Maggie talked you into this. I think she's been trying to set me up with a new wife ever since my divorce. I'm really sorry you got caught up in her matchmaking. I'm not actually looking for a new wife. I mean, not that you wouldn't be a nice wife... oh, wait, I don't mean...' He gave up and lapsed into an awkward silence.

'It's okay.' She grinned. 'I know what you're trying to say, and don't worry, I'm not exactly on the lookout for a husband myself. Let's have a nice drink and a chat and then we can tell Maggie we eloped and got married.' He laughed and she felt her shoulders drop as she relaxed. She made the decision not to mention her suspicions about Lily's death. He was nice, and she didn't want him to think she was a crackpot. Maggie would understand.

Nathan enjoyed a mouthful of his drink before saying,

'Maggie tells me you're a psychologist. Did you move up here for work?'

'Not exactly. It was time to leave my old job and I fancied a change of scenery so, here I am.' She knew she was glossing over the details but wanted to keep the conversation light. She lifted her own glass to her lips and enjoyed the first taste of the surprisingly good wine.

'What got you into psychology?'

It was nice that he was interested in her and not one of those men who only droned on about themselves. 'The short version is that I wanted to help people... and I like to sit down while doing it, hence a doctorate in clinical psychology.' Laurel was pleased to hear him chuckle at her bad joke.

'Impressive. I should call you *Doctor* Laurel, then?' He'd stopped gripping his glass with rigid fingers and had settled back into his chair. As they continued to chat, he flashed her what could only be described as a rakish grin.

'Absolutely not. I only use the title when I want a better table in a restaurant.'

'Does that work?'

'Never.' She smiled as he laughed again. 'What about you? You're a police officer?'

'Yes, just like my dad and his dad before him. Bit of a family tradition. I've enjoyed it, mostly. It's a job that allows me to feel that I'm doing some good for my community.' He dropped his gaze. 'It can wear you down, though, you know. The husbands who beat their wives, the drug users who terrorise grannies for their pension money and the senseless violence in town on almost every night of the week. Makes you wonder if there's any real good in the world anymore.' He coughed. 'Sorry. It's not something I'd usually talk about, but you being a psychologist, I think you probably understand where most people wouldn't.'

She was nodding. 'I know where you're coming from. Some of my work can be very heavy, and it's hard work to protect yourself from that.' Nathan was right. It was easier to admit these things to someone in a career that also took a hefty emotional toll.

'I knew you'd get it.' He smiled and his face brightened. 'Since my divorce, I'm a bit more prone to black dog days, but there's good stuff too. In my work I get all over the East Riding, all the villages. I couldn't hack being stuck in an office all day.'

'Is there much of a crime problem in this village?' She braced herself. Was her new home a hotbed of murder and intrigue?

'Elderwick? You must be joking! Nothing gets past the WI or Derek Fisher and his Neighbourhood Watch.' He rolled his eyes. 'You'd have to be a criminal genius to get away with anything undetected in this village.'

'And do you have many of those around here, criminal geniuses... genii?'

'Well, I've got the genius bit down, but I'm one of the good guys.'

'I'm sure you are.' *Am I flirting?*

'But seriously, no, Elderwick is very safe.'

She smiled; it was good to hear but could she believe it?. 'Have you always lived around here?'

'I grew up here, then went to Bristol University to do my degree, but I always knew I'd come back once I was finished.'

They talked for a while about his career in the police and his family, then shared memories of the places they'd both been to in Somerset. Whilst he'd been at university, Nathan had often driven out to the countryside to go walking, one of his favourite pastimes, and something else they shared in common.

'As well as walking, what else do you get up to in your spare time?' she asked.

'Well, I blame my dad for this, for as long as I can remember he's been interested in the dark side of local history and believe me, some of the bedtime stories I got as a kid... I think that's why I grew up to be a collector of Yorkshire folklore. No, no,' he held up his hands, 'I know what you're going to say, I look too young and cool for such a weird hobby.'

'Yes,' she deadpanned, 'that's exactly what I was going to say.'

'Speaking of which,' he leaned in towards her, 'how much have you heard about Elderwick's weird history?'

'Weird history? Nothing. I didn't know there was anything strange about this place.'

'Ah, then let me tell you the tale of the curse of Elderwick Hall.'

A tingle of anticipation ran down her spine.

'In 1725,' he began, 'Elderwick Hall was purchased by Archibald Hartfield for his new young wife. It had been a whirlwind courtship and Archibald, at forty-six years old, was bowled over by the beauty and innocence of seventeen-year-old Alice.'

Laurel pulled a face.

He scrunched up his nose. 'I know. Different times, et cetera, et cetera. Anyway, they moved in together, a happily married couple, but their wedded bliss lasted only a few months. You see, Archibald's two children from his first marriage were living there, too. His son, Jacob, aged nineteen and Jacob's younger sister, ten-year-old Charlotte. Their mother had died in a riding accident only a few months before Archibald remarried.

'At first, all was calm, if not exactly rosy, in the Hartfield household. Then strange things started to happen.' He lowered his voice and dropped his chin, making the light from the fire glitter in his eyes. 'First Jacob's dog was found drowned in the horses' drinking trough. Then Charlotte's cat was killed in a rabbit snare. Both *could* have been accidents. But when a fire started in the stables and a horse died, one of the grooms swore he saw someone creeping out of a stall five minutes before the blaze was discovered.'

'Three unfortunate events, doesn't sound accidental to me.' Captivated by the tale, the sounds of the pub receded as he held her eyes with his gaze.

He nodded. 'It gets worse. Charlotte went missing from her bed one night. The entire household staff searched the house, outbuildings, and grounds for hours before her little body was found at the foot of the Apple Tree Man, the oldest apple tree in the Hartfield's orchard.'

Laurel gasped. It had happened almost three hundred years ago, but a shiver ran through her as she imagined the scene.

'Archibald was a broken man,' continued Nathan. 'Especially when the finger of suspicion was pointed at his new wife, Alice. At first, he defended her. Said it couldn't have been her, that she was too small and fragile to commit such a crime. But the rumours gained ground. Whispers circulated that she wanted rid of his children so she could start a new family with him. When no other suspects could be found, he started to listen to the gossips and began to believe their claims.

'One night, tortured by grief, and in a fit of anguish and rage, Archibald beat Alice with a fire iron, demanding she confess. She refused, so he dragged her to the door and heaved her outside, leaving her lifeless body to be found the next day in a pool of her own blood. When she was discovered, so the story goes, there were bloody marks all over the door as though she had tried in the last moments of her life to get back inside.

'Archibald was acquitted of manslaughter. His lawyer successfully made the case that he had been possessed by grief and not in his right mind at the time of Alice's death. They also claimed that he didn't in fact kill Alice and that she died of exposure on the doorstep, not from his brutal beating.'

Laurel gave a snort of disgust.

'He had the orchard chopped down and the trees burnt. The area where the orchard had stood was walled up with no entrance or exit and left to go wild. He never remarried, and he never left Elderwick Hall saying he wanted to stay close to the spirit of his darling Charlotte. Jacob too stayed and grew up to be a violent and arrogant man. He married and had two children, but when their baby daughter died, his wife, Bethany, ran away, leaving their son to be raised by Jacob alone. Over the years, there were other deaths, disappearances and one young housemaid who was sent to jail for theft. Eventually, female servants were hard to retain and for many years, there was not one single woman who lived or worked in the house.

'Naturally, as time went by, questions were asked about Jacob and whether he was the one who murdered his sister. But,' Nathan whispered the final words, 'nothing was ever proven.'

Laurel rubbed at the goosebumps that had broken out on her arms despite the warmth. 'That's one heck of a macabre tale.'

'That's not all. It must have been forty-five or fifty years ago, they found old bones in the walled-up orchard. There was a whole thing about who they belonged to, but to this day they remain unidentified.'

Laurel grimaced. 'It sounds like a horrible place, Elderwick Hall.'

'It's actually a beautiful building, but ever since Charlotte's death, no woman has ever lived happily in that house.'

'Poor Petra,' she mumbled, remembering Marcus Hartfield's wife, the striking woman she'd met in the beer garden.

'Sorry, this isn't exactly first date conversation material, is it?'

'Not really.' She took another sip of her wine. 'But it is interesting in a ghoulish way.'

'If you ever feel up to hearing more, you only have to say the word. Or ask Albert. He's another one round here that knows all the dark secrets.' He waggled his eyebrows. 'Right, enough of that. Let me get some more drinks and put something upbeat on the jukebox and we can talk about more pleasant topics. Back in a tick.'

Laurel watched him wander back to the bar before staring into the lively flames in the fireplace. First Lily's death, now this horrible story, and coming so soon after her run-in with Derek. There was darkness in Elderwick.

A server arrived at the table with a bowl that he plopped down on the table.

Pulled from her gloom, she said, 'I'm not sure they're for us. We didn't–'

'Nathan ordered them at the bar,' he explained.

She hadn't been thinking about food but on seeing the crisp, golden fries, her stomach woke with a growl. She inhaled. 'Is that rosemary?'

'Yep, and sea salt. Enjoy.' He darted away, collecting empty glasses on his way to the bar.

Good manners dictated she wait, but Nathan wouldn't miss one... or two. She'd eaten five when the first notes of a new song spilled from the jukebox, and she caught sight of Nathan coming back. She stuck her greasy fingers under the table and hoped he wouldn't notice. 'Did you seriously just put on "Smooth Criminal"?' she asked when he reached her.

'It's a great song.' Nathan shrugged with a grin as he placed their drinks on the table. 'Dig in.' He nodded to the bowl.

She ate a couple more fries before saying, 'You mentioned

Derek Fisher earlier. I had a rather unpleasant conversation with him the other day. He seemed to be telling me I can't do what I want in my own home.'

'Derek's had *issues* with about everyone round here.' Nathan scowled. 'He's one of those people who believes he should be the judge of everything that goes on in Elderwick. Sees himself as the... I don't know... guardian of the village. He has a habit of collaring me, wanting me to look in to non-existent crimes. He actually spoke to me about you, and I think it might have been after your, um, clash.' Nathan hung his head and peered at her through his lashes again.

'What about me?' Laurel asked, wondering who else Derek had been speaking to about her.

'He wanted me to check you out. He seems to have the idea that you're about to invite all kinds of "psychos and nut jobs" – his words – to come and see you for therapy. I mean, it's all nonsense, of course, and I told him I wasn't about to run a background check on you or whatever it was he was getting at.'

'Wait.' A nasty thought had crawled into her mind. 'Is that why you agreed to meet me?' Was this all a setup by Derek? What had started out as a pleasant evening was taking an unwelcome turn.

'No! No way.'

Laurel was gratified to see that Nathan looked uncomfortable and flustered. 'Why should I believe you?' she asked.

'First, I don't take orders from Derek, and second, why would it matter to me what you do in your professional life? Derek has got some bee up his bum about it, and I haven't the faintest idea why.'

The idea of a bee up Derek's backside was too much and made Laurel giggle. Nathan looked relieved and the sudden chill thawed.

'I think you mean a bee in his bonnet or a stick up his behind.'

'I don't know, a bee up his bum would explain a lot. Once he gets on to something, he's like a terrier with a rat, if you'll forgive the mixed animal metaphors. That's how he's been since this whole Elderwick Hall project was announced. He's convinced there's something criminal going on.'

'And is there?' Laurel was curious to know what the police thought.

'I very much doubt it. Nothing *criminal*-criminal at any rate. The usual backhanders and the like, I'm sure, but nothing we could ever prove. His latest *evidence* is that he's found out the development company buying the Hall is the same as the one Nicholas Wright the councillor used to work for, and Nicholas is a major investor in the project, so stands to make a killing.'

'Well, you've got to admit that doesn't look good.'

'But it's not illegal. Anyway, Marcus was always going to sell the place off sooner or later. He and Petra have never lived there. They only ever stay for a couple of weeks at a time. They have a house in London.'

'As a woman I wouldn't be clamouring to live at the Hall, but I'm kind of looking forward to seeing inside. Do you know about the open house this Saturday? Mind you, after hearing about your curse, maybe I should give it a miss.'

'Really? You'd miss it?'

'No, of course not.'

He laughed again. He did have a lovely smile. 'A couple of lads from my team have been asked to go along to keep the peace in case of unruly locals.'

'Will you be there?' It slipped out before she could bite her tongue. She didn't want him to think she was angling to see him again. Not that she wouldn't like to.

'Afraid not. I'm giving a talk to a local social group that day. Talking to seventeen- and eighteen-year-olds about staying safe on nights out.'

'Very civic minded.'

'Just doin' my job, ma'am.'

Smiling, she reached for the fries, but the pot was empty. It was probably time to head off, anyway. They'd long finished their drinks and the evening felt like it was coming to a natural end.

'I had best be off soon,' Nathan said. 'Laurel, it's been a pleasure to spend an evening with you and I'm pleased Maggie set this up. Would you like to do it again sometime?' He was determinedly looking somewhere over her head as he asked.

Why was dating so awkward, even as an adult? He was a police officer, and she was a clinical psychologist. They were both used to tough conversations, yet here they were acting like gauche teenagers.

Was it time to take a leap, say to hell with being coy? 'That would be wonderful.' She beamed at him as he finally made eye contact.

Nathan offered to walk her home, but she waved him off, so he gave her his number and they arranged to meet again the following Tuesday.

'I'll need a drink that evening. I'm due at the village hall beforehand for a meeting with the infamous Derek and his Neighbourhood Watch.'

'Good luck.' She laughed.

'And you be careful at Elderwick Hall on Saturday.'

Laurel joked, 'I ain't afraid of no curse.'

Chapter Fifteen

It was sunny out but there was a bitter wind blowing. When Laurel opened the door to admit Maggie, curling leaves swept inside and down the hallway. 'Go on through and sit down. I've misplaced my jar of regular, so I hope you don't mind decaf?' She knew Maggie was bursting to ask her about the date, so took her time making the coffee and arranging a selection of biscuits on a plate before joining her in the living room.

'Tell me everything.' Maggie could barely contain herself.

Laurel took a moment to settle herself in her chair. 'Well, Nathan is lovely, very attractive. He's got an infectious smile...'

'There's a but coming, isn't there?' Maggie's face fell. 'Oh, I'm so sorry. You didn't like him, did you?'

'No, I did.' She bit into a gingernut and crunched, prolonging the suspense just that bit longer. 'We had a great evening and talked for ages.'

'And?'

'We've arranged to meet up again.' She grinned, knowing Maggie would be thrilled.

'Oh, that's perfect.'

'Don't get carried away, it's only for another drink.' It had been so long since she'd had any kind of date, Laurel was convinced her ability to know if someone was genuinely attracted to her was on the blink and whilst Maggie's enthusiasm was contagious, she didn't want to get swept up into believing something that might not be real.

'We'll see.'

'Whether anything comes of it or not, no more dates, please. I know you said that you believe women need a husband and children to be happy in life, but I don't. We're different, you and I, that's all, and that's okay. You're happy with Nicholas and I'm happy being single.'

Maggie murmured, 'I'm not happy though.'

'Maggie? Oh Maggie.' Laurel tried to gather her in to a hug, but Maggie waved her off as she searched for a tissue in her pocket.

'Do you want to talk about it?'

'No, no, I'm fine. Ignore me, it's the menopause. I have nothing to be unhappy about; Nicholas is a wonderful husband. We have two beautiful children and a lovely home.'

Those words, almost identical to the ones Maggie had used when she and Laurel first met at the café, sounded like a mantra and Laurel wondered who Maggie was trying to convince.

Maggie sniffed and dashed away a few last tears. 'Enough of that. What did Nathan have to say about our theory?'

'Ah, about that, I didn't mention it in the end. We were having a pleasant chat and then he told me about Elderwick Hall, and Derek, and it didn't feel like the right time to bring it up.'

'Okay, I suppose we haven't got much to tell yet, anyway. Saying that, I should update you on my conversations at the WI meeting last night. I didn't tell anyone what we're looking in to so I couldn't ask direct questions, but I think I may have some more clues.'

'Excellent work, Holmes. Let me grab my notebook.'

Maggie looked pleased at the comparison but insisted, 'You're Holmes. The one with the brains. I'm more of a Watson.'

'Maybe we're closer to Miss Marple and Jessica Fletcher, but younger, hotter versions.'

That brought a smile to Maggie's face. 'Younger maybe...'

Laurel swatted her on the shoulder.

'Back to the WI. We had a full house last night, so I was able to chat with everyone and I wrote up some notes when I got home. Let's see.' Maggie opened her own notebook. 'There wasn't a lot, but these snippets might be useful. Pratiksha, who lives over the road from Lily on Wayback Lane, said Hitesh and Lily were very good friends, and he was over at least twice a week helping her out in the garden. That is, up until a week or so before Lily died. Pratiksha said she didn't see Hitesh at all for around five or six days.'

'That's interesting; I wonder if he was away?'

'Dorothy,' continued Maggie, 'who you met in the bakery, she said she thinks the secret ingredient Lily used to use in her strawberry jam was nutmeg. I don't agree, I'm sure I would have noticed that. Babs, she–'

'Wait, why would a secret jam ingredient be a clue?' asked Laurel, lifting her pen from the page and squinting at Maggie.

'It's probably not, but for the sake of considering all eventualities, I made a note of it. Nutmeg is poisonous if eaten in large enough quantities. I shouldn't imagine Lily deliberately ate lots of nutmeg, but what if she got it mixed up with something else?'

'Hmm. It's a thought.' She didn't write it down.

'Babs, from Manor Road, she's doing a painting for the Autumn Festival competition, and she said Lily mentioned how she was also going to enter a painting this year. Lily once brought some of her work to a WI meeting and we've all seen how good she is. She was an art teacher, after all. The prize is five hundred pounds. What if there's someone who's desperate for money and wanted to stop her from entering?'

'It's quite extreme to murder someone for five hundred pounds.'

'People do go to extraordinary lengths in extreme circumstances.'

'True, I suppose. Sorry, carry on.'

'Finally, and this is the most interesting, Brenda – lives round the corner from you – saw Derek coming out of Lily's front door the same day we were there, but early in the morning, with a stack of letters. She was walking along the little footpath that runs past the end of the churchyard, along the back wall of Lily's garden and once over the road, it goes behind some trees directly opposite Lily's front door. Chances are Derek doesn't know she was there to see him.'

'Now, that is interesting.' Laurel made a note. 'Quite bold though, to let himself in and out of the front door.'

'Wayback Lane is very quiet and if anyone had been around, he could have just said he was out walking. I bet he waited until he thought he was alone.'

'That would explain why there was nothing on the mat when we were there. The first time I went round I didn't look, but thinking about it now there can't have been any post then either, I would have noticed it when I went upstairs. Derek must have a key.'

'He could have used the one Lily kept under the flowerpot. Oh no, wait, you've had that since the day after she died.'

'And it's a back door key.' She thought for a moment. 'You said that Derek and Lily got on well. Could she have given him a key?'

'I don't know why she would. He lives almost at the other

end of the village in the newish bungalows on The Rise and–
Oh my giddy aunt!' Maggie clapped her hand to her forehead.

'What?'

'I can't believe I forgot! Derek's brother used to live at
Church View. He's the one who sold it to Lily.'

'Meaning Derek could have had a key for years and Lily
wouldn't necessarily have known. Now we're getting
somewhere.'

'Why would Derek have wanted to hurt Lily, though? I
mean, he can be a disagreeable sort, but I've never thought he'd
be the type to harm someone, and he liked Lily.'

'He's got a temper. I didn't mention it before, but I had a
run-in with Derek a few nights ago. He turned up at the door
and got really quite angry.'

'Oh Laurel, that's awful. What was he angry about?'

'I have no idea. He just showed up and started shouting
about me not being allowed to set up a private practice from my
home. But you know, I don't think that's what he was really
angry about and having reflected on it, I know it can't have been
personal.' Insight notwithstanding, she felt irritation rise in her
again, provoked by the memory.

'Best not take any notice. He's always on about something.
He accused me and the WI of inappropriate use of the village
hall once all because we left the chairs out after the meeting ran
late. I would still have put them away, but I knew that the
history club had the hall booked for Friday morning, so they'd
need the chairs out, anyway.' Maggie sounded as peeved as
Laurel felt.

Laurel closed her notebook and looked at her friend 'Well,
cantankerous old know-it-all or not, we need to talk to Derek
about Lily's missing post.'

Chapter Sixteen

Laurel was enjoying the sunshine as she and Maggie strolled between the ancient oaks lining the approach to Elderwick Hall. There were other villagers around them, some on their way up to the big house, others already heading for home.

'How shall we do this?' asked Maggie, tilting her face toward the sun.

'Let's see how it goes,' replied Laurel. 'We can mingle, chat, have a look at these development plans, and when we find Derek, see what you can get out of him.'

'Me?'

'I don't think he's going to open up to me after our little contretemps.' And Laurel wasn't sure she could trust herself to be civil to him.

'But I don't know what to say.' Maggie looked stricken.

'Relax, you'll be fine. Maybe start by asking after his brother and ask how he likes it wherever it is he lives now. Then get round to talking about when he lived here at Church View, or something like that.'

'I'll do my best, but stay close.'

Laurel nodded. They wandered on and gradually Elderwick Hall came into view. A Georgian property, built of grey brick, dull in comparison to the warm red-orange of the modest homes in the village. Three storeys tall, it was topped by an aged but trim slate roof rising up behind a balustrade parapet with a weathervane in the shape of a stag standing proud on the gable end of a south facing extension. Laurel gaped. It was impressive but forbidding, especially having heard some of the history attached to the place. 'Kind of gives me the creeps,' she murmured.

'Has Albert been telling you about all the terrible things that have happened here?' Maggie asked.

'No, it was Nathan. It's horrible about that poor woman, Alice, and her step-daughter, Charlotte.'

'Wasn't it? Even with it taking place so long ago, I still shudder to think about it.'

'Do you think the walled-up orchard is still here?'

Maggie shrugged. 'Maybe. Albert will know, he's always been very interested in local history. Or Marcus, I suppose, since this is his house. Of course, he might not want to talk about that chapter of his family history.'

'What's he like, Marcus? I met him at the pub the other day. We only said a quick hello, but he came across as very pleasant.' She blushed at the memory, and at how she'd stumbled over her words when introducing herself to him.

'Nicholas and I have had him round to dinner now and again, with Petra, too, of course. He's polite enough and he puts on the charm, but... I don't know...' Maggie waved her hand in the air. 'I don't trust him.'

'I can imagine he's pretty slick. Petra seems fun, though. Have you ever seen her vlog?'

'Her what?'

'Her vlog. It's a video-blog, like a website where someone

posts short videos of themselves. Petra does ones where she talks about strategies and techniques to help young women in business.'

'I've seen it. It's very good,' chimed a voice from behind them.

Maggie smiled. 'Albert, you keep surprising us.'

Laurel was pleased to see him. 'Actually, we were just talking about you. Maggie said you're the person to ask about the history of this place.'

Albert looked off, squinting into the sun before nodding. 'I suspect you've already heard about some of the diabolical doings, then?'

Laurel bobbed her head in acknowledgement.

'Fascinating as it is, folk forget that behind all the rumours and lurid details, the Hartfields have suffered many losses. Did you know that Marcus' mother died in childbirth, and his father, Clement, was abandoned by *his* mother? Then there was a maid who – if village gossip was to be believed – was taken advantage of by Randolph, Marcus' grandfather. The story goes she fell pregnant but disappeared one day and was never seen again, and no-one knows what happened to the baby.'

Laurel winced; the women of the Hartfield family truly were burdened by misfortune. Marcus too, he might be rich in money and property, but what child could fail to be impacted by the loss of their mother? 'I didn't know all that.'

'I can't blame Petra for staying in London most of the time. I'm feeling funny about just visiting today.' Maggie stared up at the building.

'Ah now, dear ladies, let's shake off this melancholy air.' Albert gestured to the house. 'I am sure we'll be safe in our capacity as mere visitors for a brief window of time. Shall we go along in and see what it's all about?'

The driveway led them into a cobbled courtyard partially

enclosed by low walls topped with iron railings. To the left were stables and other outbuildings, while a gateway on the right led into a garden. The ghost of ivy marked the Hall's façade; an afterimage where life had once clung to the stones.

The grand entrance yawned open atop a sweep of steps. As she mounted them, Laurel experienced a second of queasiness to know she was treading upon stones that bore witness to the dreadful death of a young woman so many years ago.

They crossed the threshold, and it took her eyes a moment to adjust to the relative gloom inside. Just inside the door was a table of drinks for guests. She took a glass of orange juice for herself and handed one each to Maggie and Albert.

'Not exactly a champagne reception,' sniped a woman, passing within earshot.

They shuffled forward, into the general jumble of visitors and gaped at the glossy banners promoting Marcus' development: the golf course; the personal development centre; the luxury destination hotel; the executive homes. In the centre of the hall, on prominent display, a model of the grounds as they would be on completion of the project. Rendered in intricate detail were tiny trees and houses, miniature gardens, and even a doll-sized golf buggy on the fairway. No prices mentioned anywhere though, Laurel noted.

'What do you think?' asked Maggie, pulling a face when she tasted the warm juice.

She pursed her lips. 'I dislike it on principle, but I have to admit, it's attractive. If I had the money, I could be tempted by the houses they're going to build. Marcus might convince a few people here today if he's telling the truth about locals being able to make use of the facilities like the spa and these classes I keep hearing about.' She pointed to a large photo. 'Tai chi in the orangery sounds a heck of a lot sexier than Legs, Bums and Tums in the village hall.'

Maggie sniggered. 'I bet the houses will be super expensive. Nicholas has talked about us buying one with a view of the golf course. He said that we'd get it for an excellent price because he's one of the investors.'

'Isn't there a conflict of interest for Nicholas to be an investor?'

She watched Maggie's smile fade. Her reply was sharp. 'I'm sure Nicholas wouldn't do anything improper.'

'Oh no, of course. I'm sure it was all done properly.' A prickly silence descended between them. As she searched for the right words to thaw the chill, she saw Derek and gave Maggie a nudge. 'Look, Derek's here. Do you feel up to talking to him?'

'I guess so.' Maggie wrung her hands. 'Now?'

'No time like the present.'

'Okay, okay, I can do this.' She took a deep breath, and after a final beat of hesitation, headed in his direction.

Laurel had intended to keep watch over her friend as promised, but out of the corner of her eye, she spotted Marcus in an adjoining room. Dressed in a beautifully cut grey suit, a pale blue tie and darker blue pocket square, he was staring out of a window. Glancing back at Maggie, she saw her chatting away with Derek, so she thought it worth the risk to slip away.

She strolled into the room pretending to admire the décor, all the while moving closer to Marcus, but she didn't have chance to engage him before he disappeared through a second exit. She huffed and was about to leave when she heard his raised voice. She moved closer to listen.

'Just take the modelling job.'

'Why should I? It's not what I do. I'm a businesswoman, not just a pretty face.'

That had to be Petra.

'We need money to tide us over and I haven't got anything

coming in because it's all tied up. I thought we were in this together, you and me? But I've got to be honest, Petra, it hasn't felt like that for a long time now.'

'I–'

'Forget it. Now's not the time. I've got to find Barclay.' The floorboards creaked. Someone was heading back towards the door.

Laurel scurried to the window and stared intently outside, only turning when she was sure he was back in the room. 'Mr Hartfield, hi.'

He gave a start but recovered quickly. 'Hello, I didn't realise... Nice to see you again. It's Laurel, isn't it?' He treated her to a wide smile. 'Welcome to our little open day. I hope we can count on your support? Everything we're doing will benefit the community.'

This guy doesn't miss a beat.

'Do take time to look at the displays and don't forget the gardens are open for people to enjoy.' He was already turning to leave as he finished speaking.

'Marcus, do you have the keys to the Rangie?' called Petra, joining her husband and planting a swift kiss on his cheek. He handed her some keys, excused himself once more, and left.

Petra turned to Laurel. 'Are you enjoying the show?' She raised a sculpted eyebrow.

'It's quite the project,' she offered. She was dying to ask about the conversation she'd accidentally overheard – *eavesdropped* – and who was this Barclay, whose acquaintance she had yet to make?

'You could say that.' Petra sighed. 'Have you seen Albert, by any chance?' She smoothed her already smooth ponytail. 'I told him I'd show him some of the Hartfield oils if he was here today, but I have to pop out. If you bump into him, tell him they're in the gallery on the first floor and I've told the security chap at the bottom of the stairs to let him up.'

'He's around here somewhere.'

'Fab, go up with him if you like.' Petra jangled the keys. 'I'd better run. See you around.'

With Petra and Marcus both gone, she drifted back to the entrance hall. Maggie and Derek were still chatting away, so she went to find Albert, keen to poke around a bit more herself.

'This is a treat,' said Albert as they walked up the stairs. 'A glimpse of how the other half live.'

When they found it, she was reminded of the National Trust properties she'd visited over the years, but without the velvet ropes and watchful attendants. Rugs lined the wooden corridor, heavy curtains partially covered the large windows, and the walls were crammed with landscapes and portraits. Laurel's artistic preference was for contemporary art like the work of Kehinde Wiley and David Hockney, but she was captivated by the sheer range of the Hartfield's collection. In silence, she and Albert absorbed the works.

As she wandered past a Stubbs, towards the far end of the gallery, she found a series of paintings of severe looking dark-haired men with a definite family resemblance. Plaques told her these were the Hartfield patriarchs of years past. Feeling the thrill of morbid curiosity, she found the portrait of Archibald, the man who had beaten his wife almost to death and left her to die frozen and alone outside that very building.

'Sinister-looking fellow, isn't he? You can see his likeness in the current steward of Elderwick, I fancy.'

Seeing all the pictures together, Laurel *could* see, and it made Marcus seem that bit less handsome. It was the coldness of the eyes and the thin, pinched look of distaste on the lips. These men who sneered at all observers. How the different artists had each captured the same essence was unnerving. She moved away.

The gallery was at the back of the house and the view over the formal gardens from the windows was a welcome palate cleanser. Despite not having green fingers, she was still able to pick out the lavender, roses, dahlias, and lisianthus in manicured beds. Raising her gaze, she traced the line of the dense border hedge, beyond which she could see a rolling expanse of lawn stretching towards the distant tree line. Dotted here and there were enterprising people who had come prepared with picnic blankets and lunch.

'Oh, I wonder...' Albert mused, joining her as he admired the view. 'Ah, yes. You were mentioning the dark history of this place when we arrived. Well, that's the old orchard.' He pointed to a stone wall just visible.

She stood on tiptoes but couldn't see what was contained within the enclosure. Perhaps she would have the opportunity to explore up close before they left.

'There you are,' called a voice. Maggie bustled up with Derek in tow.

Laurel wasn't sure what reception she was about to get. Derek scowled at her, then nodded at Albert. A terse acknowledgement. Was there history there?

'I was just saying to Maggie here,' said Derek, crossing his arms and raising his chin, 'that I don't for one second approve of this development, but it's quite a thing to see inside Elderwick Hall. At least they know how to keep a property looking its best, unlike some houses in our village. Not to mention the state of the pond and village green. I'm going to have to have a word with the council department who maintains these public spaces. They're not up to the job at all, from what I've seen. They might think they need those big ride-on mowers, but they churn up the mud under the trees something awful. And don't get me started on whoever it is keeps messing up the village flower displays!'

Laurel bit her tongue hard to stop from saying something rude to the self-righteous windbag.

With a gentle deflection, Maggie curtailed Derek's rant. 'Will you be exploring the gardens today, Derek? I know you keep *your* garden beautifully.'

He huffed for a moment and looked out of the window. 'Perhaps, but I don't think I have the time today...' His words fell away and he paled.

'You all right, old chap?' enquired Albert.

'Hmm, yes, fine.' Derek took a step back. 'I've just remembered, I have to get back. I'm expecting a delivery I'd forgotten about.' He strode off, his hands balled into fists at his side.

'What was that about?' Laurel whispered, staring after him.

'He was fine a minute ago. Telling me he's been trying to get answers out of the council about why approval for the development was given so quickly. Then we saw you two slip up here and he insisted we follow so he could have a poke around too.'

Albert tapped a finger against his lips. 'I'll see if I can catch him, check he's all right.'

With Albert gone too, Laurel took the opportunity to ask Maggie, 'Did you find out about the key?'

'I did, but I had to lie. I told him Rose had asked me to collect some papers, but the back door key was missing from its hiding place, and did he know where it could be? He just came out with and said that he still had a key from when his brother lived there.'

'So, he sees no reason to hide the fact.' She chewed a fingernail as she thought. 'Did he mention using it to go in and take the post?'

'No, but I couldn't see how to ask without him knowing he'd been seen or that we'd been inside. Sorry.'

'No, Maggie, no need for sorry. It's more information than we had before, but I don't know if it makes him a more likely suspect, or less?'

'I'm not sure, but given the way he left just now, something is definitely up with that man.'

Chapter Seventeen

Laurel spent the Sunday pottering in the garden, raking up leaves, and flitting between reading and listening to music during the afternoon. She couldn't settle; she was too busy turning everything over in her mind. That night she slept fitfully, in the grips of another nightmare. This time she was being chased by Archibald Hartfield, who had crawled out of his portrait and was pursuing her along the unlit lanes of the village. She awoke, sweating and tense, tangled once again in her bed covers.

With a need to shake off the lingering effects of the dream, she dressed in comfortable clothes and headed out for a walk. It had been a clear night, and the world sparkled as dew caught the early morning sun. The clocks would go back soon, the nights would draw in and the mornings would stay darker longer with each day that passed. Laurel preferred autumn and there was much to enjoy in her new home and surroundings, but despite all that, she was mired in a melancholy mood.

A twig snapped beneath her foot, startling a crow that cawed in indignation. Her attention was on the bird, so she didn't immediately see the bright red van that came hurtling round the corner. A blur of colour caught her eye and she leapt into the verge. Engulfed in hawthorn and holly, her breath was ragged as her heart stuttered in her chest.

The van juddered to a halt twenty metres up the road and started backing up. *Blimey, they're taking another run at me*, she thought as she untangled a twig from her hair. She could see now it was the post van. It drew level with her, stopped, and the window came down.

'Lou?'

'I'm so sorry, me love, I'm used to these lanes being pretty empty this time in the morning. Most of the dog walkers go over on the hill, and those that don't use the footpath just over the other side of hedge there. It goes off through Birchwitch Wood, lovely walk.' She paused and looked Laurel up and down. 'Are you okay?'

'Yes, I think so. You gave me a bit of a fright.' She brushed a squashed berry off her sleeve. 'How are you?'

'I am well indeed. I'm doing the round up in Walkington and there abouts these days. How are you, after... you know, finding Lily?'

The road remained free of other traffic, so Laurel went to stand closer to the van. 'I'm okay. It was a bit of a shock, but I work in healthcare so... you know. Listen, since you mention it, and this is probably going to sound odd, but Lily's daughter is worried. I don't mean to sound melodramatic, but she's asked if I would check a couple of things out for her. Do you mind if I ask you what you saw when you found Lily? Before I got there? If it's not too upsetting?' Laurel watched Lou's face carefully.

'You ask away, me love. Delivering the post, you'd be surprised how often it's us posties that raises the alarm when the grim reaper has called for some old dear.'

'Can you talk me through what happened from when you first arrived?'

Lou thought for a second. 'Like I told the police, I was doing me usual round and when there was no answer at the door, I looked in the front window. Lily had been expecting the parcel I was delivering. She were meant to be in, and we usually have a few minutes' natter. Anyway, when I looked, I could see someone was lying on the floor and they weren't moving at all.'

Laurel's eyes narrowed. 'On the floor? But she was in her the chair when we found her.'

Lou chuckled. 'Ah. Whoops, might have given something away there. Still, can't see as it did any harm.'

'What do you mean?'

She flashed a crooked grin and turned off the engine. 'Thing is, when I first looked through into the living room, Lily was on the floor, all bent around like, and her dress had come up over her knickers. It wasn't dignified. I could tell she was gone even from outside, so I didn't think it would do any harm to pop round the back and let meself in so I could sort her out, Make her look decent, like she would have wanted.'

'So, you knew where to find the key?'

'Course, Lily told me to use it if ever she was out and I needed to use the facilities or had a parcel that wouldn't fit through the letterbox. A rare gem, that woman.'

'And when you were in there, you picked her up off the floor and sat her in the chair?' Laurel couldn't believe what Lou was telling her.

'I did.'

That explained the mystery of why Lily was sitting in the wrong chair. But it opened up a whole raft of other possibilities.

'Did you do anything else?' Laurel bit back her exasperation.

'Nope, I left the parcel on the kitchen table, locked up behind me, put the key back, and I'd just gone round the front again when you arrived.'

So many questions. 'Anything else?'

'Well, only later, when I'd finished me round. I nipped back once everyone had gone and cleared up a bit. Didn't want to leave the place a mess for when her daughter gets here.'

Laurel considered that Lou might be having her on, but she was afraid the woman was being completely serious.

'Lily had been eating, so I cleared away her plate and emptied the bin. That's all.'

'She'd been eating?' This could be crucial. 'Do you remember what she'd been eating?'

'Yes, it was one of them tarts with all fruits, blackberry, red currant, and whatnot. Got to tell you, I've not been able to face one meself since I saw poor Lily like that. She was such a friendly old dear, and she was like me, she liked her treats. I know that much. Every week she'd treat herself, "Just the one, Mrs Wembley," she'd say.' Lou chuckled at the memory.

Laurel must have looked confused, because Lou explained.

'It's from an old show on telly with Joan Sims and Sam Kelly. That's what he used to say, Dennis Waterman did.'

Laurel was getting more perplexed, but the television show really wasn't the salient point. Aiming for a neutral tone, she said, 'Lou, you've been extremely helpful.' At utterly destroying a potential crime scene, she didn't say. 'One last thing.' Now she sounded like Columbo. 'Why didn't you call for help on Lily's phone? Why wait until I'd arrived and then send me up to the school to make the call?'

Lou finally had the decency to look sheepish. 'I guess it didn't occur to me.'

Laurel was speechless.

Lou looked at her watch. 'Sorry, love, best be off, and sorry again for giving you a bit of a scare. I'd be using the footpaths if I were you.' She started the engine and raced away up the lane, leaving Laurel open-mouthed in the dust stirred up by the van's speedy departure.

Confused, astounded, and frustrated, Laurel continued the rest of her walk in a fizz of agitation. She ought to pass this information on to the police. Perhaps Nathan would help her get it to the right person.

As she neared the path that would take her past Wayback Lane and Lily's cottage, her feet started to ache and the sun vanished behind a veil of dishwater drizzle. She was desperate to get home and change into dry clothes, but when she spied Hitesh and his basket, she couldn't pass up the chance to question him, too. Goodness only knows what else she might discover.

'Hitesh,' she called.

He smiled and wandered over. The basket was empty, so he must have been coming rather than going.

'Hello again, how are you today?' he asked.

'I'm well, thank you.' She plastered on a smile. 'And you?'

'Good, very good. The weather is perfect now for mushrooms and I am looking forward to doing some foraging.'

Mushrooms! There were so many gastronomic hazards once you got thinking about it. 'Hitesh, you knew Lily well, would you mind if I ask you a couple of questions?'

'Of course. Can I pick as you ask?' He walked over to the gate and unlatched it, holding it open for Laurel to go ahead of him.

She ignored the stab of apprehension at entering a secluded area with someone who was on her suspect list and went ahead, anyway.

'Is this about the worry that she was poisoned?'

How did he know?

He must have seen her shock, because he explained, 'This is a small village with a very good network of ladies who like to stay well informed. I do a lot of odd jobs and they supply me with tea, cake and much information.' He laughed.

Laurel felt her nerves settle a little. She should have known better than to presume anything would stay secret in the village for long. It probably made for a supportive community, but it made her wonder again what stories were circulating about her.

'I hope very much that she wasn't killed. She was a lovely lady, and it would make me very sad to think someone wanted to harm her.'

'Me too, Hitesh. I didn't know her, but... me too.'

'So, what can I tell you?'

Thinking back to the list she and Maggie had drawn up after their clue-seeking visit, she lit first on the puzzle of the mint tea. 'There was an empty box of mint tea in Lily's recycling, but I understand Lily hated the stuff. Do you know anything about it?'

There was a brief hesitation before Hitesh replied, 'That was for me. Lily was so kind as to buy some for me, but I told her I could bring with me mint we grow at the commune and make my own very simply.'

Okay, that was a reasonable explanation, but why the pause before he answered? Preoccupied, she didn't see the loose rock that tripped her. As it caught on the toe of her shoe, she stumbled but managed to get out her hands to break her fall. Still, she collapsed heavily onto the gravel path and came up with her skin bloodied and torn. Tears pricked – it had been a lousy day – but she blinked them away as Hitesh helped her up with his surprisingly muscular arms.

'Come with me. Lily has a first aid kit, and we'll need to wash out those scrapes with some water. Are you all right to walk?'

She nodded and, supported by Hitesh, wobbled on shaky legs to the back door, where she realised with dismay that she had the key back at her house. She was about to tell him when he pulled a key from his own pocket and unlocked the door. Inside, he sat her down on a chair at the table, found the first aid kit in one of the cupboards, and filled a bowl with water. There was a little piece of soap by the sink which he brought over and used to wash the scratches, which were stinging.

'There, I don't think there's any grit or dirt still in the wounds, but I'll put some antiseptic cream on and cover them with a bandage for you. You'll need to watch that they don't become infected, and you should get a tetanus shot as soon as you can if you're not up to date.'

'Thank you, Dr Hitesh,' she said, impressed by his ministrations, not to mention embarrassed at her clumsiness.

He laughed. 'It's funny you should say that, I was at med school before I dropped out and came to Drumble's Hive. I can cope with a little scratch like this, but I discovered I am not great with blood, open wounds, fractures...' He ran a hand through his hair. 'I know, I know, you'd never guess a hippy like me was once on course to be a doctor.'

Laurel stiffened in her chair. 'What brought you here, to Elderwick?'

'I just thought I would like a change.' He fiddled with the tube of cream. 'And you, what is your profession?'

She strove to keep her tone light and shaped her lips into a wry grin. 'You mean you don't already know?'

He clearly understood her reference. 'I try not to take part in *all* the gossip the people in this village appear to enjoy.'

Meaning Hitesh must be the only local she'd met so far who didn't know, or who claimed not to know, her background and occupation. 'I needed a change too.' *Two can play at that game.* He'd even employed her own trick of diverting attention from himself by asking her a question in return. Clever. Or suspicious? If she gave a little more, might he reciprocate? 'I worked as a psychologist in palliative care, so we have hospital work in common.' She smiled at him and waited to see how he'd respond.

He busied himself in finishing up with the bandaging of her hands and went to pour away the water. He was just at the sink when he stopped and turned back to stare at the vase on the table.

'Now that is most strange.'

'What?'

'This vase. What is in it, this is from the yew tree. It's all dried up, but you can tell it's yew.'

Laurel gasped, her fishing for personal information forgotten as her thoughts raced. She looked at the little shrivelled berries dotting the table. Cogs were turning. Something about the berries, they were important. Her eyes darted about the room as the pieces fell in to place. Everything she had learned that day, a picture, a clear sequence of events, was coming in to focus. The explanation that was coalescing in her mind as Hitesh spoke made sense of all the facts, didn't it? Yes, she thought, well, most of them anyway. That's it! She had solved the mystery.

Hitesh observed her with concern clouding his face.

'Hitesh,' she asked, 'can you meet me in the pub tomorrow night? I think you might have just provided an answer to this whole business of Lily's death.'

Chapter Eighteen

Laurel's mind whirled as she hurried home. It had been fortuitous to bump into both Lou and Hitesh; hearing their accounts meant everything about Lily's death had become clear. She felt vindicated, elated even, and couldn't wait to share the news.

She reached the end of School Lane, glanced to her right, and stopped in her tracks. Derek was sitting alone on a bench, looking out over the pond where a few woebegone ducks paddled through the murky green waters. The drizzle was a mist in his sparse hair and his tapping foot beat a desultory rhythm.

Knowing that she should leave well enough alone, but on a roll, she altered her course and strolled towards the solitary figure.

'Derek, hi.' She smiled. 'Mind if I sit?'

He glanced at her. 'Not like I can stop you.' He'd been absently running a feather through his fingers, and his hands stilled as she approached.

'Look, I think we got off on the wrong foot the other day.

Sorry about that.' She thought an apology might disarm him, not that she had anything to apologise for.

He just grunted.

She tried another tack. 'I understand you've lived in Elderwick for quite some time and you're the authority on the history of the village.'

'Really, and who told you that?' He shifted his position to look at her.

'Well,' she faltered, 'Albert, I think.'

He made another non-committal noise and returned to observing the ducks.

'I was wondering,' she pushed on, 'if you could tell me what you know about Elderwick Hall sometime? You know, the history, the architecture, the gardens, and so on?' She didn't want to come straight out and ask about the murders, bones, and the orchard, but hoped to steer the conversation in that direction if she could get him talking.

He turned to face her. 'Dr Nightingale, I don't know what you're getting at, but I'm not just sitting here waiting to give you a personal history lesson on the unsavoury past of Elderwick Hall. Oh yes, I'm sure you've heard all the rumours and ghost stories, so I don't for a second think you are in fact interested in the *architecture*.'

'Well, I am,' she shot back, nettled by his accusation. 'But yes, I've heard about the walled-up orchard in the grounds of the Hall. Albert was pointing it out to me the other day just before you came up to the gallery. But I'm not a ghoul, if that's what you're implying?'

Derek's face reddened. 'I know nothing about the orchard,' he snapped.

His vehemence unnerved her. 'Sorry, you're right. I'm interrupting you, sitting here quietly. I'm keen to get to know you and to know more about my new home, that's all. But I'll leave you in peace.'

For a split second, as she stood and looked down at him, she thought she saw anguish in his features, and she felt a twinge of sympathy for the man.

Continuing to stare across the water, Derek spoke. 'What you can do for your new home is to put out and take in your bins on time, keep your house and garden in good order and ensure that your chickens don't encourage vermin, or you will be required to dispose of the filthy birds. Finally, yes, please leave me alone. I've got important things to think about.' He waved his hand, dismissing her.

The fragile sympathy evaporated. *What an annoying man.* There was just no use trying with some people. Whatever was his problem?

Chapter Nineteen

Thick fog swirled in the door alongside her as she entered The Snooty Fox. She was going to share her conclusion about Lily's death with her new friends to see if it held water. She'd already left messages inviting Albert and Maggie along, so she hoped Nathan wouldn't mind their planned drink à deux becoming a group event.

They'd said 7pm, she was a bit early but found Nathan waiting. 'Another pint of Bumblehoney?' she asked with a smile, nodding towards his glass.

'Nope, this one's called Cloud Spotting, and I got you a Chardonnay.' He slid the glass over to her.

She flashed him a grin, then broke the news. 'Look, I hope you don't mind, but I've invited a couple of other people to join us this evening.'

'Safety in numbers, eh?' He performed a slow wink, then becoming serious he said, 'I would have understood if you wanted to cancel.'

'No, it's not that. I've been looking forward to it. The thing is... actually, do you mind if we wait for the others? There's something I want to discuss, and your input will be really helpful.'

'Okay.' He drew out the word and straightened up, head cocked to one side.

A server walked past them with plates of food and Laurel inhaled. 'I'm starving, do you fancy getting something to eat?' He declined, saying he'd already had tea. Rather than eat a proper meal alone, she bought a packet of salt and vinegar crisps for herself at the bar and returned to slide onto the bench seat beside him, leaving plenty of room for the others when they arrived.

'Oh, your poor hands,' he said as she opened the packet. 'What happened?'

She glanced at them. They did look a bit gruesome. Although they were very sore, they'd started to heal, so she'd taken off most of the dressings Hitesh had insisted on. Left with only a couple of plasters, the vivid red scrapes were visible.

'I had a bit of a tumble but it's worse than it looks... no wait, I mean, it looks worse than it is.'

As she was speaking, she clocked Albert strolling into the bar. He arrived at the table and asked the same question about her hands just as Maggie and – to Laurel's dismay – Nicholas came through the door.

Nicholas nodded to Albert, ignored Nathan, and turned to Laurel. 'And you are?'

She bristled. 'Dr Laurel Nightingale, nice to meet you.' She felt silly using her title, but made exceptions for people like Councillor Wright.

'I see. You're Maggie's new friend who's had her running around in the rain on some ridiculous *investigation*? Laurel, you say, as in Laurel and Hardy?' He smirked.

Ha ha, great one, Nicholas, I haven't heard that one before.

'I hear you're one of those psychiatrists. Got to say, I rather think our hospitals need more nurses and doctors than they do your lot. No offence.'

'Steady on, that's uncalled for,' said Albert.

Determined not to bite back with something that would upset Maggie, Laurel took a breath before replying. 'In fact, I was named after Laurel Thatcher Ulrich after she published her Pulitzer Prize-winning book, *A Midwife's Tale*. And I'm a clinical psychologist, not a psychiatrist.' She didn't have the inclination or the energy to explain the difference between the two professions to Nicholas; he was only trying to get under her skin.

'Are you staying?' she asked.

Nicholas glared for a second, then spoke to Maggie. 'I'll be heading home after my meeting with Marcus. I'll let you know when we're leaving.'

'Of course,' Maggie mumbled.

'Speak of the devil.' Nicholas spotted Marcus and Petra. 'Good to see you,' he called. 'No Barclay tonight?'

'Not tonight, just us,' replied Marcus.

Marcus was as impeccable as ever in a casual tweed jacket worn over a black T-shirt and blue jeans. Petra, in contrast, looked like she'd just come from a yoga class in her tight and very flattering gym gear. Laurel thought Petra might come to join them, but she headed for the bar where Sam was on duty and Nicholas stalked away to join Marcus. Laurel heaved a sigh of relief, which she changed into a cough when Maggie shot her a pained glance.

'Oh, my!' Maggie caught sight of her hands.

Laurel explained about her fall for the third time while Albert volunteered to get the drinks and Hitesh, the last of the party, arrived. She was pleased to see him. She hadn't been sure about him when they first met, but she couldn't have solved the case without him, and she knew he'd want to hear what had happened to his friend.

Waiting for Albert, she reached for her crisps to get a few in at least. Her stomach was protesting the lack of food, but the bag was suspiciously light.

Next to her, Nathan winced. 'Sorry, I'm a bit of a mindless eater.'

She rolled her eyes at him, but he'd probably done her a favour. What with all the cake encouragement from Maggie, junk food was the last thing she needed.

Albert returned and handed round the glasses. The group got themselves settled and looked expectantly at Laurel. She cleared her throat, a nervous tic, and started. 'I wonder if I could take a minute to talk about Lily?' She was excited to share her thoughts, but wanted to be respectful. Everyone present had known Lily and at least two had been her close friends.

'As some of you know,' she continued, 'there's been speculation regarding how Lily died: whether she took her own life or accidentally poisoned herself. But neither of those explanations fit the evidence. Hence, Maggie and I have been doing a little checking around on behalf of Rose, Lily's daughter.'

Nathan looked baffled. She hadn't mentioned any of this to him before, but she was happy he was there. He might even be able to feed this back to the authorities, who could confirm her conclusions.

Eager to get to the grand reveal, she gave a brief recap of the events surrounding Lily's passing away.

Nathan interrupted her. 'I know you mean well, but if there had been any reason for concern over the cause of death, we would have looked into it. It was an accident, most likely.'

'You're probably right,' Maggie agreed.

Now was the moment. 'Actually, I have some new evidence and I may be able to explain exactly what happened.'

Maggie drew back, a deep line appearing between her eyes.

'I'm really sorry, Maggie, I tried calling to tell you.'

'Oh, it's okay.' Maggie brushed it off, but Laurel resolved to apologise again later.

Looking around the table, all eyes were on her. 'I feel like Hercule Poirot.'

'So, you will be revealing to us a murderer, *n'est-ce pas?*' Albert put on a dreadful accent that might have passed for Belgian if the listener were feeling generous.

Now was her moment. 'Some of the evidence, such as it is, seems to point towards foul play: mail missing from the house; broken glasses; Lily in the wrong chair; an empty box of mint tea when we know Lily hated mint tea.'

'She got it for me, the tea.' Hitesh held up his hand.

'Yes, and the missing post was Derek, and the rest was mostly Lou, who was helping, sort of.'

'Laurel, there really was never any reason to think of the death as suspicious,' Nathan cut in. 'I know the officers who were called that day, DI Coral and DS Hill. They know what they're doing. Why would you think otherwise?'

Laurel clucked her tongue. 'No, I agree, it wasn't murder. I know that now. But I believe I can explain exactly what did happen. When Lou found Lily, there was a piece of fruit tart left on a plate next to her in the living room. This tallies with The Plump Tart cake boxes Maggie and I found in the kitchen. Importantly, Lou noticed that it was a fruits of the forest tart, with blackberries and red currants and stuff.

'Now, the last time I was in Lily's kitchen, Hitesh cleverly spotted that in a vase on the kitchen table were some sprigs from a yew tree, all dried out now, but identifiable. As you'll know, yew often grows in churchyards, like the one adjoining Lily's garden. Sadly, I believe Lily had cut some to put in a vase because of the pretty red berries. Later, when she was fixing herself a snack – the fruit tart – she must have put her plate on the table and knocked some berries off onto the tart. She didn't notice because they would have blended in with the red currants and her glasses were broken. We found them in the living room, all bent out of shape, and a lens was missing.

'I looked it up to double check, and I was right, yew is extremely poisonous and can cause heart attacks quite quickly if ingested. Not the berries themselves. They're the only part of the yew that isn't poisonous, but the seeds inside them are deadly. Lily must have eaten the berries along with her tart, and Lou inadvertently cleaned up all the evidence before anyone knew to look for it. It muddied the picture for a while. But there you go. It was a very unfortunate accident. Not murder, and not suicide.'

'Wow,' said Maggie after a pause, as everyone digested the revelation. 'That's incredibly clever that you worked all that out. Well done.'

Albert shuffled in his chair and Nathan scrubbed his face with his hands.

'Thanks, Maggie, but it was just a matter of having the right clues. Anyone would have figured it out, eventually.'

'One thing though–' began Hitesh.

The door of the pub crashed open. Maggie yelped and Laurel knocked over a glass in her haste to turn and see what was happening.

A man, his skin bone white, stumbled inside. 'It's Derek,' he gasped. 'He's dead.'

Chapter Twenty

The patrons of the pub followed the pale man as he cut across the corner of the green and led them round the back of the hall. No-one spoke. To repeat the horrifying news was to make it real. Hushed, they gathered to gaze at the figure slumped in front of the door. The fog, thick and heavy, could not disguise the bright splash of crimson nor the vacant eyes in the slack, drained skin of the face. Of Derek's face.

After a beat, Nathan stepped forward and took charge of the scene. He urged everyone to back up, then approached and knelt before the body. With a clean handkerchief donated by Albert, he reached out and placed a hand on Derek's wrist, searching for a pulse. A moment later, he gave a shake of his head and a sigh escaped the crowd.

From where Laurel stood, huddled together with Maggie and Albert, it was impossible to miss the arrow protruding from Derek's chest and the slick of crimson that had spread below.

'Maybe it was another accident?' murmured Maggie. She was looking pasty and swayed on her feet.

Albert offered her his arm, and she slumped against him.

'Perhaps you should get home and sit down with a nice hot cup of sweet tea,' he suggested to her. 'Where's Nicholas?'

They looked around, but Nicholas had disappeared, along with Marcus and Petra.

Laurel felt she could do with a bit of a sit down herself. She'd only spoken to Derek the day before, and now he was gone. Her stomach churned. It wasn't the sight of the blood, it was the shock of how quickly a living, breathing, frustrating person could be forced from the world through a violent act. 'It's probably best if we all head home.' Her breathing was rapid and the ground felt unsteady.

Albert rallied. 'Hitesh, would you see Maggie home? I know it's in the wrong direction for you, but would you mind? I'll see you home, Laurel. It looks like Nathan is going to be tied up here for now.'

At the sound of his name, Nathan left the body and walked over. 'Sorry, guys, I'm going to be here a while so I can hand over to CID, and I'm going to have to ask you to stick around, too. I need you to give your names and details to Ben – Sergeant Templeton. That's him there.' He pointed to a familiar-looking man with silver hair milling amongst the spectators. 'Best wait back in the pub. Ben will walk you all over now and he'll tell you when it's okay to leave.' He turned again to regard the body. 'Do you know someone tried to break into Derek's house just yesterday? They think it was this group of teens who've given him trouble before. Poor bloke. It never rains...' Shaking his head, Nathan walked away.

———

'Thanks for seeing me home, Albert, I feel... well, I don't know how I feel. I've never seen someone who's been murdered before.' Laurel blinked rapidly to stem the tears threatening to fall. 'That's two dead bodies since I moved in. What's that all about? Seriously, I just... I just...' She stopped and tried to take some slower breaths to stave off hyperventilation.

It had taken a while for them each to relate their information to Sergeant Templeton, and from what she could glean, no-one had seen or heard anything suspicious. The sombre atmosphere whilst they all waited their turn had shifted from shock and disbelief to unease and agitation. When Ben finally said they could leave, she felt a certain reluctance to part company with the other witnesses and was glad not to be walking home alone.

When she'd recovered her breath, and the swimming sensation in her head eased, she persuaded Albert she was okay to carry on. They passed the village pond and turned onto West Street. Any other time, Laurel would have gone via the attractive Manor Road, but that night it felt necessary to stick to the well-lit West Street.

There was a sinister undertone to the familiar streets. Every shadow could be hiding a malevolent assassin drawing back a bowstring, tracking her, waiting for the perfect moment to let fly the arrow. She shivered. Laurel had never really believed Lily had been murdered, but there was no doubt about Derek's death. No matter what Maggie wanted to think, no way was Derek being shot through the chest with an arrow an accident.

An icy finger ran down her spine. She looked around, trying to see into the darkness crowding in on every side. The lamps valiantly cast their light, but everything outside their glow was hidden and threatening.

'Laurel,' Albert's voice broke into her paranoia, 'maybe now isn't the time, but I hope you don't mind my asking, you weren't really named for Laurel Thatcher Ulrich, were you? If I recall correctly, her famous book wasn't published until around 1990 and she wasn't very well known before that.'

The laugh that escaped her lips felt good, even if the sound was immediately swallowed by the insidious fog. 'No, I just said it to shut Nicholas up. I didn't think he was likely to know anything about her or her book. I've got a few alternative famous Laurels that I use whenever someone trots out the obvious joke about Laurel and Hardy. I was actually named after Lauren Bacall. Mum loved old films, *To Have and Have Not* with Bacall and Bogie was one of her favourites. She always claimed that it was my dad's fault for not paying attention when Lauren got written down incorrectly on my birth certificate. Which is how I became Laurel.'

Albert chuckled. 'Funny things names. I've always been fascinated by their meanings. Which as a matter of fact led me to discover the great love of my life, linguistics: the study of language. You may already know that one meaning of your intended name, Lauren, is wisdom. Quite apt, I feel. And in case you were wondering, Albert means noble and bright. Just so you know.' He twinkled at her.

'Then it's well chosen,' said Laurel.

Albert inclined his head in gracious response.

'Linguistics, is that what you taught at university?'

'It was, and I still dabble. I am enchanted by how language evolves, as it should, and it's a wonderful thing. However, it's a shame when older words slip out of usage. I like to do my bit to keep them alive, so we don't lose them.'

Laurel smiled. It explained a lot.

'Nothing that promotes prejudice or that has become a term of oppression or subjugation, of course. Because language is in a constant state of change, there's always something new to learn and that nourishes my spirit. I'll never be finished. There's always more for me to discover. Somewhat like psychology, I imagine? Our knowledge of the brain and mind–body relationship is ever developing.'

Laurel nodded. 'I know a lot of people think it's a quack science – or not a science at all – but one of the things which so inspires me is the acceptance that nothing is definite, nor can always be proven, but a mind open to learning and discovery is the only way we advance our understanding. After all, even in physics, new discoveries often lead to revisions of previously known *facts*. We live in an incredible world. We are unfathomably complex beings; how can anyone claim to know anything for certain?'

'Quite.'

Their conversation was helping to take Laurel's mind off would-be assassins lurking beyond the light, but the fact of Derek's death hung heavy. She knew he'd rubbed people up the wrong way and had been rather full of himself, but those weren't motives for putting an arrow through him. She blanched at the image of his slumped body that reappeared unbidden in her mind.

She thought about his manner of death. Did it suggest premeditation? Generally, people didn't walk around toting bows and arrows, so it must have been planned. Not a crime of passion or sudden rage then, but calculated and organised.

For it to happen early in the evening was strange, too. The hall was just over the green from the pub, and although you couldn't see the back door from the road, anyone sneaking round there risked being noticed. There would have been a fair few people passing since the pub had been busy. Maggie and Nicholas, for instance, would have passed the hall. Perhaps they had noticed something or someone unusual.

Albert derailed her speculation. 'I wasn't a great admirer of Derek in these later years – he'd become quite the cockalorum – but I'm saddened at his death. I think he was an unhappy man, and he wasn't always likeable, but I think he meant well.' He nodded to himself.

'I've heard he has a brother, but does he– Did he have other family?'

'His parents are gone and Derek, well, he wasn't the marrying type, if you understand? I don't think he ever felt he could have any kind of romantic relationship, which is a shame.' He clucked his tongue.

'As to why he has been killed, I'm wracking my brain but can't imagine any reason someone could have wanted him dead unless, possibly...'

'The development?'

'Hmm, yes. That's the only thing that occurs to me. Derek did say he was going to look into the planning approval. He was simply a local parish councillor though, and had no proper authority or clout to uncover discrepancies in *county* council affairs.'

Laurel pursed her lips. 'Since we know he suspected dodgy dealings, what if he was close enough to the truth and talked about it to the wrong person?'

'Perhaps, but these days not much merits scandal. Even bribes and deals with friends are regularly exposed as happening in our own government.'

With a deepening frown, Laurel wondered aloud, 'I'm not an expert in forensic psychology by any means, but the method used to kill him – a bow and arrow – it doesn't feel... personal. It's more cold-blooded.'

They walked on, each lost in their own thoughts as they turned down Birch Lane and approached Laurel's cottage. The dark lane was hushed, the sound of their soft footsteps muffled by the vapour laden air. Trees loomed from the sides of the narrow lane and the houses were indistinct outlines.

If she didn't know an entire village was mere metres behind them, Laurel could believe she and Albert were miles from anywhere, isolated in a sea of white out of which might come terrible danger. She was anxious to get inside, close and lock the door, then crawl into bed and pull the covers over her head.

It began so softly that at first, she thought she must be mistaken; a faint click, click, click, moving closer. She stopped and Albert came to a sudden halt beside her. They listened, ears straining, eyes peering into the impenetrable gloom. Click, click, click... Getting faster. Coming closer!

A strangled, torturous cry split the night.

Laurel recoiled and shrieked, clutching at Albert. She could feel him shaking against her, and it took a second for her to realise that he was shaking with laughter.

He disentangled himself and made a soft clucking sound to the darkness. The cry cut off and the clicking resumed coming straight for them, materialising into a flurry of ginger feathers.

'Ah, you naughty rooster! You nearly took ten years off my life, you mischievous bird,' Albert scolded Aroon, who was now purring round his ankles.

Laurel had no idea cockerels could make any of the sounds she'd just heard from Aroon, and she wasn't appreciating the discovery given the frantic beating of her heart as she sucked in deep breaths and tried to calm herself.

'I'm sorry about that.' Albert was still chuckling. 'I should have known. He likes to wait for me on the gate to make sure I come home safe.'

'Come along, Aroon, let's see this young lady safely to her door and then get you tucked up with your hens.'

'Don't think that calling me a young lady makes up for your rooster scaring me half to death.' She gave Aroon a scowl. 'Bird brain,' she muttered. He clucked at her in return.

'He likes you. Great guard animals, you know. Now, in you go and I'll wait until you've locked the door.'

'Thank you, Albert. Despite this,' she pointed an accusatory finger at Aroon, 'I don't know what I'd have done if I'd had to walk home alone tonight.'

'Think nothing of it. Now, "There is a time for many words, and there is also a time for sleep".'

'Shakespeare?'

'Homer.'

'Simpson?'

'Very funny.' He chuckled. 'Goodnight.'

'Night, Albert.'

Chapter Twenty One

'I can't believe there's been an actual murder.' Maggie perched on the sofa in Laurel's front room. She was still pale but had come armed with her favourite chocolate éclairs. 'It makes you appraise your own life. Don't you find?'

Maggie was right. Home alone, once Albert had left the night before, Laurel had made herself some cheese on toast, grabbed a glass of wine and examined her reaction to Derek's murder. Her reflex response – in addition to the understandable shock and sadness – was to jump online and begin a new property search. Her fingers had all but itched to get at the keys on her laptop.

'I run away, you know,' she said, breaking the silence between them. 'When anything gets tricky in my life, I disappear. When Mum died, I buried myself in work. It kept me away from my feelings. It's a habit I need to change.' She studied her hands, tracing the faint scratches from her fall. 'Six months ago, I messed up at work and a man died.' She focused on keeping her breathing steady. 'That's why I'm here in Yorkshire, and why I'm not working. You might have noticed I don't give much away about my past.'

Maggie inclined her head and gave her a sympathetic smile. 'I had noticed.'

Laurel loved her for not jumping on the detail of the man who'd died. 'The man who...'

'You don't need to tell me.'

'It'll help to tell you, I think.' Now she'd started, she wanted to get it all out there, almost all of it. If Maggie rejected her once she knew, well, she'd cross that bridge when... if she came to it. Laurel was tired of giving half answers to someone she had come to consider a good, albeit new, friend.

She took a deep breath and broke eye contact. 'I have to be careful with confidentiality. He was my patient, and he had a brain tumour. I'd already seen some evidence of confusion and paranoia, so when he told me his brother was going to kill him, I wasn't as concerned as I should have been. His nurse and I spent time helping him to understand the effect of his brain tumour and how it wasn't unusual for him to have these scary thoughts. He seemed to improve and the staff caring for him reported a reduction in his anxiety.

'It was a shock then, when only a couple of weeks later, he died.' She pulled a tissue from her sleeve and pressed it to her nose. 'It happened a lot sooner than was expected. Prognosis is never an exact science, but it felt wrong. I couldn't stop questioning myself, going over and over the sessions we'd had together and what I should have done differently.' She shifted in her seat. 'What if I'd dismissed a genuine fear? What if his brother really did kill him? I followed up with his doctors, but I was told there were no grounds to believe his death was anything but natural.

'Soon, the stress, the self-doubt began to affect my work with new patients. I was second guessing myself all the time. I was starting to hate going to work.'

'You poor thing, but it really doesn't sound like you did

anything wrong.' Maggie gave a vigorous shake of her head. 'What did the brother say about it?'

'I never met him in person, and I couldn't have discussed it with him if I had, but the other family members and the community nurses all loved him. They said he was a bit of a new-age hippy, a gentle soul.

'Despite everything, and I didn't understand it, he was always the one my patient wanted with him on the most difficult days. I had no evidence beyond my patient's concerns. There was an inquest and the coroner ruled it death due to complications of his cancer, but I'll never be one hundred percent sure. I'm so cautious now of missing something that I suspect murder even when a death is obviously from natural causes. Shades of Lily, huh?

'In the end, the only solution I could imagine was to leave my job, the local area and move far, far away. *Et voilà*, here I am. What sort of psychologist does that make me?'

Maggie took Laurel's hands and held them tight. 'I know there's nothing I can say to make this better, but thank you for trusting me and sharing this with me.'

Not typically a tactile person, Laurel freed her hands, slipped them around Maggie's waist instead and held tightly. She felt lighter than she had for months. 'Thank you,' she mumbled into Maggie's shoulder.

With a final squeeze, Maggie drew back. 'Now, have an éclair. Pastry *can* make things better.'

In a voice still cut with emotion, Laurel asked, 'I know Derek's death isn't the same, but last night... Elderwick hasn't exactly provided the untroubled life I was desperate to find.'

'You must feel you've stumbled into one of those *Midsomer Murders* villages. This isn't usual, I promise.'

They laughed and the final knots in Laurel's stomach

slipped free. The self-reproach would always be a voice in her mind, but today, for now, it was quieter.

'Thinking Lily might have been murdered, I can see that's on me, but I'm glad I listened to my instincts instead of doing nothing again. I'm happy I was wrong.'

'Derek, though, did not die accidentally,' declared Maggie.

For all that had gone before, Laurel's appetite for puzzles and thirst for answers evidently wasn't satisfied because she jumped on the statement. 'Who do you think killed him? Whoever it was, they were taking quite a risk. The pub was really busy.'

Maggie nodded. 'It must have happened between six thirty, when the Neighbourhood Watch meeting finished in the village hall and, what was it, eight-ish, when that guy burst in? That gave me quite a shock, I can tell you. His face was so white.'

Laurel put her hand to her mouth. 'Seeing Derek... it's an image I'll find hard to forget.' She gave her head a shake as though she could dislodge the memory by force. 'There was the fog, that would have helped, but a bow and arrow isn't something you can casually carry around or hide down your trousers.' She contemplated the pastry Maggie had put in front of her and the éclair won the battle over her nausea. She enjoyed an indecently large bite, then wiped cream from her lips.

'True.'

'It is a weapon you can use from a distance, though. Maybe the killer used it so they wouldn't get any blood on them.' She took another mouthful and ignored the guilt of eating whilst discussing murder. 'Oh...' She held up a finger until she'd swallowed and could speak again. 'Do you remember, there's a bunch of archery equipment in the village hall for the Autumn Festival? I know Derek said he'd lock it away, but if someone was determined, I bet it wouldn't be that hard to break in.'

'It's possible.'

'It definitely looks like it was premeditated then. Someone needed to kill Derek, and they needed to walk away like nothing had happened. But why do it round the back of the village hall? It's out of sight, but I mean, it's hardly private. Why not go to Derek's house?'

'Well, he lives up on The Rise where it's all bungalows with low hedges, bright lights and mostly elderly residents.' Maggie heaved a great sigh. 'I heard Derek even persuaded a couple of people to get CCTV cameras by their doors. Nothing happens there that at least one person doesn't know about, and if one person on The Rise knows, everyone knows.'

That made sense. Anyone waving around a bow and arrow would have been spotted immediately. 'All right, that's something else to add to the picture. The killer must have known about that *and* where they could get their hands on a bow and arrow, which means he or she is local. That's good, Maggie. What else?'

'Why *would* someone kill Derek?'

They sat in silence, each chewing over the scant details. Laurel glanced at Maggie. Having been so self-absorbed, it was only now she noticed something was wrong; Maggie had barely touched her éclair.

'Are you all right?'

Maggie gave a small start. 'Yes, I'm feeling a bit under the weather. It must be the shock, and then walking home in the damp air last night.' She prodded at the pastry on her plate.

Reaching over, Laurel gave Maggie's arm a pat. She did look rather tired and drawn, and the dark crescents under her eyes suggested she too had suffered a sleepless night. 'Would you prefer it if we talked about something else?'

'No, I'm okay, and you've got a knack for this. Maybe if we

can work out who killed Derek, we can put it behind us and forget the whole thing.'

'All right, if you're sure? Let's go through who we saw last night and see if we can't eliminate some possibilities. We can jot down our thoughts as we go.' Laurel looked around for her notebook – it was never where she thought she'd left it. After locating it, she paused, pen poised above a fresh page. She pictured the pub in her mind. 'I suppose we should include ourselves. We were both in the pub, but we can go right ahead and rule out you and Nicholas because you arrived together.' She wrote their names, then crossed them out.

Maggie gave a brief nod.

Laurel carried on, 'I'd like to exclude myself because I didn't do it, but if you want to question me, Maggie, I have to admit I don't have an alibi. I walked up School Lane to Church Lane and didn't see another soul before I met Nathan in the pub. Speaking of Nathan, we can probably count him out as he's a police officer and what reason could he have?'

'We should add Hetty, too. I didn't see her in the pub but because of The Plump Tart she and her sister, Constance, stand to benefit from the new restaurants up at the hall.'

Laurel wrote down Hetty's name. 'What about Constance?'

'She's against the development, so probably wouldn't want Derek dead, but she could have a different motive?'

Laurel pictured the scene of Derek's death. 'Then again, because she's in a wheelchair, I don't think she could have fired the arrow that killed him. The angle's wrong. She would have been too low down. Let's leave her off the list. Who else was there? Albert arrived before you, didn't he?'

'Yes, he was there when Nicholas and I came in. I'm sure I saw him going in the door just as we were crossing the green, but Albert wouldn't hurt a fly, literally.'

'He and Derek didn't see eye to eye.' Laurel remembered

their behaviour on the stage at the village meeting and later the cool greeting at Elderwick Hall. They were civil to each other, but there was no love lost.

'It's true that Albert didn't like Derek's way of doing things. Derek could be a right fusspot bossy-boots, but that's not the reason they didn't get on. They used to be friends, but Albert had a cockerel–'

'Aroon, yes, I've met him,' Laurel interrupted with a grimace, remembering her last run-in with the bird.

'No, this was Aroon's predecessor, a cockerel called Aman. Albert raised him from a chick and let me tell you, this bird was the love of Albert's life. It used to follow him around his garden and even in the house. He would perch on Albert's shoulder when he was little enough. He was a noisy thing too and would crow at all hours of the day and night. With the wind blowing in the right direction, I could even hear him up at The Grange. Funny thing, I looked up the name Aman once – Albert always gives his animals such wonderful names – Aman evidently means the one who is peaceful.' She rolled her eyes.

Knowing what she now did about him, Laurel bet Albert had chosen the name deliberately, and it had probably tickled him every time Aman had made a din.

'A few people commented on the noise, but no-one seemed all that bothered until Derek took up the cause. He made a point of bringing it up with Albert at every opportunity. Telling him that if he didn't shut Aman up, then something would have to be done. No-one thought anything would come of it. I mean, what can you do about a cockerel? Then, a few months ago, Aman was outside the gate scratching around in the road... well, you can imagine what came next. Someone, I don't remember who, told Albert that Derek had been seen driving down Birch Lane at about the right time. Derek always swore it wasn't him, but I don't think Albert ever quite believed him... or forgave him.'

'Oh, poor Aman, and Albert. No wonder he and Derek fell out. Okay, for the sake of thoroughness, we should make a note of it, but I don't really see Albert wielding a bow and arrow in vengeance, do you?'

'I suppose not, but people get very attached to their pets.'

Laurel couldn't see Albert as a killer no matter what, so she moved the conversation on. 'How about Hitesh?'

'Hitesh? I think Lily was a good judge of character and she liked him.'

'Enough to give him his own key, even. I found out the other day when I fell over and he helped me wash and bandage my hands.' She glanced down at them again. They were healing up nicely. 'I agree. I don't see him as a killer. He told me he can't stomach blood and wounds and stuff.' He'd been so gentle with her she didn't want to believe he could be the savage felon they were seeking, the killer she'd suspected.

'He could have been lying, though, and as you pointed out, shooting someone with an arrow means you don't have to get in close to the gory bits. Let's keep him in mind.'

'We should find out if it's the residents of Drumble's Hive Marcus has earmarked for the foraging workshops in that... what on earth is it called? Professional something, something?'

'The personal development centre,' said Maggie. 'It sounds pretentious.'

'Bit like Marcus.'

Maggie chuckled, fished her own notebook out of her handbag, and made a note to check on the foraging courses. 'You can say that again.' Looking down at Laurel's list, she said, 'That gives us a few people who stood to lose out if Derek had got the development halted. Anyone else?'

Laurel ran through the remaining events of the previous

evening. 'Marcus and Petra arrived after you. We know Derek and Marcus were pitted against each other. Albert dismissed Derek's crusade as motive but it's the best one we've got.' Laurel remembered something she'd neglected to tell Maggie. 'And, when we were at Elderwick Hall for the open house I overheard Marcus telling Petra that they needed money so anything that might derail or delay the building work would be a problem for him.'

She wrote the name *Marcus*.

'Does that put Petra in the frame, too? She seems like a lovely young woman, but no-one knows much about her. She could be an expert with a crossbow.'

'Yes, let's add her to the list. After all, Marcus' money is her money. If the development were to fall through, she would lose out and–' Laurel broke off. There was something about what Maggie had just said. 'What makes you think it was a crossbow specifically that killed Derek?'

Maggie's face flushed bright red. 'I don't... I don't know, I'm just guessing. Crossbow, bow and arrow it could have been either, couldn't it?'

'Maggie,' she softened her voice, 'do you know something?'

She deflated before Laurel's eyes. Laurel stayed quiet, waiting until she was ready to speak.

'Derek was shot with an arrow – or bolt – from a crossbow, not a regular bow, and I know that because Nicholas has a crossbow.' Maggie whispered the words as the colour that had flushed her cheeks drained.

Laurel absorbed the information and then brightened. 'But Nicholas couldn't have done it because you were with him...' The look on Maggie's face told Laurel she'd made a very foolish assumption. 'You weren't together, were you?'

'No.' Maggie clasped her hands until her knuckles were white. 'He caught up to me just outside the pub. He'd been out since around four and I don't know where he went. He said he was going for a walk. He disappeared after we found Derek, too, and didn't get home until midnight. He probably thought I was asleep, but I was so rattled from seeing Derek and the arrow there was no way I could sleep. I heard the back door when he came in and he was on his phone, but I couldn't hear anything he said. Then he came upstairs and went to bed.'

'Did you ask him where he'd been when he got into bed?'

She shook her head. 'We have separate bedrooms, have had for years. I didn't speak to him, and he was gone before I got up this morning.' There was another moment of silence before Maggie gathered herself. 'Nicholas didn't do this. I don't believe it. You can't be married to a man for as long as I've been married to Nicholas and not know that he's not a murderer.'

Laurel didn't like to push it, but couldn't ignore what Maggie had disclosed. 'If we're being objective, we have to admit that Nicholas has an excellent motive for wanting rid of Derek. He is an investor.'

'No, Nicholas would never do something like that.' Maggie bridled.

'But you just told me about the crossbow.'

'Yes, but not because... not because I think he did it.'

'But you don't know for certain.'

Maggie stood up and glared at Laurel. 'I know my husband.'

'Do any of us really know what goes on in someone else's mind?' Laurel knew she'd said the wrong thing even as the words were coming out of her mouth.

Maggie threw up her hands. 'Don't give me that psychologist claptrap. I know my husband and I'm sorry you don't have faith in my judgement, but he is not a murderer!'

'Maggie, I'm not saying that he is, just that we should consider–'

Maggie didn't let her finish. 'Since you're always right about everything, you're going to have to include me as a suspect along with Nicholas, since what's his is mine, isn't that right? What's more,' she said, snatching up her notebook and handbag, 'I have access to his crossbow, too, and I know how to use it.' She marched from the room and out the front door, slamming it behind her.

Laurel stared at the closed door. Maggie had never so much as raised her voice before. She sat there, stunned, and a touch annoyed. It was only reasonable to consider all the possibilities, and there was a pretty good case that Nicholas could be guilty. Especially if he had been involved in some corrupt scheme with Marcus and thought Derek might expose him. If that were true, he had the perfect motive for murder. Which was why, despite her loyalty to her friend, she felt she had no choice but to contact the police to tell them what Maggie had disclosed.

Chapter Twenty-Two

Someone, in their infinite wisdom, had decided the Autumn Festival should go ahead despite Derek's murder. Laurel wasn't sure it was the best decision, but as a recent interloper it was hardly her place to say.

Dawn brought low cloud and a chilly drizzle, but by midmorning it had cleared to leave a bright and crisp day of fiery autumn shades. The marquee was set up on the south side of the green, probably to block the view of the village hall; no-one would want to be reminded about Derek's blood-soaked corpse when there was fun to be had.

Colourful stalls decked with bunting and balloons selling everything from pottery and handicrafts to cakes and jams were dotted around the village green. Excited laughter from children bubbled above the hum of conversation and the smell of frying sausages curled through the air. Keen to support local causes and a sucker for the cute kids, Laurel wandered over to inspect the cake stall selling baked goods made by the primary school pupils. She scanned the treats on offer. Most of them looked edible, if not entirely appetising. She bought a cupcake iced in snot green and a butterfly bun with no wings from an angelic little girl with crumbs around her mouth.

As the sun shone, more happy families descended in search of candyfloss, rides on the swing-boats, and a chance to win a random bottle in the tombola. Laurel considered a flutter but wasn't all that excited about winning washing-up liquid or low-calorie tonic water. There was champagne, but she didn't fancy her chances. She dropped a five-pound note in the collection tin and waved off the tickets.

She wandered off, keeping an eye out for Maggie. Since their conversation concerning Nicholas' weaponry, Maggie had been unreachable, making it a surprise when she'd telephoned the night before. Initially buoyed by the call, Laurel was disappointed to realise Maggie only wanted to ask if she could help out at the festival. Still feeling guilty for grassing up Nicholas, she'd swallowed her dismay and said yes. Neither of them mentioned crossbows or the police.

As she was scanning faces, she sensed eyes fixed in her direction, but when she looked, there was no-one and the crowds were shifting, making it impossible to pinpoint the source. Shaking off the discomfort, she caught the sound of Maggie's voice from behind her and turned with a smile.

'Laurel, thank you for helping today.' Maggie bustled over, looking officious with a clipboard under her arm. 'Let me show you where you're going to be.'

Glad to see her friend again, Laurel made small talk as they walked into the marquee, where around twenty paintings were on display under a banner reading: *Inspiring Women*. They were an odd assortment, but she was sure love and care had been poured into the works. Laurel admired the bravery of the artists and lamented her lack of the same; if she had any courage, she wouldn't shy away from the unspoken conversation that was hanging in the musty air of the tent.

Maggie took a minute to explain what she needed doing and made to head off.

Laurel called to her. 'Are we okay?'

'Of course,' she replied through a brittle smile. 'Why wouldn't we be?' And then she was gone, back into the sunshine.

Laurel rearranged the supplies of pencils, voting slips and ballot box. It wasn't necessary, but it made her feel better to be doing something. She unfolded four chairs from those stacked against the canvas walls with the idea people might sit and chat.

'Laurel? Laurel Nightingale?'

Her heart jumped as she swung round to see a tall, dark-haired woman in loose trousers and a soft green embroidered tunic moving towards her.

'Yes?'

'I'm Rose.' The stranger beamed as she abandoned the suitcase she was pulling and enveloped Laurel in a hug. 'It's so great to finally meet you. I wish it wasn't because of what happened with Mum and all that...'

As the greeting sank in, Laurel relaxed and hugged her back. 'Rose, it's lovely to meet you. I didn't know you were arriving today. I could have picked you up from the station.'

'It was no bother. I just hopped in a taxi and when I saw this going on,' she gestured around her, 'I figured I might find you here.'

'Come, sit down.' She guided her to one of the chairs. 'You must need a drink. Can I get you a cup of tea?'

Rose took her seat and arranged herself. 'You know what, I'd kill for a bacon sandwich. I've not had a decent one since I emigrated.'

Laurel winced at the turn of phrase but smiled and said, 'I know just where to get one.'

She kept a fruitless watch for a reappearance from Maggie

as she collected the sandwiches from Jo's stall. No matter what was going on between them, Maggie would want to welcome Rose. With that in mind, she dug out her phone, but true to form, there was no signal. Then she remembered, Maggie didn't even have a mobile. *Why do I even bother toting this thing around?*

Back in the marquee, Rose devoured the sandwich like a rabbit set loose in a vegetable patch. 'I needed that.' She moaned as she finished the final bite and licked her fingers. 'At least there's something good to being back in the UK.'

'How are you doing?' Laurel didn't know if Rose would want to talk about her mum yet, but she couldn't leave the elephant in the room unacknowledged.

Rose brushed breadcrumbs from her lap and dabbed her lips with a napkin. 'I'm okay. Being back here is making Mum's passing pretty real. Last time I was in the village was when I helped Mum move in.' Her voice hitched. 'She was so happy here; she loved village life, and she always enjoyed the Autumn Festival.' She swallowed a mouthful of her tea and gestured at the display. 'She was doing a painting for today, you know? Last time we spoke, she told me she was almost finished, and I bet she would have won, too. If I had arrived earlier, maybe I could have entered it on her behalf, a kind of tribute.' She pulled a tissue out of her sleeve and gave her nose a good blow. Her eyes were pink around the edges, but she smiled back at Laurel's concerned expression.

Laurel chewed on her thumbnail as something occurred to her. 'Rose, where is your mum's painting?'

'It'll be at the cottage. You probably saw it when you were there.'

'No, I don't think we did. We looked in her art room, but there was no painting that would match the theme of inspiring women, and it wasn't anywhere else in the house.'

'It should be there. Where else would it be?'

Laurel shrugged. It probably wasn't important. There were enough people with keys and access to the cottage that any one of them could have taken it. But would any of them do that, and if so, why? She should ask Hitesh if he'd seen it.

As if he'd known she was thinking about him, Hitesh wandered in, accompanied by Albert. They made a beeline for the tables crammed with glossy purple aubergines, huge golden pumpkins, punnets of blackberries, and masses of apples, waiting to be judged. Laurel had also spied some red currants. Bright shiny red jewels, quite unlike dull waxy yew berries. She'd felt a flicker of doubt about her accidental poisoning theory.

On spotting the two women, the men came over.

'Rose.' Albert took off his flat cap. 'How lovely to see you again, but I'm dreadfully sorry it is under such circumstances.' She stood and gave him a hug, her tall frame engulfing him.

'It's good to see you again. Mum always spoke so fondly of you and your menagerie.' She had a twinkle in her eye that wasn't from tears.

Hitesh then took her hand. 'I knew your mother well. She was a wonderful friend, and I am sorry for your loss. I lost a brother not so long ago and I know grief. Please tell me if there is anything I can do for you while you are here.'

'It's a pleasure to meet you and thank you; your friendship meant a lot to Mum.'

He blushed and shuffled to an empty chair.

Rose continued, 'Assuming the body is released, the funeral will be in a couple of weeks at Saint Stephen's. Mum loved that church even though she was an atheist. You'll all be there, won't you?'

'My dear, the whole village will want to give Lily a fitting send off. We'll be there. Don't you worry about that.' Albert patted her on the shoulder.

Mindful that a lot had happened since she and Rose had last spoken on the phone, Laurel was anxious to update her but didn't want to sour the mood. Rose, however, raised the question herself.

'Laurel, the more I've thought about it since our phone conversations, the more I'm positive she didn't take her own life. However, I just can't believe she might have been deliberately harmed.'

'I might have an explanation for you. It's just a theory... but are you okay with talking about it here?'

'May as well. It's not going to be any easier hearing it somewhere else.'

Laurel saw Albert and Hitesh exchange glances, but it was Rose's call and if she said she was all right, then she would tell her what had been uncovered. 'Well, it seems as though it was an accident, after all. We now know your mum had eaten a fruit tart before she died, and in the kitchen she had a vase of yew cuttings... small branches, twig type things. She must have put her plate on the table near the vase and knocked one or two yew berries onto the tart. Her glasses were broken, so she didn't notice and then–'

'Oh no, that's not right,' Rose interrupted. 'That couldn't have happened. Mum would never bring yew into the house. It's connected with death, sorrow, and mourning. Mum knew about that kind of thing, bits of old knowledge and beliefs to help her live in harmony with the land sort of thing.'

'But maybe–'

'That's what I was going to say the other night in the pub,' said Hitesh. 'Lily loved the yew trees in the churchyard but would never cut some to bring indoors.'

'Perhaps someone else–'

Albert delivered the final blow. 'The ones in the graveyard are all male, they don't bear berries so it couldn't have come from there, and Lily doesn't have any yews in her garden. I meant to tell you when we were walking home after Derek... but what with everything, I was distracted and out of sorts.'

Hitesh was nodding.

Laurel was baffled. It had made such sense to her. She felt her face colouring. She'd made such a big deal out of revealing her explanation in the pub the other night. She groaned and tried to voice the obvious question, 'So, if...'

Rose put down her cup and picked up the thread. 'So, if it wasn't accidental poisoning, what was it? And where did the yew come from?'

Chapter Twenty-Three

By late afternoon, the festival was winding down. Laurel still hadn't had the chance to speak to Maggie, and Rose had left to get herself settled at Church View. Whilst helping to pack up, Laurel was reflecting on the new information about Lily, when the blip of a siren disrupted the clatter of folding chairs. She whipped round to watch a police car speed along West Street with a distinctive Range Rover hurtling along in its wake.

In groups of one or two, then five and six, those left on the green congregated to mutter. Someone suggested they should check out what was going on. With recent events fresh in their minds, there was speculation there might have been another murder. Nobody stopped to ask if they would be welcome as, en masse, they began to march up the long drive to Elderwick Hall. Laurel found herself swept along in apprehensive curiosity.

Cresting the rise, she could see two police officers flanking Marcus as he and a man in a high-vis vest shouted and gesticulated at each other.

'You can't hold my team responsible, *sir*. When we dig up bones, we are required to stop and call the police. If you'd been here, we would have told you first, but you weren't, and your wife said you weren't answering your phone.'

'Is this some kind of joke? Did someone plant them?' Marcus was red in the face and a vein was pulsing on his temple.

'Why on earth would anyone do that?' The foreman's brow drew down into a deep frown.

'Even if they didn't, this place is going to be littered with animal bones. There used to be a deer park here, for heaven's sake. In your business, I'd expect you to take the time to look and realise it's a damn animal before you call the cops.' Marcus was shaking his finger under the man's nose and Laurel thought it would most likely have earned him a punch to the face if the police hadn't been there.

'Gentlemen, please. Mr Hartfield,' the officer speaking approached Marcus, 'Mr Huntley did the right thing and from what he told our dispatch, it is possible that these are human remains.'

It was Nathan doing the placating. Laurel hadn't recognised him at first; she hadn't seen him in uniform before. He looked good, better than good. *Blimey*, she scolded, *get a grip of yourself.*

Intent on hearing more, the huddle pressed closer just as Nathan's colleague noticed them. She motioned to Nathan, who looked around, as did Marcus.

'Get out of here, all of you,' Marcus yelled, storming towards them. 'This is private property and you're trespassing.'

'A public footpath runs up the driveway,' called a tall and angular woman in the crowd. 'We have every right to be here.'

Nathan's colleague walked past Marcus and, with a stern glare, held out her hands. 'I'm afraid we must ask you to leave, just for now. We have, um...' she paused, 'a finding that we have to investigate, and we have the authority to restrict access, temporarily, to the public footpaths that cross this property.'

'Is that true?' Laurel asked Albert, who had appeared at her elbow.

'No idea, my dear, but I doubt from the look of her she will brook any quarrel. Don't worry,' he added in a whisper. 'You see Mr Huntley there, the foreman? He and I go back a ways. We will undoubtedly be in possession of all the morbid details by supper time.'

Muttering, the crowd dispersed, the rumour mill grinding into action. More bones, another death? Surely not.

That evening, as she waited for Albert back at her cottage, Laurel busied herself in the kitchen. When she'd ducked out of joining the WI, she hadn't been lying when she bemoaned her culinary skills, but since her move north she was determined to learn to cook some new dishes. Like other areas of her life, the time was ripe for some variety. When Albert knocked on the door, she was searching for her best paring knife so she could dice a chilli for a spicy chicken laksa.

'Would you like to join me? There's more than enough for two.'

Albert sniffed the air like an aged bloodhound. 'How could I refuse?'

She set the table and busied round getting plates and cutlery whilst Albert settled himself down with a glass of cider.

'I didn't realise they were so far on with the process that the building had started up at the Hall,' she called over her shoulder to him from the hob as she stirred the aromatic soup, her face enveloped in cumin and lemongrass scented steam. The impression she'd gleaned from the community meeting and the open day at the Hall was that there was yet a way to go before breaking ground.

'No, no-one did. I'm not sure everything *is* finalised, but Marcus has been pushing to get the preliminary clearance underway. That's why he's had William Huntley's lads make a start by clearing out the areas beyond the formal gardens, taking down old walls and whatnot.'

'Was it in the orchard that they found the bones?'

'From what I gather, it could well have been, but don't quote me on that. What I do know is they'd moved most of the stones from a long section of wall when one of them spotted an object sticking out of the ground. Evidently, this chap first thought it was a bit of tree root or random detritus but when he gave it a tug, it became obvious it was a bone. They dug around a bit more and found other, smaller bones. At this point they called William, who shut the work down and called the police.' Albert spread his hands.

Laurel had questions. 'Do the police think they're human bones?'

'They sent all the workers home and have called in an expert to take a look. Even if they are human, they could be what I believe is called *of antiquity*. However, William saw them and whilst he thinks they're old, old enough that there's no flesh left on them, he doesn't think they're ancient.'

'Bones have been found at Elderwick Hall before, haven't they? Nathan told me that the first time I met him.'

'Indeed, and it's an interesting thing. I hadn't thought of it for a long time, but this has brought it back. Derek was one of the youngsters who found them. It would have been, oh I don't know, around 1974 or 1975 when he was about ten or eleven.'

'Those bones *were* human, weren't they?'

'They were. It was quite a scandal. The bones were from a woman aged between fifteen and twenty, and it was estimated that they'd been in the ground for around forty or fifty years. Naturally, an investigation was begun, but Marcus' grandfather, Randolph, who was a powerful man around here, was also a close friend of those with influence, including the chief of police. Nathan's dad as it happens.

'The general belief is that Randolph got things hushed up. The veracity of that has never been proven, but since very little ever came of the investigation...'

Albert really is the font of all knowledge, Laurel thought. 'Fifty years isn't that long. There must have been people in the village who had some ideas as to whose bones they were?' she queried.

'Yes, there were lots of ideas about the identity of the poor girl. Almost every conversation that summer was about the bones. Randolph was insistent it must have been one of the young people who were hired between the wars as seasonal labour to bring in the apple harvest. He said it was probably an accident or a fight amongst the workers, something he'd had no knowledge of at the time, naturally.'

'Naturally,' echoed Laurel, thinking how it was always the way when rich and powerful men were involved.

'There was a fair amount of speculation amongst the rest of us that they could have been the bones of Harriet, Randolph's wife, who abandoned him and her son, Clement. We only ever had Randolph's word for it she actually left Elderwick and that she left alive. Then, of course, there was the maid who went missing and who was, according to gossip, pregnant with Randolph's child. Randolph, sad to say, was very much a Hartfield like his ancestor, Archibald. Both nitheful men and known bedswervers.'

'I'm going to need to draw a family tree to keep all these Hartfields in order.'

Albert's mouth quirked in a wry smile.

She had another question, a grim one, but it felt relevant, 'With the bones, you said the maid was pregnant... was there... I mean, could they...'

'No.' Albert rescued her from having to ask it outright. 'There was no evidence of a baby.'

'So, in summary, it could have been any one of a number of women buried up there in a shallow grave?' It was shocking to know there were so many possible candidates. The history of the Hartfields was as murky as the village pond. 'I'm beginning to think it was a serious error of judgement for me to move here. That's a lot of death for such a little village.'

Albert shrugged. 'If you dig deep enough – excuse the pun – most old towns and villages will have their fair share of dark and disturbing affairs.'

'I suppose.' Her thoughts lingered on an image of bones in freshly disturbed earth. 'How did Derek come to find the bones?'

Albert harrumphed. 'Derek got himself trapped in the orchard one night. He claimed Marcus had been trying to scare him by saying that the ghost of little Charlotte Hartfield haunted the orchard where she was killed. Marcus apparently dared him to climb the wall. Derek was a boisterous child growing up, always getting into scrapes and up to mischief, so up and over he went and then he couldn't get back out.'

'Hold on.' This didn't add up. 'How could Marcus have been there? He must have been a toddler?'

Albert flashed a wicked grin. 'Marcus likes to shave a few years off his age, and I imagine that Botox and fillers play their part, and yes, Derek looked older than his years, but I can assure you, they were contemporaries.'

She couldn't see it, but she believed him. 'I don't mean to be callous, but being boisterous and mischievous doesn't sound anything like the Derek I met?'

He gave a heavy sigh. 'Finding the bones disturbed Derek, and it changed him. Marcus had given him a boost to get over the wall in the first place, but they'd given no thought to how he'd get back. So, he's in there kicking about, trying to climb back out when he falls over what looks like a bone. He digs around a bit and uncovers some more bones, some jewellery, and finally a human skull. He shouts to Marcus to tell him to get him out of there, and Marcus heads off to find a ladder.

'The thing is, Marcus never went back. All night, Derek was trapped in that orchard. It was summer, so he wasn't going to freeze, but bravado in the bright light of day quickly vanishes when the moon rises and you're ten years old and alone with a skeleton in a haunted place. It wasn't until the next day that he was found by the gamekeeper.

'Derek told me all this years later, we'd become pals of a sort and would meet for a drink in The Snooty Fox now and again after I'd moved back from London. One night he'd imbibed a few pints, and it all came out. It'd haunted him ever since, the sight of the skull grinning at him with the glint of moonlight making the shadows seem alive.'

'Poor kid.' Despite her unpleasant run-ins with the adult, Laurel's heart went out to the scared little boy he once was. 'These days, what he experienced would be considered a trauma and ideally, he would have been offered help and support.'

'I suppose now that he's no longer with us, he can't mind me sharing with you that he did seek therapy when he was in his thirties. Unfortunately, the person he saw did something that triggered a recurrence of his nightmares. He became severely depressed for some time after.'

She nodded to herself. No wonder Derek had balked at the idea of a psychologist practising in the village after such a harrowing experience of therapy. 'It sounds as though he was re-traumatised.'

'I bow to your superior knowledge of psychology, but that would fit with his reaction.'

'I wonder if these new bones are linked to the ones he found?'

'I expect we shall find out in due course.'

The timer pinged on the oven, interrupting the gloom that had descended. Laurel stood to dish up, topping up their glasses of cider along the way. With an unspoken agreement, they talked about less grisly subjects whilst they ate. Namely, the vexing question of why her hens still weren't laying any eggs.

Chapter Twenty-Four

Laurel was desperate to call Maggie and share Albert's news about the latest bones. There was a chance that she would have already heard, but at least they could put their heads together to try to work out what it all meant and perhaps put their falling out behind them.

She picked up the phone to dial, wishing again Maggie had a mobile so she wouldn't have to risk speaking with Nicholas. She punched in the numbers and heard it ringing and ringing, but no-one answered. It was nine on a Saturday evening, so it was possible they were out at some council dinner or were entertaining friends. Possible yes, but a little voice in her head piped up to ask if Maggie might be avoiding her and was screening her calls. What if she'd blown her friendship with Maggie before it had begun?

A worse explanation muscled its way in to her thoughts. What if Maggie had confronted Nicholas about the crossbow and he'd harmed her to keep her quiet? What if, even as the phone was ringing, her lifeless body lay wrapped in an old carpet in the boot of his car while he waited for an opportunity to bury her deep in deserted woodland?

Laurel hung up and massaged her temples. There was no evidence that anything was wrong. Besides, after her tip-off, if Nicholas were guilty of murder, the police would have arrested him by now, wouldn't they? The logic did little to shift the cold lump of dread sitting in her stomach.

She spent the rest of the evening stewing over what state Maggie might be in and trying to make some sense of the recent deaths: an accidental poisoning that was looking less accidental by the day; a murder by crossbow; and now bones found at the site of a nearly three-hundred-year-old murder of a child. The same site where another collection of bones had been found by Derek and Marcus as children. Sleep eluded her for hours as images kept popping unbidden into her head. First, she saw the terrified face of ten-year-old Derek alone in the dead of night. Then Nicholas pointing his crossbow at Maggie. She tried reading for a little while and when that didn't help, she retrieved her notebook from the living room and wrote down all the ideas and half-baked theories she could imagine. Finally, she resolved the best plan was to call Maggie again the next morning and if there was no answer she would go round in person. In all likelihood, she'd find Maggie safe and well and she'd feel silly for worrying.

As early the next day as seemed polite, she called The Grange again. Over and over she heard the phone ring, but no-one ever answered.

She pulled on her boots and a jacket and snagged her umbrella from its place by the door and went out into the muted, damp landscape. The misty drizzle clung to her hair and clothes. It was gone nine, but the world felt murky and indistinct, fuzzy at the edges. The few leaves left on the trees drooped, pulled towards the ground laden with the weight of water.

Approaching The Grange, Laurel could see the wrought-iron gates were closed. She couldn't recall them ever having been so before. Despite the gloom, no lights were on inside; the house looked abandoned and shuttered, as though the occupants had packed up and left for the winter.

She held down the buzzer on the intercom for a second, already convinced there would be no answer, and she was right. Frustrated, she set her finger on the button once more and held it. Ten seconds. Twenty. Thirty. Her count was approaching forty when a voice burst from the intercom.

'Who the hell is it and what the hell do you want?'

'It's Laurel. I need to speak to Maggie, please.' She tried to keep her tone civil.

'She's not here. Go away.'

'Where is she?' There was no answer, so she pressed on the buzzer again, knowing it would rile him further, but not content to leave without speaking to Maggie, or at least knowing where to find her.

'I swear I'm going to come out there and—'

She cut him off, giving up on politeness. 'Tell me where she is, and I'll go away.'

There was a pause so long she was reaching to buzz for a fourth time.

'She's gone away for a few days. Now get lost.'

'When will she be back?'

'None of your damn business.'

'Is there a number I can reach her on?'

No answer, and this time there was still no response after a full two minutes of buzzing. Short of climbing over the gates or scaling the wall, neither of which Laurel thought she could do, there was nothing else for it but to leave.

Dejected and not in the least reassured, Laurel trudged back up Whirligig Lane – the delightful name for once failing to raise a smile – and crossed South Street, taking the path round the back of the churchyard and past Lily's garden. The church glowered from behind a waist-high wall. She remembered reading that unusually for a church, its main door sat on the north side, a side for centuries regarded as the 'Devil's side'. There had been no explanation Laurel could find to explain why Saint Stephen's had been designed that way, but that morning, in the grey and drizzle, scared for Maggie, it felt appropriate. *This place and everything that's gone on here*, she thought, *it's corrupted.*

Being too short to see over the wall as it grew to enclose Lily's garden, she didn't know if Rose was up and about yet. She thought about calling in but dismissed the idea and instead crossed the road to where the footpath continued and would eventually bring her out at the far end of School Lane and only a short stretch from her own front door.

She was swallowed by the trees crowding in on either side of the trail, their roots breaking the surface of the compacted dirt ever ready to trip the unwary. In her darkened mood, this usually pleasant shortcut felt threatening. She should go back, take the long way round. Instead, she plodded on, desperate to get home and shut out the world. With each step, she listened for an echo, worried she was being followed.

An indistinct sound, not from behind but ahead, brought her to a halt. She listened, breathless, until it came again, laughter, soft and quickly stifled. Probably a couple out early walking the dog. She took a few steps more, placing her feet quietly until she could see who it was before they saw her.

'Hitesh, wait.' A woman's voice.

She stopped and held still. Was Hitesh with a girlfriend?

'What if he finds out what we've done?'

'Honestly, Marcus has no idea. There's no way he could know, and it had to be done. I had no other choice but to get rid of him.'

Was that Petra?

'You know he'll find out eventually.'

'Not necessarily. We need to keep quiet.'

'I know.'

Fading footsteps told her they were moving away in the opposite direction. Laurel let out a shaky breath. She'd spent years helping her patients to change their habits of jumping to conclusions, of making assumptions, but after overhearing this exchange, she couldn't help but question: were Petra and Hitesh romantically involved with each other? And who was the *he* they had got rid of? Were Petra and Hitesh involved in Derek's murder?

Chapter Twenty-Five

Despite all attempts at distraction, Laurel's thoughts were drawn back relentlessly to the conversation in the woods. She wondered if she should report what she'd heard? What had she actually heard, though? Neither Petra nor Hitesh had mentioned Derek by name, they had only referred to *he*. Hardly conclusive evidence. They'd spoken of Petra having *got rid* of someone though, and who else could they have meant but Derek?

What about the other question raised by her eavesdropping? Were Petra and Hitesh involved with each other? That could be a motive for murder. If Derek had found out and threatened to tell Marcus, might they have felt compelled to silence him? Laurel couldn't see Marcus taking lightly the news his wife was having an affair. Petra could have been scared for her safety, and the same for Hitesh. Based on her own experience with Derek, Laurel could easily imagine him running to Marcus with news of the infidelity.

She switched off the television programme she was failing to watch and slumped back on the sofa. She was going round in circles over Derek's murder and Maggie's disappearance, and the speculation was getting her nowhere. Maybe reading would be a more effective distraction. She reached for the book she'd left on the side table, but her hand met empty air. Frowning, she stood and turned in a circle, casting her eye over every surface. It took two revolutions before she spied it nestled in amongst others on the bookcase. She had no recollection of putting it there.

Rubbing her temples, she admitted she might need a break. A break from constantly thinking about death, clues, and motives. But she couldn't forget Maggie. She wouldn't relax until she knew she was okay, even if her friend never wanted to speak to her again.

Nicholas was likely to call the police on her if she went back to The Grange, so that wouldn't achieve much. What else could she do? Biting her lip, she reached for the phone and dialled. 'Nathan? Hi, it's Laurel. Look, I don't know if you're at work or busy, but I'm worried about Maggie and I'm hoping you can either put my mind at rest or you can talk me down if you think I'm getting carried away?' The poor guy was probably ruing the day he let Maggie talk him into a date with her.

After a second of silence, Nathan replied. 'Let me go in another room. I'm round at my mum's.'

She suppressed her urge to apologise and tell him she would call back later. If she did that and it turned out her good manners made the difference between life and death for Maggie, she'd never forgive herself. It felt melodramatic to think that way, but then, it wouldn't exactly be the first murder in the village that year.

'Right, I'm back. What's up? Are you okay?'

'It's not me, I'm fine. It's... I know I'm being overwrought, and I'm sure it's nothing...'

'But...?'

'But I haven't seen Maggie since yesterday morning, and I

can't get her on the phone. I'm worried she confronted Nicholas about his crossbow and he's done something to her.'

'Let me check I've got this right.' Nathan's calm manner was helping already. 'You saw Maggie yesterday and now you're worried her husband is a killer and he's done something to Maggie, since you saw her... yesterday?'

When he said it like that, it did sound like she was an over-imaginative worrywart. 'I know it sounds ridiculous...'

'It's okay, I know people are on edge after Derek. It's understandable, but you can't go jumping at shadows all the time. It's like the Mrs Armitage business again. You need to trust the professionals. Look, I shouldn't tell you, but we talked to Nicholas about his crossbow – I'm glad you called me about it – and I can't say much, but there is nothing to suggest Nicholas was involved. Maybe he and Maggie have had a fight. Maybe she's gone to stay with a family member or a friend?'

'I'm sure you're right, but I'm worried and I thought if I did nothing and Maggie had been hurt, then...' she let her sentence ebb into silence.

Nathan lowered his voice. 'Confidentially, I can tell you that as a precaution we asked Nicholas if we could take one of his crossbow bolts to compare it with the murder weapon and he gave his permission freely.'

'And was it a match?'

'We don't have the results back yet.'

Laurel felt the hairs on her arms stand on end. 'How do you even know Nicholas hasn't got other bolts hidden somewhere?'

'What he gave us, he gave voluntarily. We had no reason to search his property. I don't know what you want me to say?'

'So, I'm just supposed to wait? That doesn't reassure me much,' she snapped.

He sighed. 'Look, we need to follow up on a couple of things with him anyway, so how about I offer to be the one who goes round, and I can have a chat and see if I can find out where Maggie has gone? It'll be informal though. I'm not officially working this case. I'll be doing this as a favour to you, so if he doesn't want to talk, there's nothing I can do.'

'That would be great. Thank you so, so much. Can you go today, and can you call me as soon as you've been?'

'I'll go as soon as I can, I promise.'

He hung up, leaving Laurel alone with the dial tone. Having come to Elderwick wary of forming friendships and being vulnerable, Maggie had breached her defences with astonishing rapidity and Laurel was surprised to find that she was glad. Now she just needed Maggie to return home safe.

She still had the phone in her hand, as if expecting Nathan to call back already. At least knowing he was following up on Maggie's disappearance, she was free to pursue her suspicions about Petra and Hitesh. An idea was forming of how she could do her own bit of detecting with Mrs Hartfield. It could be risky, but it was Petra. What was the worst that could happen?

Chapter Twenty-Six

Laurel knew she couldn't very well rock up at the front door of Elderwick Hall and ask if Petra was available without some kind of reason. She didn't know Petra or Marcus well enough for it to be a casual visit from a friend. So, she would have to engineer a meeting. She happened to know there was a yoga class held every Tuesday in the village hall at 11am. Petra struck her as having a flexible work schedule, and she already knew she went to yoga classes, so conceivably it was a place she might find her. It was a stretch, but worth a try.

There was a time early in her career when Laurel had kept space in her routine to practice yoga, go swimming, and hiking, but as she'd become more senior at work, her scant free time had been eaten up by all the extra hours demanded by her role. Another example of not practising the self-care she encouraged in therapy. *Bad psychologist.*

Unfortunately, a pre-yoga shopping trip was required since her gym gear no longer fit. She'd been able to get it on but wouldn't trust the seams to survive the first downward dog. Her yoga poses would be an embarrassment by themselves without flashing extra flesh to all and sundry.

Monday had been taken up with house-move admin, meaning it was early Tuesday that she got in her car for the short trip into Beverley. Before leaving Elderwick, she did a slow drive-by of The Grange, but there was no sign of Maggie or Nicholas. Nathan hadn't got back to her yet, and she was loath to hassle him again in case he cut her off. She would have to trust he'd let her know any news, even if the not-knowing was sending her crazy.

Once in town, it didn't take her long to grab a few pieces in the athletic-wear store. She hadn't wanted to spend any more time there than necessary. Already self-conscious about her body, those kinds of shops added a whole new layer to her inadequacy. The staff were invariably super fit, and she felt like such a fraud: a lumpy, middle-aged gym-dodger.

On her way back to her car, she saw the library and the temptation to do extra digging into the dark secrets of her new home was too much to resist. A quick look and she'd still have time to get back for the yoga class. Stepping inside the grandly named Treasure House was like going back to her childhood. It had everything she loved: shelves packed with books; worn yet comfortable-looking chairs in corners; a cheery children's section with bean bags and posters for story time; and the cocooned hush of every good library.

Much as she would have enjoyed losing herself amongst the stacks, she was on a mission, one with which the knowledgeable librarian, Dakila, was only too happy to assist. He suggested Laurel start with the microfiche of old local newspapers. Using the information from Albert about the bones uncovered in the 1970s as a starting point, Laurel uncovered a trove of information. Mindful of time, she printed off a bunch to read later. Dakila was kind enough to locate an older piece about Marcus' grandmother, Bethany, who had vanished following the death of her baby girl from pneumonia. Giving it a quick scan there and then, Laurel could see the reporter was hinting at Bethany having taken her own life. She arranged to have a few more of the most intriguing pages printed out to read later.

She caught sight of the time on a silent wall clock, reluctantly gathered up her belongings, and thanked Dakila, who had taken the liberty of signing her up for a library card. On her way out, seeing a display of crime novels, she decided to put it to immediate use and, despite still not having finished *Murder is Easy*, grabbed a copy of another Agatha Christie, *The Body in the Library*, as her first book to borrow. She would suggest it to Maggie as their next read.

At ten minutes to eleven, Laurel was back in Elderwick and standing outside the village hall. If Petra didn't turn up, she might give the class a go, anyway. It would do her good to get a bit of exercise. Luck was on her side though, when with a minute to spare, the black Range Rover pulled up and Petra hopped out looking perfect in navy-blue Lycra. Laurel tugged self-consciously at her new leggings and adjusted her sports bra, hoping nobody would notice her unlovely effort at rearrangement.

'Laurel?' Petra called as she saw her. 'I've not seen you here before. Nice to have you join us. Are you going in? It's not a very challenging class, but it's convenient and a break from my ashtanga.'

They walked up the steps together and into a space the same as every other village hall she'd ever been in: scuffed wooden floor; peeling white paint on the walls with brown patches of damp; the smells of sweat and stewed tea. Petra made directly for the front, situating herself in a prime position, but Laurel hung back, taking a spot in the last row. She laid out her mat, adjusting the position so she was as far away from everyone as possible. In an approximation of cobbler's pose, she took a deep cleansing breath and tried to look like she was a yogic regular, not an out of shape imposter. She scanned the room and saw a mixed bunch: a couple of women in their early twenties, at a guess; some middle-aged chatty types; and a lady who must have been seventy if she was a day.

The instructor, Caitlyn, started the class with sun salutations, a gentle start, but the undemanding soon gave way to what could only be described as slow torture. After ten minutes, sweat dripped down Laurel's back and muscles she hadn't used in years woke up, then gave up. Forget triangle pose, she couldn't even manage child's pose. Every attempt to sit her back on her heels and then walk her hands forward just left her with her bum sticking in the air. Caitlyn was kind and kept coming over to assist, but by about the midway point she must have reached her limit because after an awkward flailing arm half-moon pose, Laurel was left to her own devices.

Hot and embarrassed at the end of the ordeal, she gave her face a wipe with the edge of her T-shirt and ran her fingers through her damp hair. She didn't have time to nip into the loos for a refreshing splash of water, not if she wanted to catch Petra again and invite her for a drink – the whole purpose of the endeavour. The scone she'd been dreaming of was out, though. She couldn't show herself up in class and compound it by eating a scone with cream and jam. It would be quinoa salads and lentil soup from here on.

She mumbled goodbye to the others, lying through her teeth about seeing them the same time next week, and caught up with Petra by the Range Rover. With crossed fingers she invited her for a chat, to which Petra readily agreed, and they wandered over the green to The Pleasant Pheasant.

'I usually fast until dinner, but I don't think one treat will kill me.' Petra laughed, once seated. She asked Jo for sparkling water and a bowl of muesli with almond milk.

Laurel had mentally settled on avocado toast as a compromise between her stomach and her minimal self-restraint, but switched to raspberry tea and a natural yoghurt instead.

'Is that all you're having?' queried Jo.

'To be honest, I'm not very hungry.' Her stomach rumbled.

Petra grinned, but was good enough not to comment. 'It's nice to have the chance to sit down and get to know you a bit. I don't have many girlfriends I can gossip with in the village.'

'Speaking of gossip,' Laurel seized the opening. 'I heard about the bones. Doesn't it creep you out staying at Elderwick Hall with the history of the place, the curse, and now more... old... new-old bones showing up?'

'Oh no, I'm not a believer in that curse nonsense.' Petra waved her hands around. 'I've heard all the stories, but it's only an unfortunate series of events, nothing more. Marcus and I aren't even at the Hall much, but I've always felt very at home when we do stay.'

Jo delivered their refreshments and Laurel tasted her tea, leaving space for Petra to keep talking.

'I would have liked to make it a proper home, but I would miss the city too much to live here permanently and you can't keep a big house like that to use only a few weeks of the year. Marcus may come from money, but I don't, and it wouldn't sit right with me.

'What about you, Laurel? I thought you'd be the sceptical type, not into ghost stories and curses?'

Petra's blunt curiosity surprised Laurel into giving a candid answer. 'I was a total sceptic growing up, but then I experienced something inexplicable. I won't say it made me a believer, but I can admit there are things we don't yet understand about this world.'

'What was it? What happened?' Petra leaned forward.

Laurel had never told anyone the story before, but if opening up was what it took to endear herself to Petra, then it would be worth it. 'It was the day after my mum died.' The heaviness of her loss sprang to life once more. 'I was exhausted when I went to bed, but I woke up around 3am and I knew my mum was there with me. I can't explain how I knew. I couldn't see her or anything, but I felt her presence and all my sadness and grief went away. Only for a moment, but in that moment, I could tell she was happy that she'd left behind the pain of her failing body, and she was at rest.' Speaking it out loud wasn't so bad.

'If that had been all, I would have thought it was a dream or wishful thinking, even though it felt as real to me as it feels sitting here now talking to you, but there was something else. When I went downstairs the next day, there was a ring on my dining table. It was a ring Mum had given me when I was ten, but I thought I'd lost it. I had been looking for it the day she died and then there it was. No-one but Mum knew I was looking for it. No-one else had been in the house. I have never been able to come up with another explanation for it other than my mum put it there for me.' Laurel was surprised at herself, she hadn't planned on telling the part about the ring. She fiddled with her cup.

'So, I don't believe in ghosts as such. You know, spirits that wander the earth and haunt old houses. But I do think something of us lingers a little after our death before moving on.'

Petra reached out and gave her hand a quick squeeze. 'I don't know what I'd do if I lost my mum.' She reached for a napkin and dabbed at her eyes.

'Are you close?' Laurel shifted back into her comfort zone as the one who asked the questions.

'We were. She doesn't approve of Marcus, so we've not been in touch as much lately. Every time I speak to her, she always has to throw something in about how he's too old or that he'll just want me to pop out babies for him. Last time, I told her it was my life and I love Marcus, so she needs to get used to it.' Petra's tone was angry, but the tears remained.

'Say no if you like, but why don't I give you my number, in case you ever need someone to talk to about it? Not as a therapist, just, you know.' It felt premature to say friend.

'Thank you.' Petra sniffed and checked her mascara in a compact mirror as Laurel wrote down her number. 'Here's mine.' Petra proffered a business card and swapped it for Laurel's note, which she dropped into her bag.

Sensing Petra would appreciate a change of direction, Laurel remarked, 'You and Marcus make a good-looking couple.'

'Thank you.' She smiled and her face brightened. 'Marcus is hot for his age and image is important for me, since a lot of what I do is online. I'd like to move away from that though, get into more serious work instead of bite-sized hints and tips in perky little TikToks. What I'd love would be to host retreats for young women starting out in business, expand on what I do already. I think there's a huge market for it.'

Laurel made a guess. 'And Elderwick Hall would be the ideal place to host retreats?'

'Yes, that's exactly what I said when I first saw the place.' Her eyes shone with enthusiasm. 'I generate more income from modelling though, and Marcus is encouraging me to pursue that rather than business, especially right now, since we need the money. I mean, we don't need it longer term. Marcus is loaded, but things will be a bit tight until the new houses start being sold.'

'So, it would be a big problem if the development didn't go ahead for any reason?'

'You could say that.' Petra bent her head to her bowl of muesli.

'Does it worry you?' She asked it casually but was intent on her companion's reaction and response.

Petra pushed the last clusters around in her bowl. 'Not really. Marcus tends to get his way, and if he wants this to happen, it will. He's out at a meeting tonight actually, finalising the last outstanding details.'

Conscious of the people at nearby tables, Laurel lowered her voice to ask, 'But was Marcus worried about Derek pursuing this thing about the planning approval being given so quickly?'

'Oh no, Derek didn't worry him. What was Derek even going to do? I know he's dead, and you shouldn't say mean things about people when they're dead, but he was a sad old busybody... not that he deserved what happened.'

It is a common misconception that psychologists were especially skilled at spotting liars, and Laurel had too much experience to flatter herself as an infallible judge of character. Nevertheless, she tried, but couldn't detect anything in Petra's voice or manner that suggested she knew more about Derek's death than anyone else.

'Who could have wanted him dead? Have you heard anything?'

Petra thought for a moment, her brow furrowed, and then with a swift glance around the room she leaned forward and beckoned Laurel closer. 'I don't know if I should say this, but I heard he was trying to have The Plump Tart closed down.'

'The bakery? Why?'

'No idea. Sam at The Snooty Fox told me, and he heard it from Hetty when she was in having a drink. Being a vegan, I'm not a big cake or pastry eater, but I love their little shop, so I'm glad he didn't get his way.'

It would be interesting to talk to Hetty to see if she could draw her on Derek's reasons for wanting to close them down. It didn't seem like much of a motive, but everything was worth checking out at this point.

Laurel had finished her yoghurt and raspberry tea, and Petra seemed to be done with her muesli. She had to introduce Hitesh to the conversation before Petra decided it was time to leave. She took a gamble. 'I bumped into Hitesh the other day. Do you know him?'

'Hitesh, yes, I think I've seen him around the village a couple of times.'

That was interesting; Petra had spoken as though they were barely passing acquaintances. 'I'm pretty sure he's vegan, too. I think that's their thing up at Drumble's. Anyway, I thought I saw the two of you chatting the other day. I called, but you can't have heard me.'

Petra's cheeks flushed. 'You can't have done.'

'Now I think about it, yes, it was definitely the two of you, Sunday morning when it was horrible with drizzle.'

'Well, it wasn't me. Just because we're both vegan doesn't mean we're in some vegan club together or something. You must have seen him with someone else.' Petra was tearing her napkin into small strips.

'I'm sorry. I didn't mean to imply anything.' Laurel held up her hands.

'There's nothing to imply.'

Laurel remembered something else. 'Who's Barclay?'

If she wasn't mistaken, she saw panic in Petra's eyes as she screwed up what was left of the napkin and threw it onto the table. 'You're being a busybody just like every other damn person in this stupid, small-minded dump. It's none of your business.'

Other customers were looking round.

'I've got to go.' Petra jumped up and bolted for the door.

Laurel sat back in her chair and ignored the stares. She might not have got an answer to what Petra and Hitesh had been discussing, but she had confirmed it was serious enough for Petra to be fearful about having been seen. Fearful enough to have forgotten her purse, and her share of the bill, in her hurry to leave. It lay on the table where Petra had placed it. She slipped it into her bag and smiled; Petra had handed the perfect excuse to go up to Elderwick Hall.

Laurel's stomach gave an audible gurgle. To heck with healthy eating. She ordered a bacon butty, and it was only as she sank her teeth into the soft white bread that an unwelcome idea occurred, one which should have been obvious: if Petra was a murderer, Laurel may have just put herself in danger.

Chapter Twenty-Seven

I n between worrying about Maggie and analysing Petra's
reactions to her questions in the café, Laurel spent the
afternoon reading the newspaper articles she'd found at the
library. As she delved further into the reports, one thing that
stood out was the local press response to the finding of the
original set of bones in the 1970s.

There were some great initial pieces and even some photos,
not of the bones themselves but of scraps of clothing, plus a
locket that had also been discovered in the grave. Then the story
just disappeared, and she hadn't been able to find any follow-up.
She knew from Nathan they'd never discovered the identity of
the deceased, but it was an abrupt end to what must have been a
huge affair. She supposed Albert was right; the incident had
been hushed up.

She'd been jotting down some notes while reading about the
most likely candidates for the bones. The papers referenced a
maid, rumoured to be pregnant by Randolph Hartfield, who she
recalled both Nathan and Albert had mentioned. A second
possibility – and the one the reporters clearly favoured – was

that the bones belonged to Bethany, Randolph's wife and Marcus's grandmother. It wasn't said outright, but the subtext was that if she hadn't committed suicide, she might have been the victim of murder. Laurel was eager to return to chat with the librarian and see what else she could uncover.

By the time she put aside her research and finished her light supper, darkness had fallen. She'd planned her visit to the mansion for when she thought Marcus would be at the meeting Petra had mentioned, leaving Petra home alone.

She gambled that six-thirty would be late enough for him to have left and too early for him to be returning. She dressed warmly, and only just remembered to grab Petra's purse, before opening the door to step into an unkind autumn night. Snug in her pocket, her fingers found her phone, and an idea presented itself, an insurance of sorts. Pulling off a glove, she typed a message to Nathan, hoping there was enough signal for a text at least to be delivered.

It would be Halloween in a week, and some households already had pumpkin lanterns and cobwebs ornamenting their hedges and doorsteps. It was a time of year that held fond memories for Laurel. Every year of her childhood, her mum had cooked a special spooky themed tea of *severed fingers* hotdogs and *fresh blood* cherryade that she and Laurel would eat together lit by candlelight in their small kitchen. It wasn't until she was much older, and alone, that Laurel properly appreciated the effort her mum had put into those grisly feasts.

A streetlight at the end of her lane cast a saffron glow, but from there on up the lengthy driveway to Elderwick Hall, all was darkness, the scudding clouds dulling the light of the full moon. Pulling her coat tightly around her against the bitter night air, she felt her nerve waver. The sensible part of her wanted to turn around and go straight back to her warm cottage rather than face a long walk alone in the dark.

She thought again of the overheard conversation and of the purse in her pocket. If not for Derek's murder, she wouldn't think twice about popping up to drop it off. It wasn't even that late, despite the dark. Spurred on, she moved through the gates and beneath the stately oaks that whispered as they danced above her. Small animals rustled in the undergrowth and gravel crunched beneath her boots.

She held her nerve and put one unseen foot in front of another until the Hall rose like an inky monolith ahead of her. The shape a deeper black than the sky. Out of the night images materialised: Alice, the young wife, cast out into the cold by an enraged Archibald. Alice, terrified and injured, clawing her way up the steps, hoping for salvation only to find the door closed to her forever. There was no need for Halloween decorations here.

She crossed the cobbles, mounted those very steps, then stood before the door. A single lighted window the only sign of life. She faltered. She raised her hand to ring the bell, then lowered it again. Her mission now felt foolhardy. Petra could be a threat. The longer she stood there, the more the cold seeped into her core. Her eyes watered and she shrugged deeper into the folds of her scarf.

It would be pointless to leave having accomplished nothing. She steeled herself, grasped the handle and tugged, setting off the pealing of bells, echoing in the space beyond. She listened for footsteps, but there were none. No-one came. An icy gust pulled at her hair. She shivered. The seconds ticked on, but her presence remained unacknowledged.

It didn't seem right to hold on to the purse, so she thrust it through the letter box and turned to leave. She looked at her phone; Nathan hadn't texted back yet. She sent another message to say that she was safe and on her way home.

Moving away through the courtyard, a flicker danced in her peripheral vision, bringing her to a halt. She stood, silently watching the space where she thought it had been. Nothing. Perhaps she had imagined it. Then, so soft, a cry. Was it the wind? It came again, a child's voice. But it couldn't be. Her heart thudded in her chest, and she was gripped by indecision. Could there be a child wandering alone up there in the blackness? What if there was? What if they were lost and afraid? She thought of Derek, trapped in the orchard, a traumatised schoolboy.

Her mind was playing tricks. Had to be. The stories, the dark, it was nothing more than a phantom conjured by her overactive imagination. No, there it was! The light was back, and it was moving. She could see it on the far side of the formal gardens. Trembling, she moved through the gateway and around the side of the Hall. She was compelled to follow but couldn't call out; her voice was frozen in her throat. Whoever, or whatever, it was, disappeared through a doorway in the far hedge.

Her footsteps were painfully loud on the pathway, and blood rushed in her ears. She reached the hedge and found a second gate leading out to the grassland beyond. It stood ajar, moving soundlessly back and forth as the wind caught it. She stepped over the threshold. The faint illumination making it through the cloud cover from the moon helped little on the vague and formless landscape ahead. For a while there was nothing, until once more the light flared, held for a moment and went out. Not a torch. A candle? Too windy. A lantern then. But how did it appear and disappear so quickly?

She remembered the view when she'd looked out of the gallery window during the open day. She tried to orient herself and guessed she was facing in the direction of the old orchard. Of course she was. A nice, haunted orchard, just what she needed.

She struck out for where she'd last seen the light. The

shapes of ancient trees loomed ahead of her. She pushed on. Each breath was frost in her throat and sharp in her nose. Wishing she'd worn a hat, she tucked her hands deeper into her pockets and hunched her shoulders. *What are you doing? What are you doing!* The thought reverberated in her head.

Conscious of roots as she neared the treeline, she edged forward gingerly. Brambles tugged at her clothing and tall nettles brushed against her. A wall faded into being. Dried moss covered crumbling dead stone. She sensed before she could properly see the gaping hole torn through its structure. She peered into the depths of the space. Where once would have been the gnarled boughs of apple trees, there was emptiness. The ground covered with scrub where nothing fruitful had thrived for many years. She ran her hand down the rough wound and dislodged a rain of small pebbles to clatter onto those already below. She strained for any noise, watching for a return of the lamp. There was nothing but the ragged in and out of her own breath.

If she was careful, it would be perfectly safe to cross the threshold, but she stayed rooted. Ice crawled down her spine, blood thundered in her ears, and her vision swam as the shadows loomed greater.

She felt a presence.

Laurel had no recollection of how she'd got back home, remembered only running, stumbling, terrified a hand would reach out to grab her shoulder. How she hadn't twisted an ankle crossing the open grassland searching for the invisible driveway was a miracle. It didn't bear thinking about what would have happened if she'd become disoriented or incapacitated.

Chest heaving, body trembling, she rummaged for her key

and unlocked her door with shaking fingers. With a final glance backwards, she slammed shut the door and locked it against the dark. She didn't know who else, or what else, had been out there, but it was no child.

She considered calling Albert but that would be pathetic. She was a grown woman. Maybe the whole thing: the light, the noises, had been an illusion. She was overtired and spooked by all the recent events, not least the bones and the eerie stories of Elderwick Hall. The last thing she should have done was to go wandering round up there at night alone. Back home in the light and warmth she could almost believe it was all down to an overwrought imagination. The village and all the stories, they were getting to her. It was the obvious explanation.

The ultimate rescue routine was called for: a hot water bottle, a good book – definitely not a murder mystery – and the safety of her bed.

She sat bolt upright and, through bleary eyes, read the bedside clock: 2.17am. She cast around for what had disturbed her. The light she had left burning in the hallway was out, its gentle glow no longer chasing away the frozen shadows of her room. A beat of fear pounded in her chest as the same sense of being watched from the orchard sluiced back over her. She held still, listening for any sign that someone was there, but she couldn't hear beyond the rush of blood in her ears.

An owl screeched, making her jump. A shaky snort of laughter escaped her mouth. The bird must have called once already; its cry had woken her. 'Another bloody bird, scaring me half to death,' she muttered. As for the lamp, the bulb had blown. That's all. Nothing sinister. She snuggled back down in her bed – they couldn't get you if you were under the covers. She'd investigate in the morning.

It was a long time before her heart stopped racing.

Chapter Twenty-Eight

The grey light of dawn crept through the curtains. Laurel's head felt muzzy, and regret lay thick. She shouldn't have pushed Petra about Hitesh. She would get in touch and apologise, see if she could mend that bridge. As soon as Maggie returned – she had to remain positive – she would apologise to her, too, and would suggest they drop their investigations and focus their energies on their original idea of a book group.

She hauled herself out of bed and plodded along the landing, stopping by the lamp. She tried the switch. The lamp came on. She flipped the switch back and forth and it switched on and off. She picked it up and gave it a shake to check for a loose connection, but it appeared to be in perfect working order.

Not awake enough yet to puzzle it out, she unplugged it and continued on her way downstairs, where she lifted up the phone to dial The Grange, hoping Maggie had returned. Once more, no-one answered. Next, she tried Nathan, but he wasn't picking up either. It was possible he was screening his calls and avoiding her. Another apology to make. Finally, knowing that putting it off would only make matters worse, she grasped the nettle and called Petra.

Laurel wasn't a great fan of most vloggers or influencers or whatever else they called themselves. From what she'd seen, many of them were peddling an unrealistic lifestyle to young, impressionable people, but Petra's videos were different. They didn't promise untold wealth and didn't push snake oil remedies. Her content was thoughtful and practical, and available to everyone, no subscription required.

'Here goes nothing,' she muttered, and dialled Petra's number.

'Hello?' The voice was hesitant.

'Hi, Petra, it's Laurel.'

'Oh.'

'Look, I want to apologise for yesterday and make sure you got your purse back? I posted it through your door.' She held her breath and crossed her fingers.

There was a long pause.

'No, I should apologise; I didn't mean to bite your head off, and I did get my purse, thank you. Sorry I missed you. I ended up popping out to a soul cycle class in town.'

So, it couldn't have been Petra skulking round in the dark.

'Actually, I'm glad you called,' Petra continued. 'You might be able to help me out with something.'

This was going better than expected. 'Happy to. What's up?'

'Actually, it's something I'd rather talk about in person. I know this is an imposition, but I don't suppose we could meet up? Not at the café, somewhere private. Maybe you could come up here? Would today be okay? Anytime.'

Despite her recent scare, Laurel was intrigued and spied an opportunity to have a bit more of a nose around Elderwick Hall. Perhaps she might even wangle an invitation to look at the orchard. In the light of day, it was unlikely to provoke such terrors as it had in the dark of night. 'No problem, I'll be along in twenty minutes.'

The walk to the hall was different in the daylight and though she had expected a bit of unease, Laurel enjoyed the stroll. Elderwick Hall was just a normal, albeit grand, house with a sad history. Nothing more. Nothing less.

Petra must have been watching for her because she opened the door as Laurel reached the steps. Her expression was cheerful, but her manner distracted. She ushered Laurel in and through to a snug off the hallway.

'I'm sorry to land this on you, but I don't know who else to talk to. I know you can't be my therapist, but maybe you can tell me what I can do?'

Feeling a little cautious since it was always a mistake to blur the friend–client boundary, Laurel settled herself into a chair. 'Why don't you tell me about it, then we'll see what we can come up with.'

Petra sank onto a sumptuous turquoise velvet sofa and put her head back for a moment as she gathered herself to speak. 'Marcus got a call first thing to say that those bones they dug up aren't human, they were from a deer after all. Probably one jumped the wall years ago and then couldn't ever get out or whatever.'

'Wow.' Laurel was taken aback. 'That was quick work by the police. I thought it'd take ages to get them analysed.'

'It's not official yet, but Marcus knows people on the force. They still have to get it verified, but his contact is absolutely certain. Anyway, the thing is, he's been really weird since the builders found them. I know having bones found in your back garden is weird and I know the history of those other bones, but his reaction was, I don't know how to describe it... epic, I guess. He's totally convinced someone buried them deliberately to get at him.'

Laurel remembered hearing him say the same thing when he was arguing with the foreman.

'He hasn't stopped ranting about it since, but he won't tell me why he thinks that. It's crazy; he's sounding paranoid. He's been talking about this ridiculous curse too, saying that we need to leave now and go back to London, maybe even abroad, to get away from it. I caught him looking at flights to Qatar. I don't want to go to Qatar. I can't even find Qatar on a map! Do you think he's having a breakdown?'

Laurel considered her words before speaking. 'I wouldn't like to speculate on someone's behaviour from a second-hand account, but it's obviously upset you. What do you think is at the bottom of this?'

'I didn't think he believed in the curse, but if you look at his family history, it hasn't gone well for any of the Hartfields. Maybe he's worried history is repeating itself. Those bones discovered years ago caused some real problems for his dad, Clement, and for Marcus' granddad, Randolph, who was still alive. Marcus could be worried the same will happen to him. But we know this time they're not human, so why he's not calmed down and who he thinks is out to get him, I don't know. I'm getting weirded out by it.'

It wouldn't be a surprise if the bones being discovered had revived the stories of the curse of Elderwick Hall for Marcus. Add to that, stress over the development, and it could explain his behaviour. 'Are *you* okay? Are you worried about your safety, or his?'

'Oh god, no. Not in the slightest.'

That was a relief. 'Has he booked any plane tickets yet or made any definite plans to leave?'

'No, and I made him promise he wouldn't without talking to me first.'

'And he only found out today that the bones are from a deer?'

'Yes.'

'Would it be okay to give it some time? See if he calms down? I'm guessing he's been under a lot of pressure with the development, especially as some locals are vocally against it. That could explain why he's feeling persecuted. Has he been sleeping well?'

'No, hardly at all. He's been working all hours and sleeping even less than usual.'

'That's not going to be helping in the slightest. I wonder if he'd be open to taking a short break. Would that be possible?'

'We could go back to London for a long weekend. Marcus is meant to be taking a back seat with the development project. He owns the house, of course, and that's his investment, but he's getting himself far more involved than was planned and I think he's annoying the other guys. He's got a meeting with Nicholas on Thursday evening so we could head off some time after that.'

'That sounds like a good plan if you can get him to go for it. And if the issue persists, do you think he would talk to someone about it?'

'You?'

'Not me, no, but a therapist, yes.'

'Probably not, but maybe a couple of days away will do the trick. Thank you for listening to me blather on.'

'Any time. I'm just glad to be of help.' Laurel hesitated before deciding that nothing ventured, nothing gained and said, 'Petra, what we disagreed about the other day. The thing is, I didn't mean to, but I did hear you and Hitesh talking.'

'Oh.'

'Yeah, and I know it's none of my concern, but...' She wondered how to phrase it delicately.

'You heard us talking about getting rid of someone, and you think we were talking about Derek?'

Laurel worried she was about to be shown the door, or worse.

Petra slumped, looking defeated but not afraid. 'I understand why you feel you have to ask. You took me by surprise when you asked me about it in the café; I had no idea anyone heard us. Sorry for biting your head off. It's something and nothing, but I promise you, we had nothing to do with Derek. I'd rather not go into detail, and I suppose you can tell the police if you think you need to, but could you consider taking my word for it and let it go, for now?' Petra pressed two fingers to the bridge of her nose and closed her eyes.

Laurel was left to mull it over. On the one hand, what had she actually heard? It was so easy to take conversations out of context. However, what if she didn't press Petra, or pass the information on to the police, and it turned out she and Hitesh had been involved?

'Even if you want me to tell you, how will you know I'm telling the truth?' Petra asked without opening her eyes.

It was a valid point. 'You've got me there. Okay, let's forget about it, but if I have to say something later, I will.'

'Fair enough.' She sat back up and made eye contact. 'I promise it wasn't about Derek. Now, shall I give you the guided tour?' She grinned. 'Come on, let's start with the grand dining hall; it's my favourite room.'

Having heard and read so much about the house and the family, Laurel was thrilled to see more of the imposing home. Whilst it wasn't what she'd imagined – the house was much lighter and less stuffy than she'd pictured – it didn't disappoint. The magnificent drawing room at the rear of the property had three seating areas, two fireplaces and immense windows looking out over the formal garden. In the opulent bedrooms, there were fraying tapestries of exquisite detail, handed down through the generations, Petra explained, and now destined for a museum in Bath.

The only incongruous room was the library. It had the expected row on row of books on polished wooden shelves, and they were impressive, but it was a room dominated by a gigantic television screen. Petra studied Laurel as Laurel looked at the monstrosity with a frown on her face.

'Yeah, kind of spoils the vibe, doesn't it?'

'Why?' Laurel asked, bewildered.

'Marcus has a lot of international business interests and when he's on a video conference call, he likes them to see him in here. If you look, the camera is there,' she pointed to a slim box affixed to the top of the TV, 'and his desk is here so anyone seeing Marcus on screen sees this view.' She turned Laurel round.

She wouldn't have noticed it otherwise, but now it had been pointed out she could see from this new angle a carefully staged set. The oldest, most impressive books were on the shelves behind the desk. There was an imposing fireplace that would be in view on the left and on the right. In a gap between the draped windows was a display of at least five awards. They'd be almost out of sight, but not quite.

'I admit I do use this TV to check out my Insta pics. Look.' Petra took her phone from the back pocket of her jeans, swiped her finger around, and there on the screen was a picture of her in an impossible yoga pose.

'Impressive,' Laurel said. 'The pose and the technology.'

'Enough of that. Let me show you the most fascinating feature of this old place.'

Walking to one of the bookcases, Petra crouched down in the corner and pushed on a book. The lower shelves swung outward to reveal a cavity behind.

Laurel looked on in wonder. As a girl, she'd always dreamed of owning a house with secret passages. 'Is that a priest hole?'

'Ha, yes!' Petra clapped her hands.

It was a cramped and dingy space and Laurel pictured a frightened priest quaking and praying to be saved as the pursuivants paced the rooms in search of hidden spaces. She crouched down to get a better look but didn't go so far as to crawl into the claustrophobic bolthole.

Shattering her romantic notions, Petra announced, with a certain glee, that it wasn't a real priest hole. 'It was added sometime in the 1940s to fool and entertain guests. Marcus shows it off to everyone who visits.'

Laurel left the library, feeling silly and disappointed, but didn't have time to wallow. She steered the conversation round to the old orchard. Unfortunately, Petra made it clear that she was loath to discuss it. Not wanting a repeat of their falling out, she moved the conversation to safer ground. *Better to keep on Petra's good side and try again later.*

'Where do you plan to live once the building work gets properly under way? Will you be going back to London for good?'

Petra wrinkled her nose and said, 'If I can talk Marcus out of moving us abroad, then yes, that's the plan. Although, I can quite see myself living in the south of France, that would be spectacular.'

They laughed, and it was good to feel that they were on friendly terms.

'Speaking of France,' said Petra with a twinkle in her eye, 'let's have a glass of wine. What do you say?'

'I say make mine a large one.'

In an ultra-stylish kitchen with quartz worktops and a huge American-style fridge-freezer, Laurel perched on a bar stool that was even less comfortable than it looked. Petra and Marcus had kitted the space out with every contraption and appliance a professional chef could dream of, despite being infrequent residents.

Taking a bottle out of a full height wine fridge, Petra hopped up next to Laurel and poured two generous glasses of pale rosé. Laurel savoured her drink while Petra talked about the small cocktail party she'd persuaded Marcus to host on Halloween.

'You will come, won't you?'

'I'd like to see someone try to stop me.'

Chapter Twenty-Nine

Laurel's phone pinged with an incoming text as she was walking up the garden path to her door. Desperate for news of Maggie and in her hurry to read the message, she almost tripped over the covered dish on her doorstep. She bent to pick up the dish whilst reading the text and was disappointed to see it wasn't the information she was hoping for, just an update from Nathan. He said he'd called round to let her know there was no news yet on Maggie.

Her shoulders fell and she slumped her way inside, depositing the dish onto the kitchen table. Lifting the cloth covering, she saw golden pastry and a sniff told her it was apple and cinnamon. Even though she disliked baked fruits, it smelled divine.

It was a lovely gesture by Nathan, or his mum at any rate; she couldn't picture her friendly local copper wielding a wooden spoon. Maybe she would pop round and see if Albert would like to have it. It would be criminal to let it go to waste.

In fact, she would go and see Albert straight away. There was always the chance he hadn't heard the latest on the bones and she might be ahead of him for once. She grabbed the pie, relocked the door, and travelled the few steps to Albert's cottage. She hadn't seen the inside yet and wondered what it would tell her about this wonderful, if slightly peculiar, man.

Albert's cottage from the outside looked very much like her own, only his woodwork was painted French blue instead of sage green. The postage-stamp front garden was given over almost entirely to ornamental grasses to striking effect. In the centre, with a dramatic splash of colour, was a hip-high Japanese maple, an extravagance of flaming red.

She knocked and found the door swinging open under her hand. Movement drew her eyes down to the threshold where it wasn't Albert greeting her, but her night-time foe, Aroon. She looked at him. He gawped back. 'Hello,' she said. The bird tilted his head as though listening and blinked.

A hand tapped her on the shoulder. 'Blimmin' heck! Albert, you gave me the fright of my life!'

With a broad smile, he apologised. 'Sorry, I heard you knock. I'm just doing a few jobs in the garden. Why don't you come on back?' He shooed Aroon outside and reached past Laurel to pull the door closed before leading the way round the side of the house.

She wouldn't be seeing the inside of his home today, then.

Albert pointed her towards a cushioned garden chair and she held out the pie. 'I was hoping that you could give this a good home?'

'Ah, my dear, I can indeed. How scrumptious,' he said, taking a peek.

Laurel held on to it. 'Let me pop it in the kitchen for you, shall I?'

'Oh no need to bother yourself, you can deposit it on the table there and I shall have some as a morning snack if you'll join me?'

'I'm not a fan, actually, but you go ahead. I hope you enjoy it.'

'I'm afraid that I don't have any delicacies to offer you in return.' He looked crestfallen. 'I'll tell you what, I promised to take Jo a couple of my fat marrows so let's take a wander to the café. We can both have something there and I shall save the pie for my tea. Hold on here for a moment and I'll be right back.'

Albert disappeared inside, leaving Laurel to admire his garden, which was crammed with fruits and vegetables. She spotted raspberry canes, pumpkins, cabbages, Brussels sprouts, cauliflowers, onions, marrows, pears and an apple tree heavy with variously shaped apples, and that was just what she could see from where she was sitting. Was that a yew tree down at the far end, tucked out of sight, bar a few branches, behind a towering oak? Not that yew trees were rare, but it was interesting. *Oh good grief, do you ever stop*, she chided.

Deliberately looking away, she smiled to glimpse a cheeky robin perched on an upturned flowerpot and, for a moment, put all her worries aside and let the sounds of the garden soothe the spikes of anxiety sparking through her mind and body.

'Gosh, this is amazing,' she said when Albert reappeared. 'You must be almost entirely self-sufficient?'

'I do well out of it, it's true. I've been meaning to say for some time, if you ever have a hunger for anything that I have here, do let me know and I will provide.'

'That's very generous, thank you. What I might ask of you as well, if it's okay, are some tips for growing such fab produce. Nothing too tricky, but I'd love to have some peas and carrots of my own.'

Albert nodded. 'It would be my pleasure. Now, as we walk, tell me, have you heard the latest? The bones were from a deer, after all.'

Reuters could learn a thing or two from the denizens of Elderwick.

They took their time wending their way to The Pleasant Pheasant, and as they walked, Albert told her snippets of village history. He pointed out where various people had lived over the years and how many of the older residents were related to each other either by birth or marriage. Pretty much every building in the village had a story connected to it, and Albert knew them all. She asked him if he'd ever considered writing them down and publishing a book on the history of Elderwick. He admitted the thought had crossed his mind, but he simply hadn't had the time since his retirement to write so much as a postcard.

The café was evidently the place to be on a Wednesday morning. Hetty was chatting in the kitchen with Jo; Petra and Marcus were sitting at a corner table, both wearing headphones and staring at their laptop screens; and Nathan was jotting things down in his notebook as he spoke to an elderly couple. Albert whispered that they were Derek's neighbours.

They squeezed themselves onto chairs at the only available table. Laurel didn't even need to pick up the menu to order when Jo rushed over. She knew what she wanted and went ahead and ordered a bacon and brie sandwich.

'Good choice,' trilled Jo, before dashing back to the kitchen.

'Albert,' Laurel said when they were alone again, 'nothing happens in this village without you knowing about it. Have you heard anything since Derek was killed that might shed light on his murder?'

'My dear, I have not. I'm sad to say. I truly wish I had. No-one deserves to have their life taken even if they are a gnashgab. Derek and I didn't always see eye to eye, but I wouldn't wish what happened to him on my worst enemy. He could be a busybody and thought he knew best, but he hadn't had an easy life.' He broke off to thank Jo when she appeared with his cup of tea. 'I hope people won't think of him unkindly now that he's passed,' he continued. 'And, for the record, I never believed Derek killed my old cockerel, Aman. Did you hear about that? Stunning bird, and friendly too. A fine specimen of a Silver Spangled Appenzeller, only one in the county, as far as I knew.'

Laurel nodded as though she understood what on earth an Appenzeller was.

'I know Nathan saw Derek driving past my place at the right time, but Derek wouldn't have lied about it if it had been him that killed the poor bird.'

They shared a moment of silence.

Laurel was about to ask him to explain gnashgab, when the ping of a text interrupted. She must have stumbled into an isolated zone of mobile coverage. She dug in her bag and fished out her phone. Squinting at the screen and vowing to get herself an appointment at the opticians she read the message aloud, 'It's from Rose. Apparently, the police found some of Lily's post round at Derek's and they've just now returned it to her. She says she thinks she's solved the mystery of Lily's missing painting, and that she's popped something through my letter box, which will explain it. All very cryptic.' As she was pondering what Rose could mean, the bell over the door jangled and Hitesh shuffled in carrying a cardboard box.

'Good morning to you all,' he announced to the room. 'Jo, I've got some more apple juice for you.'

Jo's voice rang out from the kitchen, fighting above the sound of hot fat spitting in the skillet. 'Hitesh, is that you? Bring it on through, there's a love.'

He disappeared and Jo came out to deliver their food.

'This looks divine, dear lady,' said Albert, patting his green paisley shirt over his stomach.

'It really does, thank you,' added Laurel. 'I'll tell you what, if

Hitesh's got time, perhaps he'll join us for a drink or even a bite to eat. Can you ask him if he'd like a mint tea on me?'

Hitesh's voice called out from the kitchen, 'Anything but mint! I am not a fan.'

Laurel looked pointedly at Albert and was about to voice her consternation when the door flew open and Nicholas stormed in, his face puce, his eyes bulging.

'You!' His glare settled on Laurel. He jabbed his finger at her, shouting, 'You! You devious, trouble-making little...'

'Hey!' Albert cut in.

'Stay out of this, Albert.' Nicholas didn't take his eyes from Laurel. 'You think you're so clever. You think just because you've got doctor in front of your name you can come here and start poking your nose into other peoples' lives, put all kind of nonsense into peoples' heads and then... and then you accuse me of Derek's murder! Who do you think you are?'

Laurel shrank from him.

'Maggie is gone because of you. The police,' he pointed at Nathan, who had risen from his seat, 'had me in for questioning for hours because of you. They came to my house to ask if I'd hurt my wife because of you. How dare you? If anyone should be coming under suspicion, perhaps I should tell the police about the row you had with Derek.'

He must have seen the surprise on her face. 'That's right, I know about that. I know Derek came round to your house, and you argued, and you were seen harassing him by the pond the other day.'

'But I...'

'That's not all though, is it?' Nicholas sneered. 'There's something about you that people round here should be told.'

A ball of dread hardened in Laurel's stomach.

'You had to leave your last employment, didn't you? Is that

why you're not working now?' He looked around to make sure everyone was listening. 'Got a man killed, is what I heard.'

Gasps bounced around the room.

'No, I...' What had Maggie told him?

'I bet you thought no-one would find out, but *I* know.'

Oh god.

'Now you're causing trouble here, going round claiming that Lily was murdered. Telling my poor Maggie your lies, accusing me. But wait, *you* arrived in the village the very day Lily died, and *you* happened to be the one to find her. All a bit convenient, isn't it? If she really was poisoned, as you're claiming, maybe you are the one who did it. Maybe you'd like to explain all that to the police? See how you like being under suspicion.'

Why wasn't anyone making him stop?

His mouth split into a wicked sneer and a mocking titter burst from his lips; an ugly sound made by an ugly man.

No!

'That's enough,' barked Albert.

Nicholas threw up his hands and, breathing hard, delivered his parting shot. 'I don't know about you *being* a therapist, but you sure as hell *need* one! You should be struck off, put in a padded cell, locked up forever. You're finished here in Elderwick.'

Chapter Thirty

'I'm sorry, Laurel. I'm going to have to ask you to come with me.'

'You can't think there's anything in what he just said?' How could Nathan add such indignity to the insults Nicholas had scarcely finished throwing at her? Her face was aflame, and all eyes were watching over their cups of tea and plates of sandwiches, hungry for the next act in this unexpected drama. This lovely place in which she'd started to feel at home, ruined. Everyone would be talking about her, speculating, gossiping. This is exactly what she'd been running from when she left Somerset; every day, in every hospital corridor, on each ward, she'd felt as though judging eyes were following her, radiating disapproval.

'I'm sorry,' Nathan apologised, looking about as uncomfortable as she felt. 'I'll catch up with Nicholas later and... Anyway, shall we go?'

She went with him, rather than continue the spectacle in front of witnesses. Outside, he explained he couldn't ignore what had been disclosed about her argument with Derek and whilst she wasn't under arrest, the team dealing with the murder would want to ask her some questions.

Questions she could have dealt with, she had nothing to hide, but once she arrived at the station, the police left her alone for fifty minutes in a windowless room that smelled of fear and vomit. It gave her too much time to think. She tried reviewing her situation. Could they think her guilty of being involved in some way? The room and lack of information were doing a good job of seeding fear and doubt in her mind. It was a relief when they finally got started with the interview.

She was surprised that Nathan remained in the room during the interrogation conducted by his colleagues. Detective Inspector Coral's lips were set in a permanent snarl below her sharp gaze. Detective Sergeant Hill, much older and worn around the edges, was no less intimidating. They probed into her friendship with Maggie, why she'd argued with Derek, and why she'd accused Nicholas of Derek's murder. It didn't seem to matter how often she told them they had the wrong end of the stick. She really began to come unstuck when they asked about Lily. She squirmed with embarrassment as she tried to convince them she had good reason to suspect Lily's death was suspicious. In this small room, with actual police officers, it sounded like the histrionic rambling of a fantasist.

'Please, think about it...' No, that was the wrong way to approach these officials. She modulated her tone, to speak as she would have done in her old role: a professional with genuine insight into the complexities of humans and human nature. 'Sorry. I mean, the thing is...' This was going to be harder than she'd thought. 'Lily wasn't suicidal. The post-mortem shows she'd been poisoned, and she had yew – a source of poison – in her house despite her family and friends being adamant she wouldn't have brought yew into her home. Also, a painting is missing from her house.' Her heart sank; she had nothing.

'All of that can be explained,' said the older of her two interrogators in a gentle voice. 'And what kind of person would want to kill a harmless, elderly lady?'

Desperate to rescue her reputation – and to get them to stop looking at her like she might be a sandwich short of a picnic – Laurel tried a different angle. 'What if Lily *did* accidentally eat yew berries in her tart, but what if they didn't *get there* accidentally? What if someone made sure they were in amongst the red currants, and that someone also put the yew in the vase on the table? All set up to lead us to the wrong conclusion. A murder planned with cold precision.' She was losing them. 'I think this was perpetrated by someone who has no empathy, someone charming enough to be invited into Lily's house – to be fair, she probably knew him, or her – and who could watch her eat yew berries knowing it would kill her. I don't like the term, but I think you're looking for a psychopath.'

There was a long pause.

'Why are you talking about psychopaths?' The DI glared at her before turning in her chair. 'Nathan, I'm sorry, I know you know her,' she gestured back to Laurel, 'but I think she's been watching too much TV.'

Nathan flushed. 'DI Coral's right. I'm sorry Laurel, but you have to let it go. We have an actual murder on our hands with Derek, and we need you to stop playing games. I don't mean to sound harsh, and I know you're trying to help, but please stop.'

'But that's the thing. Please, just for a second, say you believe me that Lily was murdered. Now Derek has been murdered too, there has to be a connection. What are the chances of two people being killed within days of each other in a village as small as Elderwick?'

The DI held up her hand. 'You've been doing a lot of talking, but we're yet to be persuaded you had nothing to do with it yourself, with the *actual* murder, that is.'

After another thirty unsettling minutes of questions, they let her go. They had no evidence on which to hold her, of course, but she didn't doubt they'd keep looking.

Chapter Thirty-One

Laurel was paying for the bottle and a half of wine she'd downed when she'd made it home from the police station. She threw back the covers and recoiled as the bite of wintry air assaulted her. The heating wasn't on. *Great, kick me while I'm down, why don't you.* She tried to remember if she had a number for a gas boiler engineer.

Inch by painful inch, she hauled herself upright and edged her legs out to place her feet on the floor. Her right foot grazed an unopened package. She looked down at it through blurred vision. A vague memory tried to surface, but a lurch of her stomach banished any thought of bending to retrieve it. With the cold chilling her tender bones and sorely in need of a coffee, the package could wait. She nudged it back under the bed.

Since there was no hot water, she braved a quick splash in the sink before pulling on an old pair of jogging bottoms, two T-shirts, hiking socks, a bobble hat, and her thickest jumper. Giving silent thanks to Albert, who had advised her to get her firewood topped up and ready, she made, slowly, for the living room to light the wood burner.

She sensed before she saw that her world was out of kilter. Autumn leaves decorated the floor inside, in front of the French windows, wet and slimy as though they'd been stamped and ground into the floorboards. There was no reason for them to be there.

She threw open the windows and scrutinised the paving outside, but it was being lashed by rain and there was nothing to see. She wrestled the windows closed again, but not before a flurry of wind and rain brought more leaves into the room.

In the kitchen, reaching for the dustpan and brush beneath the sink, she noticed that the glass she'd been drinking from the night before was washed and upturned on the draining board. She didn't remember doing that. Hadn't she left it on the coffee table as usual, promising herself that she'd do the washing-up first thing in the morning? She rubbed a hand across her brow and considered that maybe the wine had affected her more than she'd realised.

With the kettle filled, she addressed the boiler. It was switched off. It wasn't showing an error message or, in fact, anything on its digital display. She pushed the *On* button, and it fired up straight away. Like the lamp the day before, everything seemed to be functioning as usual. If her head weren't pounding, she might have been troubled, but it was all she could do to resist the temptation to crawl back into bed and shut out the world.

A cup of strong coffee in hand, she went back to the living room, swept up the leaves, sank on to the sofa and closed her eyes. Memories were coming back to her. Wine glass in hand, she'd made a decision the night before, but was it the right one? Should she sell up and move? Was there a problem with the village, or was there a problem with her?

She took in the surrounding room. Despite everything she loved this cottage, even though the walls all needed a fresh coat of paint, the floorboards needed re-staining, the slightly wonky oak beam that served as a mantelpiece, and...

She didn't know how she'd missed it. The glass in the framed photo of her and her parents that she kept on the mantelpiece was starred with cracks. Slivers of loose glass had fallen to the hearth below. Sitting forward on the sofa, all fatigue and brain fog left her. Her muscles were tensed on alert. Someone had been in the house, and they might still be there.

'Laurel? Whatever is the matter? Come in, come in, you'll catch your death.'

Her teeth were chattering so hard it took her a second before she could speak. 'Someone was in my house last night, Albert, and I don't know if they're still there. Oh god, I was upstairs the whole time. Oh god...'

He steered her into his kitchen and sat her down at the table. 'I'm calling the police.' He plucked his phone from its cradle.

'You'll help me?'

He hesitated for the briefest moment. Or maybe she imagined it.

'Of course I will. Why wouldn't I?'

There was a painful pause.

'Oh,' Albert blushed, 'you mean because of the nonsense Nicholas was spouting yesterday? I pay no mind to him. Now, I'm calling Nathan direct and he can come round and put your mind at rest.'

Laurel sagged, then for the second time that morning closed her eyes and put her head in her hands. She had no desire to see Nathan again, but she was too tired to think of what else she could do.

Chapter Thirty-Two

The medicinal drop of brandy Albert had added to her mug was doing its work, and he'd brought out the good chocolate biscuits. Her nervous energy abated a touch, only to spike again when the bell heralded Nathan's arrival. She needn't have worried. On hearing what had happened, he took charge, and took it seriously, instructing Laurel to stay where she was while he went to check round her cottage. He returned only ten minutes later, wet and frowning.

'There are no signs of any break-in and certainly no-one in the property. But I found this under the plant pot by the back doors.' He held out his hand. In his palm lay a key. 'If you need a spare, you should leave it with Albert or someone, and certainly not in such an obvious hiding place.'

Laurel stared at the key. 'I didn't know there was a spare.'

Nathan huffed. 'Well, perhaps the previous owner left it there.'

She took the key. 'I really appreciate you coming round so quickly. I was so scared that someone might still be there. And the thought that they were in my house while I slept is just...'

She shuddered and Albert, sitting at the table next to her, patted her shoulder.

Nathan shuffled from foot to foot. 'About that, when I say there are no signs of a break-in, I mean nothing at all. Are you... are you sure that you didn't... um... that you didn't imagine it or, I don't know, make it up?'

'No, absolutely not! I didn't put the wet leaves on the floor, and I didn't break the photo. The glass in the kitchen *could* have been me, but I really don't think so. No, I know someone was in my house.' She didn't mean to be so defensive, but she hated being vulnerable and afraid. She was aware that ending her sentence by folding her arms wasn't helping the message, but couldn't stop herself.

Albert got up to refill the kettle as the awkward silence stretched between them. Nathan took one of the biscuits and put it in his mouth whole. She could almost see the cogs turning as he chewed.

'When you say that the glass could have been you, don't you remember? I noticed it was a wine glass. Had you been drinking?' He lifted his hands in a placating gesture and added, 'I'm sorry, but I have to ask, it's not personal.'

Knowing how it would be interpreted, Laurel admitted, 'I did have a couple of glasses last night, but I wasn't blackout drunk or whatever you're insinuating!'

'I'm not insinuating anything,' Nathan snapped back, 'but...'

'But what?'

He couldn't meet her eyes. 'But nothing. Forget it.'

Albert stepped in with a diversion before the conversation became any more heated. 'Laurel, before I forget, here's your pie dish back, and thank you, it was delicious.'

'Since he's here, you can give it to Nathan,' she muttered. 'The pie was from him. Sorry, I meant to say that I didn't make it myself.'

'What pie?' asked Nathan.

'The apple pie you left on my doorstep yesterday.'

Nathan shook his head. 'It wasn't me.'

Laurel's stomach flipped over with a queasy lurch. 'Well, I can't think of anyone else who would leave me a pie.' Her chest felt tight. Someone had been in her house and now it seemed someone, probably the same person, had left a pie on her doorstep. Looking at Nathan, she could see him watching her as if he knew what was going through her mind. She could sense his scepticism before he opened his mouth.

'It was just a pie. You'll probably find it was left by a friend or put outside your door by mistake. It doesn't mean there's anything going on.'

'I'm sure that Nathan's right,' piped up Albert. 'It will all turn out to have been a mistake. And I know what it's like to live alone. Your mind can play tricks on you. Maybe that's what's happening here? You had a bad day yesterday and must have been tired and upset last night. That's not to say I don't believe you, of course I do, but I don't want you to be worrying over something and nothing. It's enough to make you mazed.'

She felt betrayed by his words, but she didn't know how to convince either of them of the truth.

'See,' Nathan said, 'Albert agrees, and since he ate the pie and isn't sick, then I think we can agree it wasn't anything sinister.'

There was a pregnant pause.

'Oh dear, I am ashamed to admit that I did not, in fact, eat the pie.' Albert wrung his hands. 'Whilst I am sure it was made and delivered with all innocence, I'm afraid that I came into the kitchen to find Aroon stamping about in the dish. Such a naughty rooster. I had to dispose of it. Laurel,' he swivelled in his chair to face her, 'I didn't like to say so in case you thought I'd been careless of your gift.'

The band around her chest loosened marginally. 'No, Albert, I'm just so relieved you didn't eat it and get sick...or worse. It would have been my fault and...' she tailed off. 'So it could have been–'

Nathan interrupted, 'It doesn't mean anything. We can't go jumping to conclusions.'

'Fine. Okay, you're probably right, both of you, but Nathan please, just to set my mind at rest, will you come back with me? I can show you myself what's out of place.'

She caught a look between the two men.

'Sure, come on. I don't want you feeling scared in your own home.'

She collected up the pie dish along with her phone and Nathan handed back her keys. 'Thank you, Albert.' The words ashes in her mouth.

Nathan let her go in first. She was inclined to tell him to get lost, but swallowed the impulse and stepped into the kitchen to put down the pie dish.

Nathan had followed. There was little room to manoeuvre and when he leaned towards her she almost panicked, thinking he was going to give her a hug, but he reached to pick a plate from the sink where it was waiting to be washed.

'Can I see the pie dish?' he asked quietly. She handed it to him, and he held both items out towards her. 'Laurel, they're from the same set. This dish is yours. What are you playing at?'

She stared. He was right. They were the same: white with a blue stripe. Why hadn't she realised?

He sighed and sat down at the table, pushing the other chair out for her to join him. She didn't want to. She wanted him out of her house. She wanted to run back to bed and pull the covers over her head and never speak to anyone again. But she sat.

'You've been through a lot,' he began. 'You left your job, moved miles away from where you grew up and all of your friends. Now there's been this murder. You're living here all alone and I can see why you might get scared, or you might want people to pay attention to you. But Laurel, I think you need to get some help.'

Her shoulders slumped and an ache rooted itself behind her eyes. 'What do you mean?' she mumbled, knowing exactly what he meant.

'It's just, well... you know. We all make mistakes but there's a real murderer out there and you're risking lives by... This is so far outside of your expertise. Leave it to the professionals, yeah?'

'I think you should leave,' was all she could manage.

He left in silence. When the door had closed behind him, she retrieved her one remaining bottle of wine from the fridge. To hell with it. Why shouldn't she drink at 10am on a Thursday morning? Elderwick had been a mistake. There was no doubt about it. After meeting Albert and Maggie, she'd started to hope, to believe even, that she could have a new start in Yorkshire. Where had that got her? Maggie had betrayed her and disappeared. Albert doubted her. Nathan was openly disbelieving, and now everyone in the village would think she was, what, a killer, or unhinged? Thanks to Nicholas.

She glugged a mouthful of wine and pulled a cushion onto her lap to hug as the tears came in earnest, turning to sobs as her breath hitched in her chest. Nicholas was right; there nothing left for her in Elderwick.

Chapter Thirty-Three

She waited two nights and two days. Hiding away, dreading another call from the police wanting to ask her more questions. The more she considered it, the more trouble she realised she might be in. She had been one of the two people to find Lily; she had been in Lily's house twice soon after; she'd argued with Derek twice; and she had no alibi for the time he was killed. Not to mention, her behaviour over the last few weeks – sneaking around in the dark for one – could easily be construed as suspicious.

Surely, though, the police would understand she wouldn't have been the one calling attention to Lily's death if she was guilty of having caused her harm? Mind you, she remembered, the police were continuing to insist Lily died accidentally so she shouldn't put too much store in them reaching any sensible conclusions. She chose to overlook the fact that she'd claimed the exact same thing only a few nights back.

If there was to be any chance of Lily's murder being solved, she would have to do it herself. Coincidences – truly unbelievable coincidences – were common in real life, she knew that, and the human mind seeks patterns in data, but she now firmly believed the answer to Lily's death would be connected to Derek's death, and Maggie's disappearance.

She swallowed a guilty lump in her throat. Maggie remained missing. She was mad at her friend for betraying her to Nicholas, but even if Maggie never wanted to see her again, she couldn't let go of her concern. The police weren't going to be any help and Nicholas was being downright obstructive. But what could she do?

Frustration was making her twitchy and although she wasn't hungry – there was a first time for everything – she knew she needed to eat. However, when she checked the cupboards, all she found was a box of Jacob's crackers, a tin of tomato soup, and some dusty muesli. She needed to go shopping, but she would drive to the supermarket open late at the far side of town, away from hostile eyes.

She grabbed her coat and car keys then moved into the dark kitchen to check through the window whether the lane was empty. It was. Now was her chance. Her car was by the kerb, only two steps beyond the garden gate. She cracked open her front door and unlocked the car with the fob. The beep sounded loud in the hush. She cringed and held her breath, but nothing stirred. With a soft tread, she slipped outside, paused, and cocked her head to listen. Her heart stuttered when an engine burst into life. It was distant, but the noise of the vehicle rolled closer through the darkness. Alarm tugged at her, but she remained rooted to the spot, holding her breath. A black Range Rover raced past the end of the lane and she caught a fleeting glimpse of the driver, Marcus. She breathed out with a whoosh, locked her door, and ran to the car. If she didn't go in that moment, her nerves would fail.

She drove to the supermarket with one eye on the road and

the other on every car and pedestrian she passed. In the car park, she stopped far from the entrance in a dark corner of the vast concrete space. If not for her chickens back at the cottage, she might have kept on driving and gone somewhere far away, never to return. Pulling a hood over her unbrushed hair, she hunched her back, eyes to the floor, and skittered inside. With haste, she filled a basket with enough provisions to hole up out of sight for a few more days, including a large jar of Nutella to replace the one she'd almost finished. There was no queue for the self-checkout, and she was back in her car ten minutes after her arrival. It took her another three minutes to calm the shaking in her hands and to focus enough to begin the drive home.

Standing at her door, with two bags of groceries on her arms, she cursed; she hadn't thought to get out her keys before leaving the concealing shadows within the car. Prickles ran across the back of her neck while she rummaged around in her handbag. Her fingers swept over an umbrella, tissues, old receipts. *Where are they?*

There was a noise behind her, a whisper of movement. Had there been any wind or rain, she would have missed it, but the night was still. Her heart thumped in her chest. She peered into the darkness but couldn't penetrate the shadows.

She renewed her search for the keys, frantic fingers becoming clumsy.

A twig snapped.

'Is there someone there?'

There was no reply.

'Oh my god, is that you, Aroon? I...'

A slender object thwacked into the wood of the door, inches from her head.

She forgot to breathe. From the corner of her eye, she could just see the arrow still vibrating.

The shock lasted only seconds, but held her immobile until she heard the slap and crunch of running footsteps and her paralysis broke. She cried out and dropped to the ground, her shopping scattered like marbles. She crawled to the shelter of the hedge and cowered in the murk of the damp undergrowth.

Chapter Thirty-Four

The police found Laurel there, huddled and shivering. She got to her feet as an officer reached her and walked on unsteady legs as he guided her to his car. He settled her in the passenger seat, told her his name was Ben, and that she was safe now. Blue lights strobed, filling the lane with dancing shapes that made her flinch.

'We don't want to use the front door just yet, not until we've had a look at the lock to make sure no-one tried to break in and then of course we'll need to remove the arrow. Is your back door key on the same keyring as is in the lock?'

Laurel nodded, not trusting her voice. She recognised him. He'd been there the night of Derek's murder. Nausea whirled in her stomach.

'You're probably experiencing a bit of shock,' he said. 'I'm going to see if I can get you a cup of tea from your neighbour over there.' He nodded toward Albert, who was hovering by his garden gate, wrapped in a tartan dressing gown. Albert saw Laurel looking and gave her a little wave. She waved back, trying to show that she was okay, which she wasn't.

After a thorough search, the police told her they'd found no

A Little Bird Told Me

evidence of anyone trying to get into her house, and they couldn't find anything in the dark to give them any clue who had taken a shot at her. They could see where the bowman had stood, but there were no useable footprints, just a flattened area of grass under the trees that faced her cottage. In daylight, anyone standing there would have been clearly visible, but at night in the deep shadows, it had been easy for her attacker to remain unseen.

When they'd finished removing the arrow – to Laurel's relief, they didn't have to remove or destroy her door – Ben asked if she had a friend she could stay with for the night.

'Do you think they'll come back?' she gasped.

'No, I very much doubt they'd risk it and given your account of what happened and how you were standing, we think that this was meant as a warning rather than an attempt on your life. We can't be sure, of course, but if...'

Saliva filled her mouth. She leaned out of the car and heaved. She breathed heavily through her mouth until the urge to vomit passed. She was sweaty and cold all at once.

'Can you manage a bit of tea? It'll warm you up.' Ben pressed a mug into her hands.

With Maggie still away and not wanting to impose on Albert, Laurel had to admit she didn't have a friend with whom she could stay. She promised Ben she would lock and bolt the door, keep the curtains closed and stay away from the windows. He gave her a number to call if there was any hint of a threat and told her that a patrol car would drive by at irregular intervals for the next couple of days to monitor the area.

'I'm sorry we can't do more.' He scuffed the ground with his well-shined shoes.

The sweet tea wasn't helping, but she drank as instructed. She was ready for the circus to leave now. Her body was jittering and her mind flighty. She needed quiet and to be alone

231

before she could process what had happened. Ben saw her inside, waiting until she'd locked the door, then one by one, her rescuers left, and the night closed back in.

She called Nathan on her landline to thank him for sending the cavalry. Against a background of drunken shouting, he apologised that he hadn't been able to get there himself; he was on duty in town.

'Call 999 if anything else happens. Promise me?' he implored. 'Even if you can't speak, they'll come and find you. I can't imagine what would have happened if I hadn't seen your message. I...' He stopped and cleared his throat. 'I'll come round as soon as my shift is over.'

Bruised by their recent encounters, Laurel put him off, saying that she was fine. He argued, but she held firm and said goodnight.

Her whole body ached, but sleep was a distant friend, unlikely to visit. She picked up a spoon and snagged the already open jar of Nutella from the pantry – a longstanding and dysfunctional coping strategy if ever there was one. She double checked the doors and windows, then climbed the stairs, pulled on her pyjamas and clambered into bed where she lay wide-eyed and wakeful until just before dawn.

Chapter Thirty-Five

Nathan's presence at her front door woke her the following morning after only an hour of sleep. She was still shaken and peered out of the upstairs window to see who it was.

He appraised her when she finally opened the door. 'How are you?'

'You know,' she said with a shrug, 'it could've been worse.' Her light tone didn't hide the quake in her voice as she edged away from the entrance, anxious not to present a target.

Nathan narrowed his eyes and studied the street behind him, perhaps realising her concern. She invited him in and he closed the door behind him, but not before Laurel had seen the wound left by the arrow.

'Sorry to drop by so early. I wanted to check you're okay. I wish I'd been able to come over last night. I am really sorry this happened to you.'

For a moment Laurel, despite everything, was overcome with a longing for him to put his arms around her, to bury her head in his chest and have him hold her and promise to keep her safe. Then she remembered what he'd said to her the last time he'd been in her home, and the desire vanished as quickly as it had arrived. She led him through to the kitchen and put the kettle on to boil.

'I don't expect you to drop everything and come running, but thank you. I appreciate your concern.' The words sounded formal and stilted. She tried again. 'Honestly, thank you for coming by.'

The whistle of the kettle stalled further conversation. She moved it from the hob and set out mugs, popping in a teabag each. She took her time spooning in sugar and fetching the milk from the fridge, her movements careful and slow to hide the trembling that wouldn't quit.

Nathan cleared his throat. 'Look, I know you've just had a shock and all, but I need to ask what this is all about?'

'What do you mean exactly?' She thrust his mug at him.

'It's just... well... look, about the... thing.'

'Not this again!'

'But you have to understand–'

'I didn't imagine it or make it up!' She was almost shouting.

'No, but...'

He didn't need to finish. 'I see. You actually think I got a crossbow, stood in the dark across from my house, shot an arrow at where my head would be if I'd been standing in front of the door, and then I hid the crossbow and called the police? Do you really think I did all that? For what? To hide the fact that I'm the one who killed Derek? Is that it? Are you hoping I'll confess now?' She intended her words to blister him.

'I'm not saying that, but there was the pie, then the break-in which we couldn't find any evidence of, so...' he trailed off.

With supreme effort, she tried to put herself in Nathan's shoes. She had to sound like a reasonable woman, not someone on the brink of a psychotic break. 'Okay, I can appreciate you have to consider all possibilities, but I can tell you, I didn't do this. I did not shoot an arrow at myself or anyone else.' Tears gathered in her lashes, she dashed them away.

'I guess,' he conceded, 'but in that case, we have to consider how you've maybe been stirring things up a bit, and I need to tell you to be careful. You've got to leave things to the police; we're the professionals.'

'You keep saying that.'

'Well...'

'Wow, so you're victim blaming now? First, I shot at myself and now it's my fault that someone else stood outside my house, concealed themselves in the bushes waiting for me to come home so that *they* could shoot an arrow at my head?'

'That's not what I meant–'

'If the police need me to give an official statement, *again*, have someone call me and I'll happily pop into the station. You need to go now.' She ground her teeth.

On the threshold, he paused. 'The thing is, I want you to stay safe, that's all. I don't want you to get hurt. I'll see you around.'

She slammed the door closed behind him and kicked it for good measure. The anger was helpful, cutting through the self-pity and doubt. This time, she wasn't going to run away; it was time to develop a new coping strategy.

Chapter Thirty-Six

'**M**aggie!' Laurel was lost for words. She couldn't decide whether to hug or berate her friend who had materialised on her doorstep.

'I am so sorry I left without telling you.' Maggie hung her head. 'The police had just been round to speak to Nicholas and I don't know what came over me. I needed to get away, to have some space.' She stopped speaking and snuck a glance at Laurel's face.

Relief won out. She flung her arms around Maggie. 'I've been so worried about you. I didn't know where you were, and Nicholas wouldn't tell me anything. And I've been mad at you for telling Nicholas about why I left Somerset.' It all came spilling out. She was churning with contradictory emotions as she stood on the doorstep looking at her friend... was she her friend?

Maggie disentangled herself. 'I heard about Nicholas and the thing in the café, but no, I would never have told him what you confided to me. I know you and I had a bit of a falling out before I left, but never in a million years would I do that to you. You're one of the best friends I've ever had. I'm looking at my life in a whole new light, thanks to you. Please, say you believe me?'

Laurel's mouth went dry. 'But if you didn't...' She leaned against the door frame.

'Are you all right?'

Not at all. 'You'd better come in.'

Laurel could hear Maggie bustling around in the kitchen where she'd gone to make them each a mug of hot chocolate. She accepted Maggie's protest of honesty without question; she was certain her friend couldn't look her in the eyes and lie. While she waited, the question played over and over: if not Maggie, then who? How could Nicholas have known about her old life and the mistake she'd made?

'Here we go.' Maggie handed Laurel her drink and retreated to the armchair by the window. 'You look like you've seen a ghost.'

There was so much she needed to tell her, but first, Laurel wanted to know what had happened to Maggie. 'Are *you* okay? Where have you been?'

Maggie rested her mug on the arm of the chair. 'I went to stay with Vanessa, my daughter. We had chance to talk a lot of things over. I never knew that she and Conner felt the way they do about me and their dad. They've both kept away since moving out because they couldn't bear to watch Nicholas bully me and see me thank him for it. I didn't realise that's what I've been doing.' Her tone dropped. 'Funny, isn't it, how something can become so it seems normal and you no longer question it?'

'Oh, Maggie.'

'Don't worry about me, that will work itself out. But what about you? What have I missed?' She lifted her drink and blew across the hot liquid before taking a mouthful.

Laurel tried to be calm in her recounting, but there were only so many ways you could talk about finding a pie that may or may not have contained poison, and having an arrow embed itself in a door inches from your face.

Maggie spluttered, and a slop of hot chocolate spilled down the side of her mug. 'You were shot?'

'Shot at, but I don't know why.'

'You were shot at!' she repeated. She half rose. 'Were you hurt?'

Laurel waved her back down. 'I'm fine. They missed.'

'Oh well, that's all right then.' Maggie shook her head.

Laurel snorted. 'Sorry, I know it's not funny, but... it's surreal. I wasn't hurt, though.'

Maggie sniffed and dabbed at the chocolate that had stained her cream blouse. 'Obviously I'm glad you weren't injured, but that's hardly the point. Whoever did it is still running around out there.' She swivelled round and stared out of the windows. 'What if he comes back? It has to be the same person who killed Derek. What are the police doing?'

'I guess they're following up. They think it was a warning and that he won't be back.' She had no idea if the archer might try again, but she refused to be cowed, and she didn't want Maggie getting more twitchy than she already was.

Maggie harrumphed. 'What does Nathan say? Does he know?'

Laurel wasn't ready to talk about him yet, so she ignored the question. 'The thing is, I've not been thinking clearly since it happened. But now you're back, we can see if we can make some sense from all of this. I think it would do me good to approach this as a puzzle to be solved. To try and get a little distance from the idea that someone tried to kill me.' Doing *something* was better than sitting passively waiting for whatever was going to happen next.

Maggie twisted her lips 'We could try, but where would we start?'

'You might not know because you've been away, but Lily's daughter, Rose, arrived the day of the Autumn Festival.' Maggie's surprise showed on her face. 'We were talking with Albert and Hitesh, and we're all sure now that Lily would never have brought yew into her house. I think it's highly improbable the yew seeds got onto her tart by accident.'

'Are you saying your theory in the pub was wrong?'

Laurel licked her lips. 'After Derek, and someone taking a shot at me... I think, maybe... Do *you* think we should work on the premise that Lily *was* murdered? Or do you think this is all because I'm scared of making the same mistake I did in Somerset – not believing my patient when he said his brother was trying to kill him – and instead I've gone too far the other way, believing everything is about murder?' There, she'd said it. The thing she was afraid of: was she creating panic out of nothing because she'd messed up in the past?

Maggie held up a hand. 'If it was just Lily who had died, I'd say maybe you're seeing shadows where there are none. But, as you rightly point out, Derek has been murdered, and what happened to you...'

'They have to be connected, right?'

'If you're sure about the yew, then you're probably right.' She placed her palm over her heart. 'It's so awful. I much preferred believing it was an accident.'

Laurel strode to her desk in the corner of the room and brought her notebook and a pen back to her place on the sofa. 'Rose, Albert, and Hitesh were adamant, Lily would never have brought yew into her house.'

'So, what was it doing there?' Maggie fished her book out of her bag and studied her notes.

'I wonder...'

'Go on.'

Buoyed by her friend's encouragement, Laurel allowed her

thoughts to settle back into the mystery that had been the catalyst for all that had happened since. She laid out the theory she'd shared at the police station. 'I think someone put yew berries onto a tart which they took to Lily's. They must have broken her glasses so she couldn't make them out from the other fruits.'

'And they were the ones who placed the sprigs of yew on the dining table so it would look like the berries dropped onto the tart by accident? That's very cunning.'

Laurel managed a wry curve of her lips. 'And very cold. Psychopathic even. How else could they serve a poisoned pastry to a defenceless elderly lady? It was entirely premeditated.'

Maggie shuddered.

'But what connects Lily's death to Derek's?' She sat forward in her chair. Maggie knew the village and residents far better than her. Was there a link she wasn't aware of?

Maggie drummed her fingers on her thighs. 'There's nothing obvious, except they both lived in Elderwick. That's no help, is it?'

Laurel massaged her temples. 'Actually,' her head snapped up, 'that could be it.' She ticked the points off on her fingers. 'Two people dead with no clear link between them; one was made to look like an accident or suicide even though it wasn't, the other was obviously murder. Lily's death would have taken significant planning. Whoever gave her the tart was someone she must have known and trusted. The murderer must have been aware that she liked cakes and treats from The Plump Tart and knew when to find her alone at home. All of which tells us this is someone local. Derek's murder required the unsub – that's a good bit of TV detective jargon for you there, Maggie – to know of a time and place when Derek would be alone and could be shot unseen. I doubt he–'

'Or she,' added Maggie.

'Or she would have been toting a crossbow around with them on the off-chance. Plus, we should consider how quickly the use of a crossbow pointed to Nicholas.'

'Lots of people know he has one and can use it well.'

'Excellent, yes, now we're getting into the mind of the killer.'

Maggie scrunched up her nose. 'I'm not sure I want to do that.'

Having been scribbling away as they talked, Laurel paused. 'Man or woman then? What do we think? I say man; statistically, most murders are committed by men and whilst poison is, according to Sherlock Holmes, a woman's weapon, that's nonsense. Both murders strike me as being expedient; deliberate, calculated, and done for practical reasons. There was no moment of rage or passion inflamed here. Two people needed to die and there you go... done.'

Maggie chewed her lip for a second. 'There could be two killers. Have we considered that? Two killers, one motive, or two killers with two different motives? The methods were very different.'

'They were, weren't they?' Laurel stood up and paced. 'It feels like it would be too much of a coincidence again for there to be two murderers in Elderwick. My instinct is that there's one person, and it's a man. But we should keep an open mind in case more evidence comes to light.'

'If we stick with it being one person, perhaps they didn't have as much time to arrange Derek's death. Or maybe Derek did something unexpected that made the killer see him as a threat?' Maggie made another note in her book. She screwed up her face before announcing, 'My head hurts. We have more to go on than before, but are we any closer to an answer?'

Laurel flopped back onto the sofa. 'No.'

'You know, I read a book recently that had a wonderful

quote in it, "If at first you don't succeed, have some cake." How about we go and get something sweet from Hetty?' She must have seen the anxiety on Laurel's face, because she added, 'Nicholas is out of town so we won't bump in to him.'

It wasn't only Nicholas: Laurel was anxious about being out in the open and around other people who might have heard what Nicholas had said, or who knew she'd been carted off by the police. 'I suppose if we go, we can ask Hetty why Derek was trying to close her down. That's something Petra mentioned the other day.'

Maggie jotted it down in her book, closed the cover with a smack, and stood. 'Everything will seem better after cake. Come on.'

Their route to the bakery took them along Manor Road, an especially attractive thoroughfare lined with more of the charming red buildings for which the area was known. Even in the weak egg yolk sun, the brick had the colour of warm embers. In contrast, the tidy front gardens they passed were looking brown and bare, ready for the fallow winter months.

'"Do not mind the snow and the frost and the ice, for winter is but spring sleeping",' recited Maggie.

'Isn't that Oscar Wilde? You're sounding like Albert.'

Maggie chuckled and linked arms with Laurel.

Laurel could smell The Plump Tart from down the street: ginger, chocolate, and freshly baked bread. The bell over the door tinkled and the warm fug of fresh-baked cookies enveloped them as they stepped inside. While she deliberated over which tasty pastry to buy for lunch – along with cake – Laurel broached the subject of Derek with Hetty.

'He did threaten something, yes.' The usually sunny-faced Hetty scowled. 'It was Constance he spoke to. Do you want me to call her? She's just in back making gingerbread non-gender specific people.' She winked at Laurel and her habitual smile was back.

At Hetty's shout, Constance popped her head round the door, then manoeuvred her wheelchair through to join them, wiping flour from her hands.

'News is out that Derek tried to close us down. What was it he said to you?' Hetty prompted.

Constance thought for a moment. 'It was a couple of weeks ago now, I think. He was all worked up and being very odd. Tried accusing us of not properly labelling our products with allergens. He said people could get hurt if they couldn't tell exactly what they were eating. I explained that we have complete lists of all the ingredients for everything we sell. We're very careful. I've got a food allergy myself and our business depends on it. He wasn't making any sense, and I told him to bugger off.'

Had Derek been thinking about Lily? 'I think I can explain. Lily Armitage was eating a tart from here just before she died. Derek must have known about it and after he heard that she might have died from poisoning, he put two and two together and made five. Maybe he thought Lily was allergic to red currants or blackberries, or whatever is on a fruits of the forest tart? I don't suppose you remember anyone buying one of them around the beginning of September?'

Hetty was shaking her head. 'We've not done a fruits of the forest tart yet. We do them from October, so if that's what she was eating, it didn't come from us. Derek was barking up completely the wrong tree.'

Laurel and Maggie looked at each other.

'Definitely wasn't from here,' Constance confirmed. 'We haven't done anything with blackberries or red currants in ages, only strawberries and raspberries.'

Laurel digested what they were saying. 'I think it confirms

our theory that Lily *was* killed deliberately, then. The killer *is* local, it *was* set up to look accidental, and The Plump Tart cake box was left on her kitchen table as a misdirection.'

Maggie nodded, while Hetty and Constance stood open-mouthed.

Chapter Thirty-Seven

Laurel was surprised to see Rose waiting on her doorstep when she and Maggie rounded the corner onto Birch Lane. She balanced her large box from the bakery on one hand and waved with the other.

'I tried calling,' Rose held up her mobile phone, 'but there's zero signal in this village. I can't stay long, but can I come in? I've got some news I think you'll want to hear.'

Once they each had a cup of tea and were settled in the living room, Laurel and Maggie looked expectantly at Rose.

'The coroner's office has been in touch again and they've confirmed that Mum died from ingesting "a poisonous substance", their words. They checked for yew specifically after I told them what you'd found in the kitchen.'

Laurel felt the thrill of vindication, but no satisfaction that her theory had been borne out. 'We've just come from the bakery. Hetty and Constance have confirmed that the fruit tart your mum ate the day she died didn't come from The Plump Tart. Even though that's what we were meant to think.'

'We're so sorry.' Maggie touched Rose's hand. 'What can we do to help? You shouldn't be on your own with all this going on.'

245

Rachael Gray

Rose sank back into the cushions of the chair and let out a long breath. 'I'm like my mum; we're made of stern stuff, independent and tough, but it really helps to have you guys around. Thank you. Mostly, I've been trying to come to terms with it all. If Mum was poisoned, then who did it and why?' She thumped her closed fist on the arm of the chair. 'Why would anyone want her dead?'

'We've been struggling with that, too. She was such a lovely woman.'

'And what's this about another murder?' Rose asked. 'A man shot with a crossbow? It's... what is going on around here?'

It came as no surprise to hear the village grapevine had been in action again. 'Derek Fisher?' Laurel shot a look at Maggie. 'We were just talking about how the two might be related.'

'Have the police been round to see you?' Maggie asked Rose.

A blush coloured Rose's cheeks. 'Nathan has. He's been round every day since I arrived, checking in on me and making sure I'm okay. I remember we met when I was over here a few years back, helping Mum move into Church View.'

Despite how angry she was with him, Laurel felt a prick of envy.

'Has he told you anything about the case?' Laurel noticed Maggie's hand straying towards her bag, but she stopped short of taking out her notebook.

'No...' She drew out the word. 'The police are still saying it was an accident. As far as I'm aware, they're not linking Mum's death to Derek's murder.'

'But you said yourself, there's no way Lily would have had yew in the house? Did you tell them that?'

'They didn't seem interested.'

'Even Nathan?' Laurel hoped Rose didn't hear the edge in her question.

'He listened to me about it and said he'd speak to the officers in charge, but I get the feeling he's on board with the accident explanation. He said there could be a million and one reasons for the yew sprigs to be there. Maybe a well-meaning friend gave her them, or she needed them for a painting.'

'But now we also know the tart didn't come from the bakery...'

'You don't have to convince me,' said Rose. 'And if someone hurt my mum on purpose, I want to know who the bastard is, but I don't think the police are going to help us.' A vein throbbed in her forehead. 'Look, I'd better get going. I've got to speak to the vicar about the funeral. After that, I'm meeting Hitesh to see if he'd be interested in being paid to keep on top of the garden until the house is sold. Oh, this'll make you laugh. Did you know he and mum smoked dope together? I'd forgotten what an old hippie she was. She told me once how he would bring some round for her every now and again, and she'd hide it in the kitchen in a box of mint tea. I think that was meant to disguise the smell or something. I don't know why. I don't know who she thought would be raiding her home looking for a bit of marijuana.'

Laurel nearly choked on her tea.

'Thanks again for your support,' said Rose, standing to leave. 'I'm not sure we can do much without the police, but if you have any other ideas, will you call me? It's going to eat me up inside until I find out exactly what happened to Mum.'

'Absolutely. We're not letting this go.' Laurel walked Rose to the door.

As she stepped outside, Rose paused. 'I almost forgot. What do you think of the photo?'

'The photo?'

'The package I dropped off the other day. It's the photo that I think Mum was using as the inspiration for her painting, the one she was doing for the Autumn Festival. Turns out she'd sent the photo off to be framed and it must have come back after... Derek must have picked it up when he was collecting her post. Let me know when you've had a look.'

'Will do,' Laurel murmured. *What package?* 'Has the painting turned up yet?'

'Actually, no. I wonder if Derek had that too?' She looked at her watch. 'Crap, I'm late. See you soon.'

The second she closed the door, Laurel hurtled up the stairs, sank to her knees and rummaged under her bed. She breathed a sigh of relief as her hand closed on the padded envelope she'd ignored the other morning. Back in the living room, she flopped onto the sofa next to Maggie and handed her the package. 'Rose dropped this round for me the other day. Lily was doing a painting for the festival but it's missing. Rose said her painting was based on the photo in there.' She tapped the envelope. 'What with everything going on, I never even opened it. I might have been a bit drunk when I put it under my bed. I'd forgotten I even had it.'

'Shall I open it?' Rose had re-wrapped it, and Maggie took care unwinding an outer layer.

'Maggie,' Laurel began as a thought bubbled up, 'do you remember when we went to Lily's? There was one thing we didn't see and have yet to locate.'

'The painting?'

'The painting.'

'Well then,' Maggie said, removing a length of bubble wrap, 'let's see what we've got.'

They bent their heads and scrutinised the framed photo Maggie had revealed. It showed a young girl, possibly mid-teens, standing by an open window. A distinctive oval gold locket hung from a slender chain around her neck, catching the light.

Beyond her, through the window, was a garden bursting with roses in shades of pink, purple, and white.

'She looks just like Rose,' breathed Laurel.

'There's a note,' said Maggie, spotting it on the floor where it had fallen. 'It's from Rose.'

> This is my paternal grandmother, Flora. I never knew her. She abandoned my dad, Sebastian, before he was two years old and left him to be raised by her sister and brother-in-law. The story passed down is that she couldn't cope with the baby, so went out to work one day and never came home. She lived near here, in fact, and for some reason that made Dad want to move back when he retired. Not sure why Mum picked this as the subject for her painting, but from sketches I've found, that's definitely what this is.

'It's a beautiful picture.'

Laurel stood and paced the room; something told her the photo was important. If only she could pull all the pieces together to understand why. Then she snagged the corner of a thought.

'Okay, Maggie, tell me what you think of this. The only thing we know of that is missing from Lily's house is her painting. So, what if whoever killed Lily was the one who removed the painting?'

'Why would they take a painting?'

'Exactly. Why would they take it?'

'Because...' Maggie's face creased, 'it must show something that they didn't want anyone to see?'

'So, our killer must have been round to Lily's and he or she saw the painting.'

'And if Lily told them it was for the Autumn Festival, the killer might have been afraid someone else might see it who would understand its significance?'

'Meaning the killer had to get rid of it before the festival.'

'And Lily too.'

'Yes, that follows.'

They looked again at the picture, but there was nothing distinctive about it. The background could have been of any country garden, the clothing worn by Flora was plain and nondescript.

'Wait, if the painting had to be got rid of, why didn't the killer take this photo too?'

That stopped Laurel in her tracks. She blew out a breath and looked at the ceiling as if she would find inspiration there. 'Oooh.' Her brain fizzed. 'It's what Rose said to me. Lily had sent the photo to be framed, so it wasn't at her house when she was killed. Maybe the killer didn't know there was a photo. Rose only has it now because the police found it at Derek's house and returned it to her. Look, the envelope's addressed to Lily.'

Maggie gasped. 'That's the link between Lily and Derek!'

'Derek picked up Lily's post after she died. He must have opened the package when it came back from the framers and saw the photo.' She backed away from the picture. 'Shit. Somehow, the killer found out Derek had seen it.' Sweat broke out under her arms. 'That's why he was killed.'

Maggie dropped Rose's note and it fluttered to the floor. 'Nathan told us the night Derek was killed that someone had tried breaking into his house. I bet it was the killer looking for the photo.'

'He obviously didn't manage to get it, but with Derek dead, that might have been enough to solve his problem.'

'And with all the police around afterwards, he wouldn't have had another chance to get it. And... oh my goodness...

could the killer know that you have the photo now? If they do, it would explain why they got desperate enough to shoot at you. It would also explain why you thought someone had broken in. They were looking for it.'

Too agitated to sit still any longer, Laurel resumed her pacing. 'They couldn't find it because I'd put it under my bed. But how did they know *I* have it now?' Seconds passed before she could order her thoughts. 'In the café,' she breathed. 'I was in the café when I got Rose's text about her dropping off the photo. I read it out loud. It didn't mean anything to me, but if the killer overheard... Maggie, it must have been someone who was there at the same time.'

'Who was there?'

Laurel thought back, bringing the scene to life in her mind's eye. 'I was with Albert. Petra and Marcus were there, but they had headphones on. Nathan was talking to a couple of Derek's neighbours. Hitesh came in, and of course Jo was around.'

'Was that everyone?'

'Well, Nicholas came in to ruin my life, but that was afterwards, so I don't see how he could have heard me. Oh, Hetty was there too. She was in the kitchen with Jo.' She groaned. 'It could have been any of them.'

Maggie bolted up from her seat and ran from the room. Laurel could hear her at the front door before she sped back into the living room and went to the French windows, pulling on them so vigorously they rattled in their frames.

'What are you doing?'

'We should have thought of this sooner. When the killer couldn't get the photo back from Derek, what happened?' She didn't wait for an answer. 'Derek got killed. The killer's already taken one shot at you.'

Once more Laurel slumped onto the sofa, her legs suddenly useless at holding her.

In a quiet voice she said, 'The pie that was left for me on my doorstep is just like the tart given to Lily, and when that didn't work, someone shot at me like they did to Derek.'

'We need to call the police.'

Laurel played in her mind how that conversation might go. Based on her recent encounters with officers of the law, Nathan included, her guess was her fear would be met with scepticism if not outright disbelief.

'We should, but what would we tell them? Nathan already thinks I'm doolally, and it's all supposition. We don't have any actual evidence unless we can explain the importance of this photo.' Her gaze kept darting to the window, checking the garden beyond for threats.

'If we can do that, we would know who the killer is.'

'We would.' Again, they were reduced to staring blankly at the photograph. Then it hit her. The key to the whole affair was right in front of her. She understood the importance of what she was looking at. She bounded over to her desk in the corner of the room and selected a piece of paper – one of the newspaper reports she'd found at the library – and laid it alongside the photo of Flora.

'Maggie, I know who the killer is.'

Chapter Thirty-Eight

In the wake of Laurel's deduction, they worked the theory over again and agreed it consisted of coincidence, guesswork, and some spectacular leaps of logic. Without solid proof, they knew the police wouldn't take them seriously. Maggie lobbied to contact Nathan anyway as a potentially more receptive officer of the law.

Still smarting for her recent run-ins with him, Laurel preferred not to. No point adding more grist to his *Laurel is crazy* mill. The best, and indeed their only practical idea, was to go to Petra's party at the Hall and in the safety of the crowd, poke, prod and see what they could shake loose. Someone must have a fragment of evidence they could use to prove the killer's identity.

Halloween dawned dull and misty to match Laurel's mood. She couldn't stomach any breakfast and wished the hours would hurry by

There was a knock at the door, which she opened cautiously – the memory of the arrow never far away – to reveal Albert with his cap literally in hand.

'Laurel, my dear, I'm so sorry that I impugned your veracity the other day. I am ashamed to say that I thought you were getting yourself all of a muddle and whatnot and had given yourself a bit of a scare. However, Maggie has been round for a quiet word and has set me straight.'

She gave him a sad smile. 'I accept your apology and it's okay. If I were you, I'd have had concerns too.' Scrutinising the tree line opposite, she judged it safe to step beyond the threshold, marginally.

He beamed back at her. 'Well, of that, I am mightily glad. I have become quite fond of my new neighbour and wish to remain her steadfast friend, if she will have me, and if she will allow me to escort her to the ball at the Hall this evening?'

'Oh, honestly, yes, to all the above.' She startled at a tickle on her shin and looked down to see her hens wandering free. 'What are you three doing out here? Albert, your Aroon must be leading my hens astray and teaching them bad habits; they've never escaped their run before.' She reached down and gave the largest of the escapees a scratch. 'Henrietta, Henny Penny, Miss Cluckington, any eggs for me today?'

'My oh my.' Albert started laughing. 'No wonder your little ones haven't been laying; they're all roosters!' He shook his head. 'My dear, I have such a lot to teach you.'

Bundled up in their winter gear against the cold and fog that pooled and drifted in tendrils, they set off for Elderwick Hall. Cold as it was, Laurel was sweating under her layers and her step faltered at every snap of a twig or distant bark of a dog.

'Mind if we join you?' a voice floated out of the dark, materialising into Nathan.

Laurel yelped and crashed into Albert, who steadied her. She wasn't thrilled Nathan had turned up, but what could she do? Then she spied Rose with him. It wasn't so long ago that, despite her protestations to Maggie, she would have liked to date Nathan. Of course, that was before he'd patronised her and as good as accused her of losing her mind. Regardless of this current opinion, she felt the return of a prickle of envy as she noticed he and Rose were holding hands.

'What are you supposed to be?' Maggie squinted and gestured to Nathan's all black outfit with little cardboard ears and yellow feathers stuck around his mouth and down the front of his sweater.

'I'm the cat that got the canary!' He grinned and did a twirl. 'I'm disappointed no-one else has bothered to dress up.'

'I didn't know it was fancy-dress,' said Laurel.

'I'm not sure it is,' Albert said.

Nathan pulled some of the feathers off his costume and let them drift to the ground. Laurel hid her smirk.

As they came into the courtyard, music flowed through the open doors and a silhouetted figure appeared atop the steps. Her gown ruffled in the slight breeze and an arm held aloft a champagne flute. But despite the gaiety, Laurel still pictured the bloodstained stone.

'Aren't you all too old to be trick or treating?' The figure revealed itself to be Petra. She ushered them inside with a laugh before waltzing away in a sparkle of diamanté.

'Oh my goodness, it's so beautiful,' whispered Rose, twisting her head back and forth to take in the view. 'I wish Mum were here to see this.'

'Shall we track down some glasses of fizz?' enquired Albert, presenting his arm to Rose and escorting her into the crowd of chattering guests.

Maggie was sticking close to Laurel. 'I'm really quite scared,' she whispered in her ear.

Laurel didn't want to admit it, but she was too. 'We'll be

fine, safety in numbers and all that. This is our best opportunity to find out all we can before we go to the police. It would be awful if they dismiss us, or if there's nothing they can make stick, and the killer gets away with it, or just plain gets away and leaves the area.'

'But it all makes sense. Surely, they would see that?'

'I don't know. They deal in proof. We don't have any and I don't have any idea how we can get some unless we get a confession, or the killer is caught in the act of having a go at me again. I have to say, I don't fancy either of those options.'

They were handed glasses of champagne by a dashing young man dressed as Dracula. Laurel, barely noticing the burst of bubbles on her tongue, knocked hers back and in the absence of a table, abandoned the empty flute in a giant plant pot. Around and above them, onyx spiders hung in gossamer cobwebs, orange and green lights transformed familiar faces into witches and pumpkins, and a giant skull carved from ice chilled blood red vodka.

'I thought this was just a little drinks thing. I feel very underdressed.' Maggie patted her hair, which she'd curled for the evening.

Laurel thought Maggie looked wonderful as ever in her pale orange tunic and black velvet trousers. 'Me too.' She looked down at her own jeans and baggy jumper.

Constance and Hetty appeared next to them, giggling. Constance controlled herself for long enough to say, 'Did you hear? This is a goodbye party. They're leaving tonight. Petra said they're flying to the UEA... no, wait, the AEU... no...'

'They're flying to the UAE in the morning,' slurred Hetty. 'Might stay forever, apparently.'

'Come on, let's dance. Maggie, Laurel, come with us.' Constance didn't wait for a reply before wheeling back to the dance floor with Hetty tripping along after her.

That was unwelcome news. When she and Petra had spoken about Marcus' sudden desire to leave the area, Petra had been less than keen. Laurel gripped Maggie's hand, tension tightening the set of her lips. The ebb and flow of music and conversation faded behind the rush of blood. Maggie squeezed back. Looking for their host, they caught her eye and waved her over.

Petra sashayed across the floor. 'Ladies, are you having a good time yet? Guess what,' she hiccupped, 'Marcus and I are going away on a little hols. He only told me this morning. It's a surprise for my birthday. Isn't that fabulous?'

'That's great, really it is.' Laurel was thinking frantically. This changed everything. If they didn't act now, they might miss the only chance they'd get. 'Petra,' she had to shout to be heard above the music, 'we need your help with something real quick. Can we use the library for ten minutes?' She wasn't sure that Petra was even listening to her anymore.

'Sure, help yourself. You know the way.' She made as though to twirl away.

'I do, but I need you and Marcus there.'

'And Nicholas,' Maggie chimed in. 'He's around here somewhere.'

'Oh,' Petra's face lit up, 'have you organised a going away gift for us? That's so sneaky. Yes, I'll get Marcus and Nic and see you in there.' She clapped her hands and pirouetted away to be swallowed by the throng.

'It's not the sort of gift you're hoping for,' Laurel muttered to her retreating back. Filling Maggie in on a plan devised on the spot, and ignoring her friend's nervous protestations, she got Maggie to search for, and round up, the others. 'Be quick. I've no idea when Petra and Marcus might head off.' She took out her phone and swiped through the photos as she made for the library to prepare. She'd only have one shot at this.

'Laurel, hello, Laurel. Excuse me!'

It was a moment before Laurel realised someone was calling her. It was the woman she'd met in the bakery. She dredged up a name. 'Dorothy? Can I catch you later?' She saw Maggie, Albert, and Marcus already disappearing up the stairs when Dorothy's hand on her sleeve pulled her back.

'I can't find that policeman friend of yours, so I need you to pass on a message. You ask him why he hasn't sorted out this vandalism problem yet.'

'Dorothy, please.' People were pressing in on them, the heat of bodies making it hard to breathe.

'I'm no gossip, but I had a gentleman staying in my holiday cottage and he saw the vandal with his own eyes, caught him in the act even. He reported it then and there, on the spot, in person. All right, the chap had his hands full at the time – it was the same day Lily was found, you know – but why hasn't he done anything? That's what I want to know.'

'Dorothy...' The woman's grip was fierce, and Laurel's clammy palms failed to dislodge her. If she didn't get away, she would miss her only window to confront their suspect.

'My gentleman guest, he even told Derek, and Derek said he'd take it up with Nathan again himself, and still nothing's been done... and Nathan's had plenty of opportunity–'

'I'll tell him, okay?'

Maggie burst through the crush of bodies. 'You need to come now. Marcus refuses to wait.'

Seizing the opportunity, Laurel prised Dorothy's hand from her jumper and rushed off after Maggie. Marcus and Nicholas were both nursing glasses of whiskey and irritated expressions as she hurried into the library and closed the doors behind her. With the tumult shut out, the quiet was jarring and her ears rang.

'What are we doing in here and why are you two looking so anxious all of a sudden?' Nathan was suspicious.

She needed to get her bearings. She was really sweating now and her head was buzzing. She looked around the room. She'd often made jokes about the gathering of the suspects at the end of a case so the canny detective could unmask the killer, but this was a long way from being funny, or glamorous.

'Okay,' she said. *Breathe!* 'Rose, I'm sorry, we didn't want to spring this on you, but we know who killed your mum and Derek.'

Shock was written across every face, except Petra's. She was pouring herself another drink with the concentration of the already tipsy. Albert helped her out, then placed the bottle out of reach.

Knowing about the technology in the room, Laurel turned on the enormous television and with a few swipes – just as Petra had done when she'd given her the tour – she made two pictures appear on the screen, larger than life. 'On the left is a photograph of a girl called Flora,' she explained. 'She's Rose's grandmother. She lived near here and disappeared one day nearly ninety years ago. And on the right, well, you can see for yourself.'

THE YORKSHIRE NEWS, 30th August 1975

Lucy Locket?

By Summer Maxwell

Could a distinctive locket provide a clue to the identity of the remains found in the grounds of Elderwick Hall?

We reported last week on the grim discovery of bones made by two children from the village of Elderwick. We can now reveal that in amongst the relics was a distinctive gold locket. The locket has been passed to the police, who are appealing to anyone who might recognise the description of this piece of jewellery to come forward.

The gold locket is adorned with a blue multi-faceted stone, green gold leaves and a rose gold violet flower.

The party, barely audible, carried on outside the doors as Laurel's audience stared in bemused silence. It was a full twenty seconds before anyone spoke again.

'Are you saying it's the same locket?' asked Hitesh. 'That the locket Flora's wearing in the photo is the same locket they found with the bones?'

'Marcus.' Laurel's voice caught in her throat. She tried again. 'Marcus, we know you killed Lily and Derek.'

He gaped at her, a vein pulsing on his forehead.

'You can't go making accusations like that,' spluttered Nathan, looking backwards and forwards between them.

She gestured at the screen. 'We don't have a photo of the locket found with the bones, but you can see the description from the newspaper clipping, and that matches the locket in Rose's photo.'

Albert stood nose to screen. 'I mean, it could be, but I don't think you can say for certain.'

Marcus' face reordered itself into a sneer. 'I think your imagination has got the better of you, Laurel. It is Laurel, isn't it? I don't know why you're here talking about murder, but I shall have to ask you to leave.'

'I'm sorry.' Hitesh raised his hand. 'I don't understand.'

'As many of you know, there are a lot of dreadful stories connected with Elderwick Hall and the Hartfield family. For instance, there was a maid who disappeared after being *taken advantage of* by Marcus' grandfather, Randolf Hartfield. We believe Flora was that maid, and we believe they were *her* bones that were found in 1975,' Maggie explained.

'I'm calling the police,' Marcus declared, making to leave the room.

'I *am* the police.' Nathan put his hand out to stay him. Marcus snarled and ripped a feather off Nathan's costume, but relented and remained where he was.

Laurel squashed a flicker of doubt and pushed on. 'Marcus, you went to see Lily to ask her to run art classes in your proposed development centre. Whilst you were there, you must have seen a painting she was doing, a copy of this photo of Flora.' To the others gathered, she said, 'Marcus recognised the locket straight away because he and Derek were the ones that found the bones and the locket. He knew what it meant, and he couldn't risk either Lily ever seeing this newspaper article or Derek ever seeing the painting or the photograph.'

'What does she mean?' demanded Petra.

'We believe Flora was pregnant by Marcus' grandfather when she went missing, and that the baby she had was Sebastian Armitage, Rose's dad.' She paused to let this sink in. 'In fact, once you know about it, you can see the family resemblance in those portraits of Randolph upstairs. I knew Sebastian looked familiar in the photo I saw of him, but I couldn't place the likeness. That means Rose is directly descended from the Hartfields.'

'Randolph was my grandfather? Is that what you're saying?' asked Rose, her face pale and drawn as she absorbed the news.

'Rose, I'm sorry again, we didn't want you to find any of this out like this.'

'No, it's okay. I want to know.' Her mouth a taut line, she glared from Marcus to Laurel and back again.

'We'll probably never know what happened,' Laurel continued, 'but I would guess Flora returned to Elderwick Hall after having her baby and whether she wanted money or just to tell Randolf about his son, Randolf killed her to keep her quiet and buried her in the old walled-up orchard. Rose, you told us your grandmother left her baby with her parents and walked out one day, never to come home. I think that's when she was killed. I don't think she meant to leave the baby, your dad.'

'And all of this means Rose has a claim to the Hartfield family money,' finished Maggie.

Anger washed like a wave over Hitesh's face. He pointed a finger at Marcus. 'You killed Lily because you thought she'd want your money?'

'I didn't kill anyone,' snapped Marcus. 'This is ridiculous. Look, I can see you've got it in your head that there are some connections here, but it's all just village rumour and come on now, we all know about your history.'

Laurel's fingernails dug into her palm, but she ignored him. 'We know Derek must have seen this photo; he recognised the locket as the one he found the night he was stuck in the orchard, and he understood the significance. Our guess is he tried to use it to blackmail Marcus and threatened to expose him if he didn't call off the development. We don't know if he realised Marcus had killed Lily.'

'And he found out too late,' said Albert. 'The silly sod.'

Petra had gone ghostly white. 'He's got a crossbow,' she murmured.

Marcus turned to scowl at his wife, then addressed the room. 'There were a bunch of bows and arrows in the village hall. Anyone could have taken one.'

'It was a crossbow, and we think you specifically used a crossbow to kill Derek so that it would put *Nicholas* in the spotlight. Probably not for long, but enough to muddy the waters.'

Laurel thought she could see in his eyes the moment Marcus realised the tide had turned against him. Petra had backed away and all eyes in the room were hostile.

'Enough,' growled Marcus. He glared at Laurel. 'I've seen you skulking around. You've been poking your nose into things that don't concern you since you arrived in this village.'

'Look, Marcus,' Nathan put a hand on Marcus' arm only to have it roughly shaken off, 'let's call the on-duty team and get this all sorted out.' He held up his mobile and pulled a face. 'Damn it, can I use the phone in here?'

Marcus gave a tight nod. 'And I want to make a complaint of harassment.' He eyed Laurel with a bitter look before barking at Petra to go downstairs and find their solicitor. 'I trust the old bastard isn't so drunk yet he can't put a stop to this nonsense because as soon as this is sorted, we're getting out of here.'

Petra hurried away and Nathan ushered everyone else out of the library, then closed the door, sealing himself and Marcus inside.

Left to hover outside on the landing, Hitesh put his arm around an unsteady Rose, as Laurel strained to hear the conversation from within. Only Nicholas stood apart, fingers dancing over the screen of his phone, ignoring Maggie, who kept glancing his way. Expectant minutes passed.

'Marcus, no!' Nathan's raised voice came from behind the door, followed by a crash and the shattering of glass. A meaty smack: a fist; skin on skin.

Hitesh rushed for the handle and pounded on the solid wood as it refused to turn. 'Nathan, let us in!'

The sound of what could have been a body hitting the floor came from inside.

Maggie's hands covered her mouth, her wide eyes dark and

panicked. 'You'll never get through,' she gasped as Hitesh began kicking at the barrier.

'There must be another key? Where is it?' Laurel pleaded.

No-one knew.

Albert drew Hitesh back from the door and got down on his knees. 'There's a little trick I know.' He put his eye to the keyhole, then fished a folded-up newspaper from his back pocket. He smoothed out a page and began to slide it through the gap under the door. From another pocket he retrieved a chewed stub of a pencil and poked it into the keyhole, waggling it about until there was a thunk from the other side. With painstaking care, he withdrew the piece of paper upon which rested the key from the lock.

'Tally-ho!' he cried as he held it aloft.

'Albert, you're a genius,' cried Maggie.

Hitesh snatched the key, unlocked the door, and burst into the room.

Cold night air seeped in through an open window. Nathan lay dazed on the floor by the desk, the large television screen in shards around him and the cardboard ears of his costume bent and torn. A thin trickle of blood marked his forehead. Laurel ran to the open window and peered down at the dizzying drop onto unyielding cobbles. There was no sign of Marcus.

'Is everyone all right?' Albert handed round a bottle of brandy. Rose and Nathan had left in an ambulance and a manhunt was underway.

Petra looked bone weary. She shrugged and opened her mouth, then closed it again before saying, 'I can't believe I didn't know.'

Maggie hugged her. 'We don't always see what's in front of

us and sometimes people are very skilled at hiding their true nature.'

Petra hugged her back, but then pulled away a little. 'Did you suspect me too?'

Feeling guilty, Laurel looked first at Maggie and then said to Petra, 'I have to admit, for a little while we thought you might have been in on it. You didn't strike us as being motivated by money, but after I overheard you and Hitesh talking the other day about having had to get rid of someone, well, even though you swore it wasn't sinister...'

Petra gave a mirthless laugh. 'Oh god, it probably doesn't even matter now. We were talking about Barclay.'

Laurel had almost forgotten about the never-seen Barclay. What was Petra about to confess to? 'Barclay?'

'Barkley, B-A-R-K-L-E-Y,' she spelt it out, 'Marcus' dog. Damn thing was getting out every five minutes. It was him digging up all the flower beds around the village that Derek was getting in such a state about. We even caught him digging in the graveyard one day. When they found those bones in the orchard, I was petrified they were real ones Barkley had brought back from an actual grave.'

'We thought he would be better off in a new home,' said Hitesh.

'Marcus thought he'd run off, he would have... he would have blown a fuse if he knew.'

Albert patted her gently on the arm. 'It's over now.'

Chapter Thirty-Nine

Laurel's thoughts churned as she tried to fit together pieces that felt as though they were from different puzzles. *It's hopeless*, she decided at 6am, as she gave up and got out of bed to clump downstairs to the living room.

A picture was trying to form. She had expected to feel vindicated when they'd exposed Marcus – she'd wanted to shout *I told you so* at Nathan – yet something wasn't sitting right. She looked for her notebook and found it shoved on top of the books in her bookcase. It wasn't where she thought she'd left it. These days, nothing ever seemed to be where she thought it would be. With a prickle of worry, she wondered if she was over-stressed. She'd been under stress many times in her old life, but her memory had never been this bad. This was new and unsettling. Could she be losing her marbles? The leaves in the living room; the broken glass in the picture frame; the boiler; the lamp?

Shrugging it off, she looked at the notes she and Maggie had jotted over the preceding weeks and sketched large question marks beside all the as yet unexplained clues and still unanswered questions. How many of them had been real and how many could she have inadvertently misconstrued or made-up? There was the arrow though, that was real, no doubt about it, and nothing to do with her getting confused or having a faulty memory.

But what of the pie left on her doorstep? It had been made in one of her own pie dishes. She'd checked after Nathan had gone, and it was hers; the small chip in the rim confirmed it. It didn't make any sense. She put the book aside, set down her pen, leaned back, closed her eyes, and tried to work, step by step, along the timeline from finding Lily's body to the present moment.

What if she and Maggie were right about the *how*, but they'd tripped up on the *why*? The *why* – protecting his inheritance – had led them to Marcus, so if they'd got the motive wrong...

Start again. What were the alternatives? Lily had been murdered. It wasn't an accident. She felt sure of that now. Derek, there'd never been any question there. What connected them? As Maggie had said the last time they discussed it, nothing significant connected them other than they both lived in Elderwick and they were friends. In all their poking, prying, and theorising, they hadn't been able to identify a single other, plausible reason for either of them to be killed. Sure, there was the development in the grounds of Elderwick Hall, and Derek wasn't the most popular person, but neither of those constituted sufficient motive for murder. The locket, the identity of Rose's grandmother, and a possible inheritance had felt right, but was it all too farfetched?

Lily's murder must have been premeditated and carefully orchestrated. Derek's was less clear cut. Though there must still have been some planning involved – no-one walked around with a crossbow, just in case – it was far less intricate. She and Maggie had speculated he could have been killed because the murderer had no choice, or felt they had no choice and was compelled to act with haste. Derek must have known something.

She was getting nowhere, going in circles.

Keeping her eyes closed, breathing slowly, trying not to think, simply letting her thoughts flow, she hoped an answer would present itself. There had to be a vital connection she was missing, but like a will-o'-the-wisp it kept dancing out of reach. Exhaling her frustration, she opened her eyes and saw the book she'd borrowed from the library: *The Body in the Library*.

'Marcus is afraid of heights!' She jerked upright. Shapes came together, slotted into place to reveal a disturbing picture. It explained everything and how it had been done. And if she was right, there was only one person who could be responsible. And if that was who was responsible, there was only one explanation, an explanation as bizarre as it was cold-blooded.

Oh no, no, no, no.

It was 9am when she made the phone call to Elderwick Hall.

'Hello,' said a voice.

'I need you to check the priest hole in the library.'

Chapter Forty

The doorbell rang. Could they have been that quick? She hurried to answer, but it wasn't who she'd been expecting. 'Nathan.' Her hand went to her hair. She wished she'd thought to do something with it. 'Come in.' She stood back and invited him through to the living room.

Sporting a wide grin, Nathan whipped out the bottle of champagne he'd been hiding behind his back. 'It's a bit early in the day, but I thought we should celebrate. I'm not ashamed to admit it. You were right about Lily, Derek, the whole thing.'

An expensive bottle, she noted, the real deal. 'Wow, thank you, but I don't think I even have any proper glasses.'

'Let me look.' He disappeared into the kitchen, returning moments later brandishing two flutes. 'Shall I do the honours?' He popped the cork, which landed somewhere on top of the bookcase, and poured. With their glasses filled, he raised his towards her. 'Laurel, I can't thank you enough. You've cleared up two murders and I get to claim a whole lot of the credit.' He winked at her.

She laughed along with him and sipped her drink. 'Sit

down.' He chose the sofa, and she picked the chair. 'Have they caught Marcus yet?'

'No, and with his money and connections, he might have made it out of the country already. We won't stop the search, though. There's a chance he might slip up and if he does, we'll be waiting.'

'I'm glad you're okay.' She studied the cut on his forehead. It wasn't deep but was an angry red. 'It sounded like quite a scuffle in the library before he jumped out of the window.' He'd have an impressive blue-black bruise within a day or so.

'Aw shucks, t'weren't nothing,' he drawled, running his fingers lightly across the wound.

She offered a weak smile at his attempt to lighten the mood. 'Was Rose okay? She went with you to the hospital, didn't she?'

'She did.' His eyes softened and a grin crowded his features. 'Actually, I know you and I had a couple of dates, so I should let you know,' he fidgeted on the sofa and looked away, 'Rose and I... we're in love.'

Her heart sank. She had figured something was going on, but it was jarring to hear it confirmed. 'That was quick.' The words slipped out. She didn't begrudge Rose happiness, but did it have to be Nathan?

'Well, we actually met a few years back.'

'When her mum moved to Elderwick? Rose mentioned it,' she explained, noticing his frown.

Like a love-struck teenager, he bobbed his head. 'It was completely by chance. I'd called in to ask if Lily wanted any advice on her security, you know, elderly lady living alone and all that. Rose was there and we hit it off, had a few drinks. I hoped it might turn into something, but she was adamant she was off to New Zealand.' He shrugged. 'After she left, I met my now ex, Sylvie. We got married, but that didn't work out. I guess

I've been waiting for Rose to come back, so I might have another chance, and here we are.' He beamed.

'Rose said you've been a fantastic support since she got back.' Laurel was aware her tone was peevish, and Nathan must have noticed.

'I didn't have you down as the jealous type, Dr Nightingale,' he teased.

How could she ever have been attracted to him?

'Excuse me a second. I need a glass of water. Nine fifteen is a bit earlier than I usually start on the fizz.' She nipped into the kitchen, but before she'd had chance to turn on the tap, Nathan's head appeared in the doorway making her jump.

'Everything okay?' He leaned against the wall by the fridge.

She ran the water and splashed some on the back of her neck. 'Yes, I think it's all catching up with me: last night, all the drama.' She didn't have to pretend to look shaken.

'Let's get you off your feet, shall we?' He placed a solicitous hand on her shoulder and guided her back to the sofa. 'Here, you can't let me drink alone.' He pressed the flute back into her hand and watched her drink.

It did feel good to sit on the soft cushions, and she was quite sleepy. To be expected, given she'd been up most of the night. The alcohol was going straight to her head, and she never did get that glass of water. She was struggling to keep her eyes open, but she needed to keep talking. 'Nathan, do you know about the psychopath test?' Her tongue wasn't working right, and she was slurring her words.

'The what?'

'The psychopath test. It's not real, it's not an official test or anything, it's a joke, I suppose.'

'No, I don't know it.' He edged forward on the sofa. 'Shall I top you up?'

She was surprised to find her glass was empty. He held her hand steady so he could refill it, then guided it to her lips.

'Wait.' She pulled her glass away and liquid sloshed onto the floorboards. 'Whoops.' She snorted. 'Let me tell you about this test. While at a funeral... at a funeral for a family member, this girl meets a guy she doesn't know.' She jabbed her finger at him. 'She thinks he's amazing, perfect man, but he leaves. Later, she kills her sister. Why does she kill her sister?' He was next to her on the sofa, she poked him in the chest. 'Why?'

He smirked.

'What's... answer, Nathan?' She tried to put down her glass but missed the table.

'Uh oh, here you go.' He handed back her glass, full once more, then lifted his own in a toast, but he didn't drink. 'You're an intelligent woman, so you know I know the answer.'

'That's why you killed Lily.' More liquid sloshed out of her glass. 'You bumped off poor Lily so Rose would come back from New Zealand for her mum's funeral so you could try again with her!' She struggled to focus. 'But you had to be clever. You had to come up with some elaborate plot.' *Stop poking the beast!* But the words kept tumbling out. 'Like many psychopaths, you're not as clever as you think.'

'You're just trying to defend that ridiculous profile of yours, the one you were spouting at the station.'

'You admit it?'

He folded his arms. 'Marcus is missing, presumed very much guilty. Why would anyone think any differently?'

'Your scapegoat, Marcus, isn't missing, though, is he?' She thought she caught a tiny twitch in his eye, but she was swaying so she couldn't be sure. 'You tucked him away in the priest hole.'

He yawned. 'Don't mind me, I'm enjoying your story. Which is all anyone will ever believe this is, after I've got rid of his body. I think I've laid sufficient groundwork for people to question your claims, your *veracity*. Not been one hundred percent lately, have you? Forgetting things, getting yourself mixed up, seeing lights in the dark, and the best one, being paranoid about a pie left on your doorstep. Not to mention it was you who just accused Marcus of murder. That was a fun surprise, but I'm nothing if not adaptable.'

Laurel heard her voice as though from a long way off. 'I know why Derek had to die, too. Poor Derek. His friend saw you the day you killed Lily. He complained to you about Barkley, Marcus' dog, digging up the flower tubs. Dorothy told me... she told me. Said you had your hands full. I thought she meant you had your hands full dealing with Lily being found, but I think you had your hands full literally. With Lily's painting. He must have told Derek and when Derek tack... tackled you about the vandalism, he told you. Did he realise the sig... ficance of you having the painting?'

Nathan's face hardened. 'You know, Derek was constantly bothering me with complaints about one thing or another. Then, once you started harping on about the painting being missing, I knew that sooner or later the gossip would get back to Derek. So that's on you. You could even say it was your fault I had to kill him.'

'No,' she whispered.

'Yeah.'

'Why take the painting?' *Curiosity killed the cat*, she thought, and giggled.

'She looked like Rose, the girl in the painting. I wanted to have it.'

'And I came up with all that stuff about Marcus and the inheritance.' She was too tipsy to care about how ridiculous she'd been.

Nathan ignored her. 'Using an arrow to kill Derek was

inspired, don't you think? After he'd gone on about how dangerous they are. Wonderful irony.'

'Nope.' She shook her head, but he was in full flow. Maybe the Bond films were right; the bad guys like the sound of their own voices too much.

Focus!

'Then, since I already had the crossbow, it amused me to take a shot at you, too. I meant to miss, of course.'

'Sure.' Her head lolled forward.

'Besides, what do you mean, poor Derek? You had him down as Lily's murderer at one point.'

'How...' Understanding dawned through the fog invading her head. 'You read my notebook! It was you! You were in my house.' Anger roused her, set her adrenaline pumping.

'Repeatedly. Your *sleuthing*, it's all rather amateur hour, but it was so helpful in concocting entertaining little storylines for you to chase your tail over. Silly me, though, I must have let slip a few things to Nicholas. I did enjoy your falling out with Maggie.' He licked his lips.

She fumed. He'd played them all so easily. But he was going to lose in the end. She had to buy herself more time. 'The bones... at Hall?' It was hard to form her words, and breathing was an effort.

'Not guilty. Serendipity, and didn't that just top it all? You're very suggestible for a psychologist. A few grisly stories about the place and you were off and running. Albert played a blinder too – not that he knows it – by telling you about Derek, Marcus and the bones. I couldn't have invented anything better.' Nathan stood, picked up her notebook from the desk and slid it into a pocket before checking the rest of her papers.

'Sucks for you that I moved here.' She let her head slump back. It felt so heavy now. Perhaps she could close her eyes for a second.

'Ah, no, no, that's the best bit.'

Now she could hear him rifling through her drawers... *rifling through her drawers*, that was funny.

'What?' She couldn't follow what he was saying. Maybe it didn't matter anymore.

'Once you arrived and stuck your nose in, it was such fun watching you chase around. I'd hoped for a slightly more worthy opponent. It's good this is ending now. I'm getting bored, and Rose and I have a new life to build.'

'Fun! You're in-insane.' She thought she saw movement outside the French windows.

'A psychopath, according to you.'

'Had to keep you talking, dummy.' Another giggle escaped her. 'Big mistake... huge.' She peeked at him through half-closed eyes. 'Not long... he's gonna get you.'

Nathan was frowning, his brow wrinkled. 'What are you talking about?'

Her eyes drifted closed.

As though from far away, she heard a pounding at the door.

And a smile played across her lips.

Epilogue

Two weeks later

'How is Aroon doing after his run-in with Nathan?'

'He has recovered very well, Laurel. Thank you for asking. Although, I rather fear his role in capturing the crazed killer of Elderwick has gone to his head; his strut is cockier than ever.'

'I saw him in the garden, before I... anyway. I heard he launched himself at Nathan and inflicted all kinds of damage. I wish I'd seen it,' she wailed.

'Well, you did. You just don't remember it. Rohypnol will do that to you. Are you feeling quite restored?' asked Albert.

'I am. I have a huge blank in my memory which is scary, but other than that, I'm fine.'

'I am so thankful he didn't...' he tailed off.

'It's okay, you can say it. He hasn't admitted anything, but I don't think he'd planned to kill me. I think he wanted to gloat; he needed me to know how clever he was. But he couldn't risk another death. This way, he could tell me everything safe in the knowledge I would never remember our conversation.' Laurel grimaced. 'I just hope he doesn't get away with it. There really isn't much evidence, especially since Marcus' head injury means he can't remember what happened in the library.'

'How did you work it all out in the end?' asked Hitesh.

She'd been over this with Maggie, but still blushed when she answered. 'That's the thing, I didn't exactly work much out, mostly it was luck. Oh and Nathan drugging me was the final giveaway. I was ninety-nine percent certain after that.' They laughed.

'There was one thing that helped me re-evaluate after accusing Marcus – I feel so bad about that, I'm not sure the grapes and flowers are nearly enough of an apology – Albert, do you remember on Halloween you pointed out my hens are in fact all cockerels? Well, that got me thinking that I might have been seeing what I expected to see, and not the truth. I saw a police officer and not an obsessed killer.'

'You might say I helped *crack* the case. You know, crack, like crack an egg. Nothing? Philistine, you don't appreciate a good joke.'

'We appreciate *good* jokes,' called Sam as he brought over their drinks.

Laurel handed Albert his drink and tasted her Red Hen, a cider Nathan would never get to try.

Hitesh touched her on the elbow. 'How is Rose doing, Laurel?'

'Did you see her at the funeral?'

He nodded.

'She's struggling, knowing she had been so close to the man who murdered her own mother.' A shudder ran down her spine. They'd all been close to Nathan and none of them had suspected a thing. 'She got back home to New Zealand yesterday. We had a quick chat on the phone before she went to sleep off her jet lag. I think she'll be okay; she's a strong, independent woman. Nathan might have been obsessed with her, but he was never the love of her life. She had always planned to go back home, to the life she's built over there.'

'She told me she is an artist,' said Hitesh. 'Like her mum. I looked her up online. Her work is amazing and she's pretty famous.'

'Good for her,' said Albert.

'Sorry we're late,' called Maggie, as she and Hetty appeared at the table.

'Maggie, my partner in crime-busting! Hetty! Come on, you can squeeze in.' Laurel greeted her friends and noted, not for the first time, that Maggie was looking healthier and happier than she'd ever seen her. She'd been spending a lot of time with Hetty since dumping Nicholas, and it looked like it was doing her the world of good.

Maggie beamed. 'I didn't think we were going to make it. We've been over in York with Petra and the roads were busier than we expected coming back. She sends her apologies, by the way. She won't be able to join us tonight. She's heading off to see her parents tomorrow and to start looking at houses near to them. It seems a family reunion is on the cards.'

'I'm not surprised Petra wants nothing to do with Elderwick Hall after everything that's happened,' said Laurel.

'The curse strikes again,' Albert intoned.

Laurel wasn't sure if he was joking or being serious. The recent events were undoubtedly another stain in the history of the grand house.

'I think Marcus got the worst of it,' said Maggie. 'He's likely to be in hospital for some time yet, and the investors have all pulled their money quicker than a politician breaks his promises.'

Albert gave a wan smile. 'Derek would be pleased to hear that the development is off.'

Maggie's lips quirked. 'I'm glad there was a good turn-out

for his funeral. He wasn't the easiest man, but we'll miss having him around.'

'Speaking of Derek,' said Hetty, 'I heard from Rose that the new bench on the village green will be in memory of both Derek and Lily. The primary school children have volunteered to plant some flowers around it, which I think would tickle them both.'

Hetty nudged Maggie. 'Shall we give them the good news about Nicholas, too?'

Maggie flushed. 'Nicholas told me I had to move out of The Grange and that I wouldn't be seeing a penny from him. Unfortunately, he underestimated me as he has always done. I know about the secret accounts he'd opened to squirrel away his dodgy money from all those bribes he took, and I found his passwords and account numbers years ago while cleaning. I wasn't sure at the time why I made a note of them, but hey-ho, they came in handy in the end.'

Laurel was uncomfortable. 'Maggie, you know that's not really legal?'

'Oh, I'm not keeping the money. I've given all the information to HMRC, who will keep Nicholas busy for many months to come.'

'Ha, just what he deserves.' Laurel blew Maggie a kiss and Hetty slung her arm round her shoulders and gave her a hug.

'And Laurel, after everything that's gone on, two deaths, an attempt on your life, being drugged, will you be–'

Laurel smiled at Maggie, her friend. 'I'm not running away this time. Elderwick is my home now, for good and bad, and I'm staying put.'

Albert lifted his glass. 'A toast, to Elderwick's very own Hetty Wain–'

'No!'

A FRESH START

'Hi, Hitesh, thank you for agreeing to meet.'

'You're most welcome. I'm very pleased to see you healthy and well after everything that has happened.'

They were walking along a quiet lane leading away from the village. Beyond the hedgerows, the fields were brown and bare, waiting for their spring blanket of new growth. Although it was mild for the time of year, Hitesh was bundled in a worn, grey coat, a blue and gold scarf about his neck. He didn't know it, but Albert was following along some way behind, ostensibly out walking Lago, his impudent rabbit, should anyone ask. Laurel wasn't scared of Hitesh, but after her brush with Nathan, she wasn't taking any chances. Plus, Albert had insisted when she'd confided in him with her plan.

Hitesh, she saw, was wringing his hands. 'It's okay,' she said. He looked at her with tears in his eyes.

'You know?' he whispered.

'I do. Can you tell me about it?'

'How did you... how?'

'You're the reason I moved to Elderwick. It's a gorgeous

village anyway, so it was no hardship, but I couldn't let it go. I needed to know.'

'And now you know.'

She nodded.

'My brother told you about me?'

'He loved you so much. You were the world to him, and I think I got you all wrong when he told me you were going to kill him.'

Hitesh stopped, curling into himself, hands covering his face.

'You did it for him, didn't you? He wasn't afraid of you. It's what he wanted.'

She waited. There was no rush, time enough for the truth.

When he regained his voice, Hitesh said, 'He was in so much pain and he begged me. For weeks he begged me, and I knew what was coming. I'd done my rotation in palliative care. I knew. And I was losing him. His brain tumour was eating away at who he was. Amit was disappearing.'

'I'm so sorry.'

'I didn't want to do it, but I had to do it, for Amit.'

'I understand.' An image of her mum swam behind her eyes. Her mum, who, towards the end, was unable to speak, reliant on others for everything, struggling to breathe. Approaching a feared death, and a blessed release.

'What will you do?'

She'd thought about it, agonised over it, but in the end, there was only ever one answer. 'You loved your brother, Hitesh. That's all I needed to know.'

THE END

Acknowledgements

I can't express enough how grateful I am to my wonderful husband, Steve, for making *A Little Bird Told Me* possible. His love, patience, and feedback on my work gave me the confidence to get serious about my dream of becoming a published author. And my heartfelt gratitude to Mum and Dad, who sparked my love of reading all those years ago. They have always been my unwavering supporters in writing and in life, and are incredible parents.

A huge thank you to my BBF (best beta friend), Jessi Porter, who is an incredible writer and who has been a stupendous companion through this crazy world of writing books. She has been there since the very early days of this manuscript, and it wouldn't be what it is without her insightful comments, eye for detail, and unerring encouragement.

I would also like to thank Mandy Gravil, Vanessa Friend and Kathy Leeman who generously gave their time to read and critique my work. As did my dear friend Emily Wood, whose kind words always lift my spirits when the writing is hard.

Thank you to everyone at Bloodhound Books for turning my long-held dream into a reality. In particular, Betsy Reavley and Fred Freeman, who took a chance on my book; Tara Lyons, for coordinating the publishing process and steering me in the right direction; Patricia Dixon, for her enthusiastic support throughout; my incredible editor, Clare Law, who whipped this manuscript into shape; and proofreader, Ian Skewis, who gave it a final polish; Hannah Deuce and Lexi Curtis for the brilliant marketing and inspired publicity; and Mel of Better Book Design for my gorgeous book cover. Not to mention my fellow Bloodhound authors for their guidance and encouragement.

This book was written during 2020/21. At the time, I was heading up the Department of Clinical Health Psychology at Airedale NHS Foundation Trust in West Yorkshire and I need to pay tribute to my fantastic team, colleagues, and patients: it was a privilege to work with you all through such a challenging time. You're amazing and I miss you.

Finally, a special mention to the Airedale Hospital and Community Charity who work tirelessly to help Airedale NHS Foundation Trust by raising funds, supporting others and championing the Airedale community. (https://airedalecharity.org/)

If you'd like to follow me, you can find me on:
Facebook: RachaelGray_Psy
Twitter: @RachaelGray_psy
https://welcometoelderwick.godaddysites.com/

About the Author

With over twenty years of experience working as a Doctor of Clinical Psychology for the NHS and healthcare charities, Rachael Gray is the author of *A Little Bird Told Me*.

Though she'll always be a Yorkshire girl at heart, Rachael now lives and writes from the home she shares with her husband in Normandy, France.

Rarely without her nose in a book, her debut novel is inspired by her love of a good whodunit.

She can be found on Twitter: @RachaelGray_psy, and Facebook: RachaelGray_Psy

A note from the publisher

Thank you for reading this book. If you enjoyed it please do consider leaving a review on Amazon to help others find it too.

We hate typos. All of our books have been rigorously edited and proofread, but sometimes mistakes do slip through. If you have spotted a typo, please do let us know and we can get it amended within hours.

info@bloodhoundbooks.com

Printed in Great Britain
by Amazon